"I know you don't want to get married, and honestly, neither do I."

When Maggie didn't say anything, Adam sighed. He reached to her and gently tilted her chin up so that she looked into his eyes.

"For the baby's sake and to repair your reputation, I will marry you. But I am not offering love. Think of it as an arrangement for the child."

"A marriage of convenience is fine by me. I don't have a choice. Pa no longer wants me in his wagon. So yes, I'll marry you, I'll be faithful and I promise not to fall in love with you or expect you to love me."

The sharpness in her words cut deep. How was it that Maggie sounded as bitter as he felt?

Adam released her chin, wishing he'd found a less blunt way to offer her marriage. "Then I'll go tell your pa and get the preacher to do a quick ceremony."

Adam felt as if the weight of the world had just been placed upon his shoulders.

Rhonda Gibson lives in Oklahoma with her husband, James. She has two children and four beautiful grandchildren. Reading is something Rhonda has enjoyed her whole life and writing stems from that love. When she isn't writing or reading, she enjoys making cards for her friends and family. Rhonda hopes her writing will entertain, encourage and bring others closer to God.

Books by Rhonda Gibson

Love Inspired Historical

Pony Express Courtship
Pony Express Hero
Pony Express Christmas Bride
Pony Express Mail-Order Bride
Pony Express Special Delivery
Baby on Her Doorstep
Wagon Train Wedding
Wagon Train Baby

Visit the Author Profile page
at LoveInspired.com for more titles.

Wagon Train Baby

RHONDA GIBSON

LOVE INSPIRED
INSPIRATIONAL ROMANCE

LOVE INSPIRED®

INSPIRATIONAL ROMANCE

ISBN-13: 978-1-335-49848-9

Wagon Train Baby

Copyright © 2023 by Rhonda Gibson

For questions and comments about the quality of this book, please contact us at CustomerService@Harlequin.com.

Love Inspired
22 Adelaide St. West, 41st Floor
Toronto, Ontario M5H 4E3, Canada
www.LoveInspired.com

Printed in U.S.A.

Being confident of this very thing,
that he which hath begun a good work in you
will perform it until the day of Jesus Christ.
—*Philippians* 1:6

Thank you to Tina James for always believing in me and my stories. To James Gibson, you are my rock. To God be the glory, without Him I cannot write.

Chapter One

⌒

Oregon Trail
June 1860

A patch of blackberry bushes caught Maggie Porter's attention as she followed behind her father's wagon. Ripe purple berries hung from thick vines, causing her mouth to water. Over the last couple of weeks, Maggie had collected greens and other plants that her pa and brother enjoyed with their simple meals. She took one last look at the wagon train, then ventured from the trail and into the bushes.

The sound of the wagons rumbling forward filled the air. Maggie gathered her apron in front, creating a bowl, and picked the fruit as fast as she could. Thankfully with only twenty-five wagons, she might have enough for each family to enjoy. She couldn't resist the urge to toss one of the plump berries into her mouth. Sweetness oozed from the soft fruit.

She heard a sound and stopped chewing, tilting her

head to the side to focus on its origin. *Is that a baby's cry?* She'd heard babies cry on the wagon train, but this cry seemed to come from behind her, not in the direction of the wagons. She tilted her head again and listened.

After several minutes of silence, Maggie continued picking the fruit, aware that the wagon train was moving farther away from her.

As they were leaving Independence, Missouri, she realized that to survive the trail, she'd need to look for wild fruits and vegetables to supplement their supply of food. Normally, it was at a rushed pace, but thankfully today they moved at a snail's pace as the men tried to avoid the chug holes concealed by the rain and mud from the night before. She realized moisture from the grass and weeds had caused the hem of her dress to become heavy as she took a step to rejoin the wagon train.

There's the cry again. This time Maggie turned and walked toward the sound. Her gaze searched the trees and bushes. She untied her apron and carefully laid it and the berries it held down. She'd pick it up on her return.

Maggie took several steps into the woods, leaving the trail farther behind. She glanced over her shoulder and in the distance she saw her brother standing on the wagon seat, looking forward. They'd stopped again for some reason or other, so she decided she'd have time to investigate a little further. As she ventured deeper into the woods, she peered closely around the base of the underbrush that covered the wooded ground, thinking she might catch sight of a baby. "I'm being ridiculous," she murmured even as she moved farther away from the wagon train.

Just when she'd decided she was hearing things, the sound of a baby's whimper snagged her attention once more. Maggie walked toward the cry. As it grew louder, she found herself running to reach the child, aware she was leaving the wagon train farther and farther behind. Still, she couldn't leave a baby out in the woods, and if she hurried, they would be back to the safety of the wagon soon.

Maggie stopped. She listened but couldn't hear the crying. Her heart beat loudly in her ears. As her breathing calmed, she became aware of a low growling to her right. She'd been warned of wild animals and even wilder men that roamed the trail. How many times had her father and brother told her not to wander off?

Time to face the foolishness of her actions. Maggie turned slowly to face either man or beast. She swallowed hard and focused on the animal before her.

A large white dog stood between her and a very small girl who looked to be less than two years old. Tears stained the baby's face as her big green eyes took in Maggie. Her little bonnet had fallen from her head revealing light brown curls. Had the dog hurt the child? Maggie didn't think so. The little girl held the dog by its fur, clinging to him as if the animal were a friend. Maggie prayed that the big beast was a friend. She'd never seen a dog this big up close.

Keeping her voice calm, Maggie knelt and held the dog's gaze. "Hello there, boy."

The dog's ears twitched back and forth. He laid his ears back but stopped growling deep in his throat. Using his body, the dog pushed the little girl back as if herding her away from danger.

The child stumbled but didn't fall. Still holding on to the dog but looking at Maggie, she asked, "Mama?"

Maggie looked about. Woods surrounded them on three sides. A rock wall stood at the dog's back. She smiled at the little girl and shook her head. "I'm sorry, little one, I don't know where your mama is, but if you come to me, I'll help you find her."

The baby took a step as if to come to her, but the dog gently pushed the child back again. She looked at her dog and then buried her face in its coat. Soft sobs shook her shoulders.

Maggie wasn't sure what to do. Without closing her eyes because she wanted to keep watch on the animal, Maggie prayed. "Lord, I know You sent me to find this little girl and I feel like You sent the dog to protect her. Father, I ask You to let the dog know I am not going to hurt him or the baby as I approach them. Keep me safe as I try to do what I feel is right, in Jesus' name. Amen."

She stood still a moment and took several deep breaths. Then she stepped forward. The dog watched her but didn't growl. "Sweet boy, I know you are trying to protect your baby and I appreciate that, but I want to help her too, and I can't do that if you don't let me near her. So, we are going to have to trust each other." Without waiting for a response, Maggie squared her shoulders and walked to the dog and little girl.

The child raised her head and looked at her. "Mama?" she asked again.

The dog scooted to the side and allowed Maggie to

pick up the little girl. "I'm sorry, honey. I still don't know where she is, but we'll find her."

Before she could move away from the dog, it began a low growl deep in its throat.

Maggie held her breath, expecting the animal to attack her. She looked at the dog and braced her legs, ready to run. Only the dog wasn't looking at her but into the woods.

The dog pushed against Maggie's legs and she realized he was trying to herd her as he'd done the little girl earlier. Maggie took a step back but kept her gaze on the tree line. She clutched the child close and looked behind her to see if there was a bush to hide behind. Seeing one, she eased back until she was within its branches. Only then did she realize the bush hid an indentation in the rock wall. Could it be a cave? A place to hide?

Adam Walker knew before he entered the camp that something was wrong. He could feel the tension in the air and hear the raised whispers as women were starting fires and the men were tending to their animals. He made his way to his own wagon and his mother.

She looked up at him as he entered their camp. "I'm glad you're back, son." His mother thrust a warm biscuit in his hands and a tin cup full of coffee. "Eat fast. The wagon master wants to see you as soon as possible. The Porter girl is missing."

Adam understood what that meant. He thrust the biscuit into his mouth and chewed. Butter oozed from between the warm bread. His gaze moved to the circle of wagons, and he found the one belonging to the Porters. Mr. Porter and his son, Martin, stood talking to the wagon master. It was obvious Mr. Porter was angry, judging by his red face and clenched fists.

Maggie Porter was quiet and tended to stay to herself. He'd learned early on that she was generous; he'd had the pleasure of enjoying the fresh greens she'd shared with his mother on several occasions. With strawberry blond hair, blue eyes and a heart-shaped face, she'd garnered looks from several of the younger, unmarried men, but her brother had shielded her from their attentions.

Adam would be leaving in a few minutes to go looking for the woman, no doubt about that. Adam had noticed her trailing behind her father's wagon earlier in the day but had thought nothing of it. His mother had called her a girl, but everyone knew she was a widow and in her early twenties. On a wagon train this small, there were very few secrets.

Except one. Why didn't she go by her married name? He shook the thought off; there were more important matters to consider now. He needed to find her before the sun went down.

His mother handed him another biscuit the moment he'd swallowed the last bite. "You better get over there. It's looking a little heated. I'll pack up a couple of biscuits and jerky for you."

Adam kissed his mother on the cheek. "Thanks, Ma." He raised his head and searched out Josiah, his hired driver.

When their gazes met, Josiah nodded his agreement to the unspoken command to watch after Adam's mother. Only then did Adam turn to the Porter wagon.

"Come on, Shadow, let's see what the hullabaloo is all about."

The solid black horse snorted and followed obediently.

He walked unhurried. Adam knew that everyone watched his every movement. "Slow and calm" was his motto. If he appeared calm, then others tended to settle down as well. He took a sip of his coffee and sighed.

A few feet away from the Porter wagon, Adam heard Maggie's father say, "We can't wait any longer. I'm going after my daughter, Cannon."

Mr. Porter stared at the wagon master, Jim Cannon. Most people just called him Mr. Cannon or Cannon; either way they said his name with respect.

Approaching from behind the Porters, Adam nodded at the wagon master as he came into speaking distance. "Good evening, Mr. Cannon."

The older gentleman tipped his head toward him. "Evening, Adam."

Mr. Porter turned to face him. "It's about time you got back." He then turned back to face Mr. Cannon. "He's here now. Let's go."

"Hold up." Adam took another sip of his mother's coffee. "Where are you rushing off to?"

Martin answered in a calm voice. "My sister is missing, Adam. Pa and I wanted to go looking for her, but Mr. Cannon advised us to wait for your return."

Adam liked Martin. He was in his midtwenties, softspoken but matter-of-fact. "I'm glad he did."

"I'm going with you." Mr. Porter turned to the horse he'd saddled up earlier.

The wagon master answered, "No, sir, you are not going. Adam is our best tracker. He'll find Miss Porter."

"How long has she been missing?" Adam asked.

Martin ran his hand over his face. "Last time I saw her was around four this afternoon. She was following the wagon as usual." He raised his gaze to Adam's. "I'd like to go with you."

"I know but I can make better time alone." Adam pulled himself onto Shadow's broad back. His gaze met Mr. Porter's. He knew the man was worried sick; any good father would be. "I'll bring her home, Mr. Porter." Adam intended to keep his word.

John Porter swallowed hard. "The sooner the better," he conceded.

Adam turned his horse back to his camp. He handed his mother the cup. "I'll be back as soon as I can."

She lifted a flour sack filled with the biscuits and jerky for him to take. "Godspeed, son." She turned to the wagon but not before he saw the mist filling her eyes.

Adam hung the bag on his saddle horn. As he traveled the way the wagon train had come, he wondered if his mother's tears were for him or the woman he'd been sent to find.

Adam studied the ground closely. The heavy storm the night before had left the ground wet. Footsteps leading from the trail would help him find her. He knew Miss Porter probably went in search of something edible.

In minutes he came across the spot where she'd left the trail. Her foot had slipped on the small slope. He slid off Shadow's back and studied the wet ground. The hem of her dress had dragged through the grass and weeds, making his job easy.

He came to the berry patch and saw where she'd stood picking the sweet fruit. Adam grabbed a handful for himself and continued following her trail. When he came to her apron lying on the ground, he stopped. Why had she left the fruit behind?

Adam took a deep breath, put the apron in the flour sack and continued his search. His heart rate quickened when he read the tracks that confirmed she'd started running. The sun was dimmer in the trees, but he could still make out that her footprints were the only human ones present. So, what was she running from or to?

Confusion filled his mind. She ran first one way and then another; he could tell when she stopped and then when she'd take off running again. Had her mind started playing tricks on her out here alone? Had she gotten lost and panicked when she realized she couldn't hear the wagon train?

He continued following her footsteps. Adam realized she'd doubled back and was heading toward the trail. Maybe she was already out of the woods and heading to the wagons. A sigh escaped him. Had he been holding his breath? He must have been.

A low growl stopped him. His gaze moved quickly to the woods around him. Had he stumbled upon a wolf pack? Or a bear? Adam pulled his gun from the holster on his hip. If he didn't have to shoot the animal, he wouldn't. But it was better to be safe than sorry.

Adam continued to search the area around him. He bent down once more and studied the ground. Paw tracks. From the looks of them, dog or wolf prints. He saw others. Were those tiny human tracks? He traced the small footprint. Maggie Porter's boot imprints were mingled in with the animal and child tracks.

He stood and began following the indentions. They went to the rock wall that stood in front of him. Adam realized that a shadow of an opening was to his left. It had been well concealed by the bush growing in front of it. The growling became deeper and louder. Was she in that indention with the animal?

Only one way to find out. He called, "Miss Porter? It's Adam Walker from the wagon train. Are you here?"

The animal growled louder at the sound of his voice. Her voice called over the animal's warning. "Mr. Walker, we're in here."

He felt sure she sounded relieved.

"Let me pass, you big brute." Maggie Porter pushed the bush aside and stepped out of the cavern's mouth. She held a little girl on her hip.

A large dog followed her, then stepped in front of her. His warning growl, and the placement of his body between them, told Adam not to make any fast moves. He stood still and asked, "Why didn't you come back?"

She brushed the hair from the child's eyes. "I'm lost. Pa always said 'if you get lost, stay put and I'll find you.'"

Adam wanted to laugh but decided that was a bad idea since the huge dog bared his teeth as if to say, "One more noise out of you and I'm going to bite first and ask questions later." In a soft voice he asked, "Where did you find her?" He nodded toward the child she held.

Maggie looked at him and grinned. "Here with this

big boy." She reached down and patted the dog between the ears.

"Where's her family?" Adam asked, though he continued to watch the dog.

"I don't know. She keeps asking for her mama."

He'd not seen any other tracks besides Maggie's and the little girl's. "Are you all right staying here a little longer with the dog?"

She nodded. "I think he's her protector."

"I believe you're right. I'm going to go look for her parents. I'll be back in a few minutes." He had no intention of leaving them alone for very long. His gut said that the little girl's parents were probably close by.

Maggie called after him. "Mr. Walker?"

Adam turned to face her.

"I don't think we are alone in these woods." Her gaze moved to the animal still standing in front of her. "He pushed us into that small cave and then I heard some men. They weren't real close but the dog didn't like it. When I sat down and cuddled the baby, he positioned himself in front of the mouth of the cave." Her pretty blue eyes searched his before she warned, "Be careful."

After half an hour, Adam spotted wagon tracks. He'd been thinking long and hard about the little girl and her family. It seemed strange the baby had been alone with a dog. The moment he'd seen the child his thoughts had turned to another wagon train that was at least a month ahead of theirs.

He knelt closer to the ground and ran his fingers through wagon wheel ruts. They were several days old and headed toward a denser thicket of trees. He tied

Shadow to a nearby tree, cradled his rifle in his arms and on silent feet made his way deeper into the thicket.

His scouting and tracking skills fell into place as he slipped around battered bushes and branches. From the boot marks, he could tell that the wagon had been tracked before. Adam counted three sets of boot prints following the ruts, much like he was doing now, only these people were more careless and had broken lower branches from the trees.

A few more feet and he saw the wagon tipped over, its contents scattered about the campsite. He remained in the trees searching the area for signs of danger. A low moan drew his attention and he slipped through the woods to the other side of the camp.

It didn't take long to spot the man and woman on the ground, their clothes soaked with blood. A glance informed him that the man was dead. Adam passed him and fell to his knees by the woman. Her tear-soaked, pale face spoke of her own impending death.

"What happened?" Adam asked.

"My baby?" she whispered between shuddering breaths.

"We found her. She's safe."

The air caught in her throat as she rasped, "And Brutus?"

Adam assumed Brutus was the big dog that had protected the child. "He is safe, too. Brutus kept her safe until they were found." He paused then asked, "How are you? And why are you here alone?"

A new tear trickled down her cheek. "My husband… sick. Train…left us." He patted her shoulder as she took another shuddering breath to say, "Here two weeks and then…they came. They killed him."

"You're safe now." He reached for a blanket that lay close by and tucked it under her head.

She shook her head. "I'm dying, too."

Adam knew her words were true. She'd lost a lot of blood. He brushed hair from her eyes.

"My baby…" Her words caught in her throat. "Lilly May James. Fifteen months old." More tears streamed from her eyes. "We have no family. Please, I need to know…you will take care of her…raise her." Her hand reached up and grabbed his wrist. "Promise me."

Adam patted her hand with his free one. "She'll be taken care of. I can assure you that."

Her grip tightened and her green eyes blazed into his. A mother's strength shone through them as she said, "Promise you will raise her."

How could he make such a promise? He wasn't even married. His mother was too old to raise another child and Adam had no intention of marrying anyone. Finding his fiancée in the arms of his brother when she'd talked of love and marriage to him had left Adam cynical regarding the faithfulness of a woman.

The baby's mother pulled hard on his wrist, bringing him closer to her. A look of determination filled her ever paling face. "I can't let go until you give me your word you will take care of Lilly May."

Adam gently freed his wrist and eased her to the ground. "I'm not married. I can't raise her." His insides trembled as the woman sobbed. "But I promise I will find her a good family. A loving family."

"Thank you." She struggled to breathe. "Take her

things. She loved listening to her pa read. Will you… read to her?"

He nodded and found himself making promises as the woman drifted away. "I'll take care of everything. Are you sure there is no one I can take her to?"

Her eyes drifted closed, and she exhaled the words, "Brutus will help. Tell Lilly May…how much we love her."

Even though he knew she'd taken her last breath, Adam answered her. "I'll make sure Lilly May knows she is loved."

Adam swallowed hard, stood and looked about. Blankets and clothing were tossed around the campsite as if someone had found no real use for them. Food storages had been rummaged through. He doubted anything of value had been left behind. Either the oxen had been taken or had run away during the attack. Adam felt that they were probably with the bandits, either to be sold or eaten.

A large chest had been turned upside down. Adam didn't know why but he walked to it and turned it right side up. Clothes and a small book with an elastic strap spilled from the chest. He picked up the book and opened it. Each page was dated and in very fine print. Adam read a few lines that told of one of the many days the family had traveled on the trail. He slipped the book inside his shirt and collected the baby's things. Then his gaze returned to Lilly May's parents. He'd give them a proper burial and then return to Maggie Porter and the child.

Two hours later, he made his way back to the cave where he'd left them. The sun had long sunk over the horizon. A full moon lit the night, casting shadows but warding off total darkness. A low growl warned him to stop. Adam knew without being told that the dog would protect the little girl with his life. The fact that Lilly May's mother had trusted the dog spoke volumes of Brutus's faithfulness to his ward.

He called the dog. "Brutus, come here, boy."

The big dog slowly ventured out of the cave.

Adam dismounted from the horse and pulled down the carpetbag that contained the baby clothes he'd taken from the campsite. After hobbling Shadow, he turned to the cave where he knew Maggie and the baby were hiding. He stopped just outside the entrance. Adam knelt in front of the big hound, wondering briefly at the breed of the dog. Adam knew he was taking a chance with the animal but if he was to keep his word to Lilly May's mother, he'd have to earn the dog's trust.

"Come, boy." He set the bag to the side and held his arms out to the dog, much like he would a small child.

Brutus tilted his head to the side. He took a tentative step toward Adam.

"Come on, Brutus. We have to learn to trust each other." Adam spoke to the dog like he did his horse. Shadow was his closest friend, and often he depended on the animal's instincts when out scouting. Adam had no doubt that Mr. James and his wife had done the same with this fine animal.

Brutus took several more steps toward Adam.

Adam reached out and touched the dog's head.

He leaned into Adam's hand, then sat down and allowed Adam to rub his head and scratch his ears. A bond slowly began to build between the two.

Lilly May let out a cry. The sound reminded Adam that he needed to get the diapers and clothes to her. Brutus also seemed to remember the girl and hurried back into the cave.

Adam picked up Lilly May's small bag and followed. In the cave, darkness enveloped him. He could make out the shape of Maggie sitting with her back against the far wall. She cuddled the baby.

The dog let him into the small space then lay down between the door and the people inside. It seemed he had decided to protect them all.

Adam frowned. "We need to quiet her down."

Maggie looked up at him. "The men I heard?"

He nodded. "Yes, they attacked her wagon and killed her parents." Adam prayed Lilly May didn't understand his words.

Maggie's gasp reached his ears.

The baby seemed to sense Maggie's fear and cried louder.

Adam knew they had to calm the child down or she would give away their hiding place. It was too dark to take them back to the wagon train now, especially since there were murderers somewhere in the area.

"I think she's hungry," Maggie said as she rocked the crying child.

He nodded, remembering Maggie's berries and the food his mother had packed. "I'll be right back." Adam slipped from the cave to where he'd tied his horse. Lilly May's cries were growing louder. He took the food and a canteen of water from the saddle, then hurried back to the cave.

Brutus growled as he rushed into the cave. He dug

into the bag and discovered his mother had packed four small biscuits, a block of cheese, two apples and a small bag of jerky. Adam pulled out a biscuit and offered it to the dog. "Enjoy, Brutus."

Lilly May sniffled. Maggie shushed and rocked the little girl.

"Give her this." Adam eased down beside Maggie and handed her one of the biscuits.

In the darkness he could hear Maggie offering the child the bread. At first Lilly May rejected the food, with a loud "No!" Adam wasn't sure what Maggie did to get the child to eat the biscuit but soon her crying ended and she began smacking her lips.

Maggie sighed. "Poor baby was just hungry."

Adam grinned. "Her name is Lilly May." He felt the dog's big head drop into his lap. "And this big fella is Brutus." He pulled apart one of the biscuits and put a piece of the cheese inside it. "I'm sure you're hungry, too. Here, take this." He placed the cheese-filled bread in Maggie's outstretched hand.

They ate in silence. Adam rubbed the dog's silky fur.

Maggie's soft voice reached out to him. "Did Lilly May's mother tell you what is to become of her?"

"She has no living relatives now. I'm to find her a good family." Adam had no idea how he was going to do such a thing. He'd talk to his mother when they got back. Maybe she'd know what to do with the baby.

"I'll keep her," Maggie announced.

Adam sighed. Why hadn't he realized Maggie would want to raise the baby? After all, she'd ventured into the woods to save her. "I can't let you have her. I promised her mother I'd find a good family to raise her."

Stubbornness filled the air as Maggie responded. "I'm keeping her."

Adam shook his head. Realizing Maggie probably couldn't see him, he said, "Her mother put her in my care. I'll decide what will become of her."

"*I* found her."

He knew there was no reason to argue about it tonight. Besides, by morning perhaps Maggie would decide that taking care of a child was more work than she'd bargained for.

Silence filled the cave.

Adam wished he could see Maggie's face. Maybe she wasn't serious. He'd heard her tone and knew that was a false hope. Weariness seemed to seep into his bones. He waited to hear her attempts to persuade him that she was the best person to raise Lilly May, but none were forthcoming. He listened and heard Lilly May's and Maggie's breathing had deepened. They were both asleep.

Leaning his head against the rock wall, he sighed. Today he'd promised to take care of Lilly May, find her a good family and let her know her parents loved her. How was he going to fulfill those promises? And what was he going to do about Maggie Porter? It was obvious the woman wanted the child, but she was lacking one necessary thing.

A husband.

Chapter Two

Maggie woke with a start. She glanced about. Beside her Lilly May still slept soundly. Adam stood in the door of the cave with Brutus at his side. He held his finger to his lips.

Her blood pulsed quickly through her veins and her hands began to shake. Oh Lord, had the bandits found them in the night? Maggie's mouth went dry. Would her brother and father come looking for them only to find they'd been murdered like the baby's family?

Adam knelt beside the dog and shushed his low growl. Brutus quieted but the hair stood up on his neck and back.

Maggie held her breath. She tilted her head to hear. Her gaze darted to the sleeping baby. Maggie prayed she wouldn't wake until whatever danger that was out there passed. Relief washed over her when she heard her father's voice calling her name. She said quietly so as not to wake the baby, "It's Pa."

Adam nodded. "So it is." He stepped out of the cave and called, "We're here."

Lilly May woke at the sound of Adam's loud call. She sat up and began to cry. Brutus hurried to her and began licking her face.

Maggie pushed the big dog to the side and scooped up the baby. "It's all right, little one. Adam was calling to my pa."

Lilly May stopped crying and her face lit up. "Pa?"

Maggie realized she'd confused the child. "No, baby, your pa isn't here."

Lilly May's lips trembled.

Maggie pulled her close and hugged her tight. "I'm sorry. I didn't mean to hurt your feelings." She rubbed the baby's back and rocked gently, all the while listening to the voices outside the cave.

As expected, her pa's voice carried over the others. She heard him ask, "Why didn't you return to the wagon after you found her?"

Adam's strong voice was lower and harder to hear.

She gathered up the baby's carpetbag and the flour sack with the remainder of their late-night supper. "Come on, Lilly May, I want to introduce you to your new family." She held Lilly May's hand and walked out to join Adam, her family and Mr. Cannon.

Her pa was protesting something Adam had said. "I don't care. You spent the night with her, so you will marry her. I won't have you dragging the family name through the mud."

What? Marry the wagon train scout? Had her father lost his mind? She shook her head. "Pa, I'm not marrying anyone." Maggie handed Adam the bags then looked to her brother. Martin was often the voice of reason for their father.

She was shocked when he crossed his arms and shook his head. What did he mean, no?

"You'll marry him," her pa insisted.

Adam was no help. He merely tied the bags onto the saddle horn and took a long drink from the water canteen.

The wagon master sighed. "We need to get back to the train. We'll continue this discussion there."

Martin motioned for Maggie to follow him to his horse. She picked up Lilly May and hurried after her brother. He swung into the saddle and extended his arm for her to ride with him. But when she held the baby up to him, he frowned down at her. What was wrong with him?

Adam came up beside her and extended his arms. "I'll take her."

Thinking he was going to hold the baby while she climbed up onto the horse, Maggie handed the little girl to him. She grinned as Lilly May snuggled against his chest. The little girl thrust two fingers into her own mouth and closed her eyes.

But Adam tucked the baby against his chest and walked away.

Maggie watched as he carried the little girl to his horse and swung up in the saddle like he'd done it a million times. She remembered him saying the night before that he'd find Lilly May a good family to take care of her.

She called to him. "Mr. Walker, I can hold her."

He grinned across at her. "I think she's content to stay with me."

As if to confirm his words, Lilly May reached up

with her small hand and caressed his stubbled chin. She looked like she'd been riding with him all her young life. Brutus too sat beside Adam's horse, looking up at him.

Martin patted her hands that were around his waist. "Looks like that's settled." He turned the horse to follow his father and the wagon master.

It was far from settled. When they got to the wagon train, she was taking her baby back. Lilly May had already captured her heart. She wasn't going to give the little girl up, and if Mr. Walker and her pa thought differently, they had another think coming.

But when they returned to the wagon train, her father continued to demand that Adam marry her. He insisted that her reputation had been compromised because of their night in the cave. Never mind that there had been a child and an oversize dog in there with them.

Adam refused to give Lilly May back to her. He insisted he'd promised to find her a good home. And a single woman was not considered a family.

The wagon train families stood about debating what should be done. From the sounds of their voices, Maggie felt that half thought she should have Lilly May and the other half felt Adam should find her a good family like he'd promised.

She stood facing both men. "Pa, you can't force us to get married. I'm a widow, after all, not a dewy-eyed schoolgirl." She turned to face the wagon scout and said, "Mr. Walker, I have more right to take the girl than you do. I found her." Maggie crossed her arms and gave them both a stern look.

Her father looked at her with the same degree of sternness that she was dishing out. "I'm still your pa and you live with me. So yes, I can insist this man do the right thing by you."

Adam shook his head. "You might have found Lilly May, but I promised her mother I'd find a good family for her."

Maggie looked to Adam's mother. "Please tell him."

His mother looked confused. "What do you want me to tell him?"

"That he can't keep Lilly May."

Mrs. Walker sighed. "I'm sorry, Maggie. I quit trying to tell him what to do years ago."

She didn't know where to turn next. No one wanted to help her keep Lilly May. Maybe she should let him try taking care of the child on his own. No, that was a ridiculous thought. As the wagon scout, he couldn't tote the baby around with him.

Maggie looked to the wagon master. "Mr. Cannon, are you going to let him keep Lilly May? If he does, he won't be able to scout for the wagon train," she pointed out.

Jim Cannon looked to Adam. "She's got you there."

Adam looked unfazed. "Ma, will you help me take care of Lilly May until we can find a good family to take her?"

She shook her head. "I'm sorry, son. I'm too old to be chasing a toddler around."

Maggie couldn't control the grin that pulled at her lips. The shock on Adam's face was priceless. What had he expected? That his aging mother would agree to take care of the baby?

Mrs. Walker laid a hand on Adam's arm. "You promised her ma a good family. If you marry Miss Porter, both of you could offer Lilly May a good family."

Maggie and Adam shook their heads.

She didn't know why he was so averse to marrying her, but Maggie knew she'd never marry again. Her last marriage had proven she was unlovable. If her husband had loved her, he'd never have chosen death over life.

"Come with me, daughter."

Maggie allowed her pa to take her elbow and pull her away from the crowd of people who had gathered. When they were standing beside their wagon, he said, "Look, I don't want to seem harsh, but I can't let you ruin this family's name. What would your ma have thought about you staying out all night with a strange man?"

She sighed. "Pa, it was innocent. I found Lilly May, and Mr. Walker found her parents murdered by bandits. By the time he'd buried her family, it was dark. With the threat of those men still out there, we decided it was better to stay concealed in the cave than to be wandering the woods at night with a child."

"Innocent or not, you spent the night alone with a man. You know that when we get to Oregon your brother and I are going to open a small store. We can't have the town folk thinking you are a loose woman. It could ruin the business." He crossed his arms once more and dared her to deny it.

So that was it. Her father was more concerned about his future business than her happiness. Maggie shook her head. "Pa, that's no reason for me to get married."

He placed both hands on her shoulders. "Daughter, you are too young not to want to marry. I have seen in your eyes that you want children, and you've proven it by demanding to keep the little girl. If you marry Mr. Walker, you could have the child and many more."

"Pa, I don't want marriage. I just want to keep Lilly May. Is that too much to ask?" She heard the pleading in her voice but didn't care. She had to reach her pa's soft spot for her.

But he just shook his head. "If you don't marry the man, you don't get the child."

Maggie couldn't believe her father would make such a demand. He knew she'd always wanted to be a mother. That she had prayed for a child before her husband's death. This was her chance to finally have a baby to love. "What? What are you saying?"

"You've already shamed me by spending the night with the man unchaperoned. I won't have you bringing that little girl into our wagon as an unwed mother."

Maggie couldn't believe her ears. Would her pa really refuse to let her and Lilly May travel in his wagon? Tears pricked the backs of her eyes. What was she going to do?

Adam watched as John Porter took Maggie to their wagon. He was very aware of everyone standing about watching as if they had nothing better to do. His gaze moved to the sun overhead. Normally, the wagon train would be heading out about now, after a quick midday meal.

Since his mother refused to help with the care of Lilly May, Adam knew he should be thinking about the different families on the wagon train, and which one might make a good family for Lilly May. It was obvious Mr. Porter expected him to marry Maggie and give the baby a home, but that was out of the question. Women expected love relationships in a marriage, and he had no intention of marrying. No, he'd find a good family for the baby.

Mentally he pictured each family. The Shorts would make a nice family for Lilly May, only they already had six children. Perhaps Mr. and Mrs. White would be interested in taking the little girl into their home. He dismissed them quickly also; they were getting on in years and their children were all above the age of ten. Lilly May deserved to live with children her own age. His mind drifted to the Merriweathers; they were a new family with only two children under the age of five years. But, as his mother pointed out, Mrs. Merriweather looked to be expecting again. Adam dismissed them as possible candidates to raise Lilly May.

His mind continued to examine each family with children on the train and none of them seemed to be suitable to bring up Lilly May. So, while he waited for Maggie's and her father's return, he rocked Lilly May and began to think of the families with no children riding in their wagons. Some were too old, and others were too young. Plus, all knew about Lilly May, and they had not come to ask to adopt her.

Maggie was the only person on the train who truly wanted the child. Maybe she was the perfect mother for the baby. He watched as Maggie talked to her father. He could see the frustration and disbelief on her face as her father confronted her.

In his arms the baby sucked hard on her fingers. In a few moments she began to cry again. First it was a small whimper, but it quickly escalated into a full-blown scream. He didn't know what to do with her. Holding on to her was becoming a challenge and no one, not even his mother, offered to help.

Maggie stomped across the way. She walked around him to where his horse still stood and pulled the last biscuit from the flour bag. Adam watched fascinated as Maggie returned to him and extended the bread to the little girl.

Lilly May took the biscuit and began gnawing on it. "Umm." She smiled around the bread. "Tantu." Lilly May extended her arms out to Maggie.

Reluctantly he released the child to Maggie. "She was hungry." He should have realized that himself, but he hadn't.

"Yes, she was." Unshed tears filled Maggie's blue eyes, but she still managed to smile at the little girl.

His heart softened toward the pretty young woman in front of him. Lilly May needed a woman to raise her and from the looks of things she was content to let Maggie be that woman.

The wagon master spoke up. "Walker, you need to figure out what's going to happen here. We have a wagon train to get to Oregon before the winter snows hit."

The wagon master was a patient man but would make the decision for them soon, if Adam couldn't decide the future of Lilly May. What other excuses could he come up with? None of the other families on the wagon train was suitable for the little girl and from the looks of her Maggie wasn't in the mood to simply give her up. He fought back the desperation that churned in his gut and took a deep breath. He turned to his mother. "Can I talk to you for a minute?" Like Mr. Porter, he really didn't want everyone on the wagon train hearing their conversation. At her nod, he led her back to their wagon.

He removed his hat and ran a hand through his hair in frustration. "If I marry her, it won't be for love."

"Lots of people don't marry for love," she reminded him.

Adam didn't want to marry at all. How could he trust Maggie Porter to be faithful to him? He didn't even know her. He'd thought he knew his fiancée, but he hadn't, and the angst from her betrayal still stung. Glancing over his shoulder, he saw Maggie cuddling the little girl. Much as he tried to deny it, the two seemed to belong together. He turned his attention back to his mother and tried another excuse. "She'd be moving into the wagon with you."

His mother grinned. "I'd welcome the company."

The wagon master called out, "All right, everyone! Break time is over—get these wagons ready to move!" He watched as the crowd began returning to their wagons. He tipped his head at Adam and then turned his horse away.

Mrs. Walker began gathering up their campsite. Josiah finished hitching up the oxen and Adam walked to where Maggie still stood. Tears trickled down her cheeks. He sighed. "Looks like you and I are in between a rock and a hard place."

She nodded.

Could he accept his fate? Was there no way around marrying Maggie Porter? He stalled by talking. "I never meant to ruin your reputation and I never dreamed this little girl would raise so many problems for us all. Lilly May has lost a lot over the last couple of days, and she seems to have taken a shine to you." Again Adam took his hat off and ran his hand through his hair. "I know you don't want to get married and honestly, neither do I."

Maggie continued to watch the little girl eating the bread. When she didn't say anything, Adam sighed. He reached out to her and gently tilted her chin up so that she looked into his eyes.

And that was when he made the decision, a decision he would probably regret in the days to come.

"For the baby's sake and to repair your reputation, I will marry you. But I am not offering love or a husband and wife relationship. Think of it as an arrangement for the child. We get married but not in the biblical sense."

Adam wasn't prepared to hear her bitter laugh. Her words and the hurt she revealed in her eyes stung when she said, "I'm not surprised, Mr. Walker." She summed his proposal up nicely with, "A marriage of convenience is fine by me."

He squared his shoulders at the sorrow that filled the space between them. Still, he pressed on. There was one more thing, something he felt he had to make her understand. "All I ask is that you be faithful to me. Can you do that?"

Maggie's eyes bored into his. "I don't have a choice. Pa no longer wants me in his wagon. So yes, I'll marry you, I'll be faithful and I promise not to fall in love with you or expect you to love me."

The sharpness in her words cut deep. How was it that Maggie sounded as bitter as he felt?

Adam released her chin, suddenly wishing he'd

found a less blunt way to offer her marriage. But he'd done the best he could under the circumstances. "Then I'll go tell your pa and get the preacher to do a quick ceremony." As he walked away, he felt as if the weight of the world had just been placed upon his shoulders.

His anger began to grow toward Mr. Porter. Maggie had said her pa wouldn't let her travel anymore in his wagon. What kind of father would cast his daughter to the side because of a ruined reputation? He approached the wagon and tried to swallow the anger building in him.

Mr. Porter turned to face him, the hard set of his jaw revealing his attitude. "Mr. Walker, I hope you have come to your senses and decided to marry my daughter."

Adam gave a curt nod. "Yes, and she's agreed to marry me."

The old man's face eased right before Adam's eyes. "That's good. Maggie deserves to marry and have children."

It wasn't what Adam expected him to say. He'd thought Mr. Porter hard-hearted and mean-spirited to treat his daughter as he had. Could it be that this father knew what his daughter needed more than she did?

Mr. Porter looked at him. "I've heard good things about you. My Maggie deserves a good man, too. All I ask is that you be patient with her. She's still hurting from the loss of her husband."

Adam didn't know what to think about the way Mr. Porter was talking. He'd been so determined to see her married and now he was giving advice on how she should be treated?

Her pa continued. "If you'd like, I'll keep her things

in our wagon until we get to Oregon. That way your wagon won't be weighed down more."

"I'd appreciate that," Adam answered. "I'm headed to Preacher Brown's wagon now. We'll be married before we head out."

Preacher Brown was a short man with a round belly. He looked up from hitching the oxen and grinned. "How are you today, Adam?"

Adam liked the preacher. He always seemed kind, never judgmental and always had a ready smile. "Busy as always, Preacher. Do you think you can return with me to my wagon really quick and marry me to Miss Porter?"

"I'd heard I might be performing a wedding today. Are you both sure this is what you want to do?" he asked, wiping his hands on his pant leg.

Was he sure? Adam took a deep breath. It wasn't a real wedding. Maggie had said she'd be faithful, and with the marriage, Lilly May would have a good family. "I'm as sure as I'll ever be," was his answer.

"And the bride? How does she feel about this marriage?" The preacher pulled on his dress jacket that his wife handed out the back of the wagon.

Adam grinned. "Well, she agreed to the wedding, so I guess she feels all right with the marriage."

The preacher's wife giggled. "Sounds like you should ask the bride, Preacher."

He patted his wife's hand. "I believe you're right. I'll be back in a few minutes."

Maggie held Lilly May close as the preacher said the words every young woman longed to hear. Words that would bind them forever in marriage. She glanced to her right where Adam stood with his hat in his hands. He was handsome. A younger, more naive Maggie would have been thrilled to marry him. But he wasn't her first husband and this wasn't her first wedding.

The little girl, cuddled against her chest, sucking her thumb, was the reason for this wedding. Lilly May closed her little eyes in contentment.

Maggie repeated the vows with the same dull tone of voice that Adam had used. Theirs wasn't a love match and never would be. Disappointment at the thought brought tears to her eyes. Maggie forced herself to not focus on the wedding but on the babe in her arms.

How long had she dreamed of being a mother? All her life. This wedding would ensure she would be a mother at last. And she intended to be the best mother any little girl could ask for.

"I now pronounce you husband and wife," the preacher intoned as the ceremony ended.

Maggie let out an inaudible sigh. She'd done it. She'd married Adam and provided a home for Lilly May.

But Preacher Brown had some last words. "You may kiss your bride."

She turned to face Adam. He stepped closer and leaned toward her. Was he about to kiss her? His head lowered and he kissed her on the forehead. Then he stepped back. "I have work to do. I'll see you tonight." And then he walked away.

Her cheeks filled with heat as the wedding party stepped away. With a bowed head, Maggie followed her new mother-in-law to the wagon. It wasn't the wedding of her dreams, but it wasn't a love match either.

She was now a mother and that had been the goal. She'd gotten what she wanted—the baby. So why did she feel hollow inside?

A married man. Adam was still amazed and dismayed as he rode away from the wagon train an hour later. The ceremony had been quick, with just the preacher, his wife, Adam's mother and Maggie's brother as witnesses to the marriage. Martin had explained that their pa was busy with the oxen, but he wouldn't miss his sister's wedding for the world. The rest of the wagon train was aware of the wedding, but they'd done as the wagon master had commanded and prepared for the rest of the day's journey.

He had then reported to Cannon all that had happened the previous night. They'd discussed that the bandits who had murdered Lilly May's parents could still be in the area causing both Adam and Cannon to worry about the safety of their passengers. Now Adam scouted ahead of the wagon train, keeping close watch out for the bandits and wild animals.

Indians weren't normally dangerous. Often, they were simply curious about the wagons and wanted to trade with them. If he ran across them today, he'd be sure and warn them of the bandits.

He spent the remainder of the day scouting the land ahead of the train. His gaze moved along the trail. Seeing a new grave off to the right, he rode Shadow over and investigated. Fresh dirt could be seen under the rocks of the small mound. A child's resting place. He sighed with sadness. Shadow stomped his right hoof against the ground, almost as if in agreement with his sorrow.

Adam pressed on and soon noticed several other graves. These too were fresh but were too large to be children. It didn't take much to figure out that these folks were probably from the wagon train ahead of them. He continued searching the trail for any signs of trouble. Seeing none, he began looking for a nice place to camp tonight and tomorrow.

Since the next day was Sunday, he knew the wagon master would halt the train until Monday morning. Sundays gave the ladies a chance to do any wash they might have. He found a good spot with a small creek off to the right. He led Shadow to the water and enjoyed the quiet of the place. "How about a long drink, ole boy? You earned it."

His thoughts turned to Maggie and Lilly May. When he'd left, Maggie had been crawling into the back of the wagon to put Lilly May down for a nap. Maggie had yawned big before disappearing within the wagon. He hoped she could rest, too. It had been a stressful night and day for both her and the child.

While his horse drank his fill, Adam's thoughts went back to the small grave he'd seen earlier. Had the child gotten caught under a wagon wheel and been crushed by the weight of the wagon? That happened a lot on the trails. He made a mental note to remind Maggie to keep Lilly May away from their wagon wheels.

What was life going to be like now that he had a wife and daughter? Would he be worried about them all the time? Not only that but now he had to rethink the house he'd planned to build for his mother and include rooms for his new spouse and child.

Before his fiancée had betrayed him, Adam had worked at the sawmill. He'd learned from the finest men in the country how to build furniture and homes. Building a slightly bigger house for his new family shouldn't be too hard. He sighed at the thought that he had a family.

What had he been thinking agreeing to marry? Would Maggie be able to keep her promise to be faithful? Or would she fall in love with another man and leave him standing in shame once again?

Chapter Three

Maggie woke with a jerk. She hadn't meant to fall asleep while putting Lilly May down for her nap. Whatever must her new mother-in-law think of her? She pulled the flap back and found the older woman walking to the left of the wagon.

"Don't try to get out while the wagon is moving, child. You might slip and fall." She grinned up at Maggie. "I can't raise that baby, so you have to stay healthy."

Maggie leaned against the wooden tailgate. "I'm sorry, Mrs. Walker. I didn't mean to fall asleep, too." Maggie pushed the loose hair from her face.

"Call me Grace. You are now Mrs. Walker too so I think first names are how we should address each other. Don't you agree?" Her warm brown eyes searched Maggie's face.

"Yes, I would like that." She also liked the way Grace reminded her of a woman from church back home in Independence. Her gray hair had been styled on the top of her head in what looked like a loose knot.

"Try to get some rest, Maggie. Lilly May will be awake soon and I'm sure she will be a handful." Grace was joined by another woman her age. Brutus walked beside her. His dark gaze assured her he'd remain close by.

Maggie slipped back inside the wagon and tied the flap closed. The wagon was packed with the mattress Lilly May and she had been resting on in the center. She knew that Adam would probably spend his nights under the wagon. As she lay back down beside the sleeping child, Maggie wondered. Would Pa give her one of the small tents so that she and Lilly May could have their own resting place at night?

She listened to the sounds around her. The wagon bumped and the wheels squished through muddy potholes. Dogs barked and children could be heard playing as they ran or walked beside their wagons. Men yelled out to each other as they moved slowly down the trail.

It felt odd to be married again. Unlike her first wedding this one held no promise of love. She sighed. Oh, she had loved Matthew, but she quickly discovered that his purported dream of a big family and spending a lifetime with her was nothing but a lie. He'd told her what she craved to hear. He'd made her feel special and wanted. Loved.

But she'd quickly learned after the wedding that Matt only loved himself. Her father offered him a job at the store and Matt had declined. He'd wanted to live on his small farm. She hadn't cared if he worked in town with her pa or on the farm. All she'd cared about was being in love and starting a family.

She later learned Matt had married her so that her

father would pay off his small farm. But that hadn't happened. That was when she discovered Matt's true feelings toward her and felt the first sting of betrayal. Matt let it be known that he did not love her or trust her. She'd quickly learned not to trust him either.

Now, sitting in the middle of nowhere, married to a man she hardly knew, she thought back to Adam's only request. It felt strange that Adam had asked her to be faithful to him and seemed to trust that she would do as she'd promised. Would he continue to trust her to keep her promise?

Lilly May woke. She looked about her and then at Maggie. "Mama?"

Maggie gently pulled the little girl into her arms. "I'm sorry, sweetie. Mama isn't here anymore."

The little girl pushed away from Maggie. She stuck her bottom lip out. It trembled and tears began to pool in her eyes.

How long would the little girl grieve for her parents? Trying to distract her, she asked, "Want to get out and walk with the wagon?"

Lilly May nodded as tears streamed down her face.

Maggie gently wiped the tears from the little girl's eyes then turned to the front of the wagon. She pulled the flap open behind the driver's seat. "Can you stop for a moment and let us get out?"

The driver was a young man with a friendly smile. "Yes, ma'am." He pulled the oxen to a stop. "Let me know when you are free of the wagon."

Maggie nodded and hurried to the back of the wagon. She picked up Lilly May, thankful the child wasn't wet after her nap, and pulled the curtain back.

Grace stood there with open arms. "Hand the child down to me."

Once the baby was safely out of the wagon, Maggie scrambled down after her. She knew the men wouldn't be happy that they'd stopped. Next, she hurried to the front of the wagon and called, "We're out."

The driver flicked his wrists and the oxen moved forward again.

Grace cuddled the baby against her chest. "It's been a long time since I've held a baby this close."

Lilly May laid her head on Grace's shoulder and sighed. The tears were no longer streaming down her face. She'd tucked a thumb into her mouth and watched the activity around her.

"She seems content," Maggie commented, looking toward her father's wagon.

Martin was driving the team and her father walked beside the wagon. Maggie hated that her last words to him had been mean-spirited. She sighed. "Grace, do you mind watching Lilly May for a few minutes while I talk to Pa? Or would you rather I take her with me?" Maggie remembered that Adam's mother had refused to keep the baby so she wasn't sure what the older woman's answer would be.

Grace rubbed her cheek across the baby's soft hair. "You go on. We'll be fine together for a few minutes."

Maggie smiled. "Thank you. I won't be long."

At Grace's nod, she hurried to catch up with her pa. When she came even with him, he glanced her way and sighed. "I'm sorry I couldn't attend your wedding."

Maggie said what she knew he wanted to hear. "That's all right, Pa. It was a simple ceremony." Though he'd insisted on the wedding, was he regretting that decision? Did it even matter now?

His Adam's apple bobbed as if he were swallowing hard. "I did it for your own good."

She loved her father and knew his disappointment in her ran deep. She'd insisted on marrying Matt even though her father and Martin had disapproved of her choice in husband. Perhaps to his way of thinking, her pa really had done the right thing by insisting she marry Adam. Adam was a good man and Maggie already knew from her brother and father's past conversations that her pa respected her new husband. "I know."

Maggie loved her father and brother. Disappointing them had never been her intention. Was she hiding her true feelings from them? Probably. Men didn't understand what was in a woman's heart. Still, like other women, she was expected to do as her father and husband told her to do, even if it wasn't fair.

They walked in silence for a few moments more before he said, "I told Adam that you can leave your things in our wagon until we get to Oregon."

"All right. But I'll still need to get my clothes and I was hoping I could use one of my tents." She held her breath as she waited for his answer.

He stopped walking and turned to face her. "Of course you can use the tent. I'm not heartless." His eyes seemed full of remorse.

"No, sir, you are not." She met his gaze and hoped he could see that she wasn't angry at him. A little hurt, yes, but not enough to withhold forgiveness for his harshness of earlier.

He nodded. "Is there anything else you need?"

She shook her head. "No, I don't think so." Maggie wanted to talk to Grace about their food supplies before she asked her pa for her share from his wagon, but for now the tent was enough.

He seemed to know what she was thinking and said, "Tonight I'll divide up the food stores and you can add them to your wagon."

Maggie impulsively hugged him around the waist like she'd done as a child. "Thank you, Pa."

John Porter hugged his daughter close then gently patted her back. "I only want you happy," he said against her head.

Lilly May chose that moment to start crying. Maggie pulled away from her father and smiled. "I know, Pa." Then she hurried back to help Grace with the baby.

Later that evening, Adam rode into the camp, his shoulders heavy. He eased out of the saddle and entered the wagon master's camp.

Cook greeted him. "Good evening, Adam. Would you like a cup of coffee?"

Adam stopped well away from him. "No thanks."

"You're back kind of late. Thanks for leaving us a marker to know where to camp," Jim Cannon said. "Have any trouble?"

The arrow made from rocks had been the two men's sign for "camp here" since he'd started scouting for Cannon over two years earlier. But normally he returned to the wagon train and rode beside the wagon master instead of leaving signs. He nodded. "Yes and no."

"Well, which is it?" Cannon came to his feet but stopped his approach when Adam held up his hand.

"Don't come any closer until I tell you what I need to say." Adam didn't know what his friend would say or do when he heard his news. But he knew the wagon master could be in danger if he came closer.

Cannon sat back down. "Then out with it."

Cook came to stand beside the wagon master.

Adam twisted his horse's reins in his leather-gloved hand. "Everything looks good for Monday's journey—that's the good news."

Cannon nodded. "Sounds like what we expected. What's the bad news?"

"Remember that wagon train ahead of us?" He waited for Cannon to nod. "Well, I found several new graves on the trail and decided to see if I could catch up to them."

"Did you?"

"Afraid so. They had stopped some time ago. They're sick. And the people are dying." He twisted the reins tighter.

"That's not the worst, is it?" Weariness lined the wagon master's craggy face. He took his hat off and laid it against his knee.

Adam sighed. "No, sir, it isn't. Lilly May's parents were from that wagon train. The wagon master, Ben, told me that he had separated them thinking it would save the train but unfortunately it did not. Diphtheria has spread through their wagons, and they have pulled far from the trail to separate themselves from other trains."

"Son, how close to the wagon master did you get?"

"He stopped me from getting too close. But I buried Lilly May's parents and brought the child back with me."

When he'd heard the news, Adam had wanted to

kick himself. The little girl's mother said her husband was sick and they'd had to pull away from the wagon train. He'd assumed it was just a regular sickness and he had focused on the bandits who had killed them. Now he'd contaminated the wagon train, including his elderly mother.

"Is the little girl sick?" Cannon asked.

Adam shook his head. "I don't know. I came straight to you so I have no idea if she is ill or not. She wasn't when I left at noon."

Cannon stood. "Well, sometimes these things hit fast. She might be sick by now. Thankfully you moved your wagon to the rear of the train, so none of the other wagons have been too close. Circle around the camp back to your wagon. Don't stop and talk to anyone. We need to find out if that baby is sick. I'll meet you there."

He pulled on Shadow's reins and did as the wagon master ordered. Cannon headed through the wagon train. Adam watched him check on each wagon he passed.

His mother and Maggie were sitting side by side, their heads bent low over their sewing when he reached his campsite. His gaze moved about the camp, but he saw no sign of Lilly May. He did see a tent set up at the edge of the wagon. Perhaps the baby was in there or inside the wagon.

"We saved you a plate, son," Grace said, turning her gaze back to the fabric in her lap.

He tied Shadow to the side of the wagon and walked toward the firepit. Maggie put her sewing aside and picked up the dinner plate. "I hope you like beans and cornbread."

He nodded and took the food. "Thank you. Where is the baby?"

"She's sleeping in the tent. I asked Pa for it so that we wouldn't be a burden on your mother during the nights." Maggie turned back to the fire and pulled the coffeepot from its edge. She poured hot coffee into a tin cup.

Worry ate at Adam. "How long ago?"

Maggie frowned as she handed him the cup. "About an hour. Why? Is something wrong?"

Grace looked up at them. When he didn't answer, she said one word. "Son?"

"I'm not sure." His gaze darted between the two women. "I found Lilly May's parents' wagon train ahead of us." He took a deep breath and then blurted, "They are all sick. With diphtheria."

Maggie gasped and her hand went to her mouth. "Oh, no, you don't think the baby is sick, do you?"

Brutus stood and stretched. He padded over to Adam and Maggie.

"I hope not." He squatted, set the tin cup down and patted the dog's head. "Please, go check and see if she is running a fever."

His mother's gaze met his as Maggie hurried to the tent and slipped inside. "We've all been exposed, haven't we?" she asked.

Adam swallowed and nodded.

Cannon stopped at the edge of their camp. "Is the babe sick?"

He stood again. "Maggie is checking now." His gaze moved to the tent flap where his new wife had disappeared.

The wagon master cleared his throat. "I've been

thinking. Since you have been exposed, I need to move your wagon away from us, and that also means I'll have to get one of the other men to scout for us for at least fourteen days. If you and your family don't show signs of illness, you can come back to the wagon train."

Brutus growled deep in his throat.

Adam's gaze followed the dog's. Maggie's father and brother stepped from the shadows. Her father spoke. "I figured something was up when you passed our wagon," he offered in way of explaining why they'd followed the wagon master. "We'll move off with them. My son and I have been with the baby. If she was exposed, then so were we."

Josiah had been eating in the shadow of the wagon. He stepped forward. "I'll be staying with them too, sir."

Cannon nodded. "Agreed, and I'll ask the preacher and his wife to join you." He looked to Adam. "Did you talk to anyone else?"

Adam shook his head, thankful that he hadn't had time before heading out to scout.

Maggie came from the tent. "She's not sick. Her fore head was cool to the touch."

"Thank the good Lord." Grace released air from her lungs as if she'd been holding it for a long time.

"Aside from the Browns, is there anyone else you all have come into contact with since Lilly May has joined our train?" Cannon asked, looking from one person to the next.

Each of them shook their heads and muttered, "No."

"Good. Adam, I want the wagons to stay at least twelve feet from ours. Stay even with us but don't get close." He stopped and pointed to the right of the train.

"I'll ask the preacher to follow your wagon, and Mr. Porter, you and your son can close up the small train."

Adam nodded. "We'll do it now."

"I'll let folks know what is going on," Cannon told them.

Mr. Porter and Martin were already returning to their wagon, while Grace and Maggie were breaking camp. He looked at the plate in his hands and sighed.

Adam ate fast and gave his plate and cup to Maggie. He turned to help Josiah hitch up the oxen.

She laid her hand on his arm as he turned to go. "I am sorry." Tears watered her eyes.

He waited for them to fall but they didn't. He patted her hand. "You aren't to blame for this."

Maggie dropped her hold on him and turned away. How could he say that? If she hadn't gone looking for the baby, none of this would be happening. She felt a warm tear slide down her cheek. Thankfully, Adam had gone and couldn't see her crying.

Once the wagon was packed and ready to move, Maggie walked toward the tent. She dreaded waking the sleeping baby. She pulled the flap back.

"Maggie, you don't have to wake her," Grace whispered from behind her. "I can hold her while you break down the tent and then as soon as we are settled again, we can put her back down." A smile touched Grace's tired face. "If we're blessed she'll sleep through the whole move."

"Thank you, Grace." Maggie couldn't stop herself from apologizing again. "I am so sorry. I've caused all this trouble."

"Nonsense, child. If you hadn't found that sweet baby, she'd probably be dead by now. You did the right thing." Grace hugged her about the shoulders.

As soon as the older woman released her, Maggie hurried inside the tent to hide the tears that threatened to flow again.

As she emptied the tent and began to break it down, she thought about the bandits. Were they still out there? Would they attack the three lone wagons? She looked at the expanse between them and the others. What kind of danger would they be in separated from the main train?

Instead of looking at the negatives, Maggie told herself to focus on the positive. Ma had always said, "Maggie, if you look to the good instead of the bad in any situation, you will find that things aren't as bad as they seem." The first positive was that no one was showing signs of sickness. The second was that instead of being alone with Adam and his mother, there were three other men to help protect them. And lastly, they had Brutus to help guard them at night. The faithful dog now trotted beside Grace as she carried a sleeping Lilly May.

Maggie returned to folding up her tent but she couldn't stop the thoughts from entering her mind. This was her wedding night. But it was nothing like her first wedding night. That night had been a celebration of love and trust. At least she'd thought so at the time. But a week into the marriage Matt had begun going to town and not returning until the wee hours of the morning and often the next day. He'd become withdrawn and sour. Over the next three weeks, she'd begun to wish he'd open up and tell her where he was going; Maggie had suspected the local saloon but hadn't wanted to think that her husband was seeing those women. He'd never come home drunk or smelling of cheap perfume. No, he'd smelled of cigar smoke and had bloodshot eyes.

Once when Martin visited, Maggie had asked if he knew where Matt had gone, but her brother only told her to ask her husband. So she had.

Matt had claimed to be visiting his parents in town, but Maggie couldn't bring herself to believe him. She'd hoped to stop him from going one afternoon but when she'd gone to the barn to intercept him before he left, she found Matt hanging from the rafters. He'd chosen to take his life, something she would never forget.

After the funeral, Maggie had gone to the bank to see how much she still owed on her small farm. She'd hoped to live there and not have to move back home with her father and brother. Only the banker told her that she no longer owned the small cabin or the land. Matt had lost it in a poker game the night before he'd hanged himself. If only he'd have talked to her, told her of his gambling problems, maybe they could have saved the farm and his life.

With her tail tucked between her legs, Maggie had returned to her father's house, and they had started their new journey from Missouri to Oregon. Her pa had told her she could find a new husband and a new life there.

Shaking off the troubling memories, she trudged toward the three isolated wagons. Would her life ever be like other women's? Would she and Adam create a home for Lilly May that looked like a real family to those around them? Maggie sighed. She'd be the best ma to Lilly May and keep her promise of faithfulness to Adam, but other than that, she didn't see how she would ever be good enough for him to confide in or fall in love with.

Chapter Four

Maggie was thankful when Adam met her halfway and took the tent from her arms. It wasn't that the tent was that heavy but with the blankets and Lilly May's bag she'd been afraid she might drop something on the damp ground. "Thank you." She adjusted the blankets, then hurried to catch up with him.

"My pleasure. I'll set the tent up if you want to help Ma with the baby."

He offered her a lopsided grin. The look sent an appreciation through Maggie of just how handsome her new husband could be. She pressed the awareness down and focused on the fact that he was walking slowly so that she wouldn't have to rush to keep up with him.

Did he know just how tired she was feeling? "I'd like it close to the wagon but not close enough that the baby will keep everyone awake if she can't sleep." Maggie wouldn't admit that she craved privacy for herself, but she did. A lot had happened in the last twenty-four hours, and she needed privacy to process it all.

"I'll set it up on the side of the wagon. I've already cleared the spot of stones." He continued, "As soon as you get the baby down again, we're going to have a quick meeting."

Maggie nodded. She saw Grace standing behind the wagon holding the sleeping baby. The older woman looked as tired as Maggie felt. "I best go relieve your mother."

As Adam walked to the spot he'd chosen, Maggie admitted she was looking forward to sleeping in that tent tonight. The days seemed to be getting longer and the nights shorter.

When she came even with Grace, Maggie apologized. "I'm sorry it took me so long to get the tent down." She laid the blankets and bag on the tailgate of the wagon and reached for Lilly May.

Grace smiled. "You didn't take any longer than need be, and the baby was no trouble at all." She laid Lilly May in Maggie's waiting arms.

"Thank you." Maggie looked down into the baby's sweet face. Moments earlier she'd been feeling guilty for all the trouble her finding the child had caused, but looking into Lilly May's sleeping face, all regret was quickly replaced with warmth and love.

"I've been thinking. We can make the baby a bed from one of my dresser drawers and that way you can have your own space in the tent, too. If you want to, I'm sure we can get something set up tonight." Grace touched the baby's cheek.

Maggie met her gaze. "Are you sure it will be no trouble?"

"I'm sure. Babies are a lot of work and at the end of

the day, you are going to need your own space to sleep. And not having to worry about rolling over on her in the night will help you sleep better."

Once more Maggie found herself thanking Grace. "I hadn't thought about that," she admitted. There were a lot of things about raising a child that Maggie realized she didn't know. Unlike other young mothers she hadn't had nine months to plan for her baby. Doubts began to plague her tired mind.

Grace patted her arm. "Don't you fret. There are a lot of things that you will think of and it will all come naturally for you. And if you ever want or need help, you have me now and I'm more than happy to be a grandmother to this sweet girl."

"The tent is up." Adam walked over and touched the baby's forehead. "Good. She's not running a temperature." Relief seemed to fill his eyes.

"No, she's just tired," Maggie assured him.

"Son, will you get the bottom drawer out of the wagon? I emptied it but didn't think I should try to climb down with it." She told him her plan. "It's right in the back of the wagon there."

He turned to grab the drawer. "Ma, I would never have thought of that." Adam smiled at his mother.

Grace gave Maggie a look that said, "See, you aren't the only one who didn't think of a drawer as a bed," then quickly picked up the blankets and bag. "Come. It won't take us but a few minutes to get her settled."

Maggie nodded. She walked to the tent with Brutus, Grace and Adam on her heels. True to his word, Adam had set the tent about four feet from the wagon. He'd faced the opening flap toward the wagon. She could see that he'd hung a lantern inside for her to see by.

Adam stepped around her and pulled the flap open. "Let me put the drawer inside and then I'll take Lilly May."

Within seconds he was back and extending his arms for the baby. Maggie carefully handed her to him and then turned to Grace for the blankets and bag. Adam carried the baby to where the other men were waiting by the coffeepot. The fire would keep the child warm until she was back under her blanket.

"We'll wait for you by the fire," Grace offered. "I've been told we are having a meeting in a few minutes." She grinned at Maggie and rolled her eyes as if to say she thought the meeting could wait until morning.

Maggie giggled. "I've been told the same thing."

Grace laughed and then followed her son. "I'll save a spot for you," she called over her shoulder.

Maggie crawled into the tent. It wasn't very big but would be sufficient for her and Lilly May's needs. She glanced up at the kerosene lantern that hung from the center of the tent. Adam had thought of her needs before she had. Maybe being married to him wouldn't be so bad after all, she thought tiredly.

Knowing the others were waiting, Maggie made the baby's bed first and then her own. She placed Lilly May's bag at the foot of the drawer and then sat back on her heels. Her own things would take up a small amount of space, but she felt she would be comfortable enough.

She pushed the flap open once more and found Adam waiting for her.

"Will you have enough room in there?" he whispered.

Maggie smiled. "We will be comfortable. Thank you for the lantern."

He handed her the baby. "You're welcome." He grinned and then turned to join the others.

Maggie laid Lilly May down gently. The baby whimpered in her sleep. Her little fingers went into her mouth and that seemed to give her some comfort. Maggie's heart went out to the baby. How confusing it must be for the little lamb. She'd lost her parents and the security of her family. Maggie knew she and Adam would become her protectors, but Lilly May would have to learn to trust them to provide what she needed.

She whispered softly as she patted Lilly May's back. "I'll not let you forget your true parents, little one. I pray in time you will learn that I love you as if you were my own flesh and blood."

As Maggie quietly exited the tent, she found Brutus standing beside the flap. His dark eyes met hers. Maggie bent down and rubbed his head. "Watch over her, sweet boy—I'll be back in a few minutes."

As if he understood, the dog moved in front of the entry and lay down. He raised his head and looked up at her once more.

"Good boy." Maggie smiled and gave him one last rub behind the ears before she went to join the others.

"How's she doing?" Adam asked as she entered their circle.

"She's sleeping and cool to the touch. I don't think she is sick." Maggie stood beside her new mother-in-law.

The older woman reached up and took her hand. "That's good." She gave it a gentle squeeze and then returned her hands to her lap.

Maggie could hear the music and laughter coming from the wagon train and she imagined they all were wishing they were with the other group, especially Josiah. In the past, she'd noticed he and Penelope White were the first ones on the dance floor every time the fiddler picked up his instrument and began playing.

Adam cleared his throat to get everyone's attention. "Well, it looks like we are going to be keeping our own company for the next two weeks."

Everyone nodded.

He continued, "We'll need to create a system like the big train. Since we have five men here, two of us can split the night watchman job each night and that way, we will all get a few nights of sleep and keep our animals safe. Is that agreeable with you, gentlemen?" Adam waited for each man to nod his head in agreement.

Maggie's gaze moved to Brutus. His head rested on his paws and his ears were up. As long as the dog remained calm, she felt confident that Lilly May still slept.

Adam's voice drew her gaze from the tent. "Ladies, I'm going to ask you not to go to the river alone. You need to go in pairs or as a small group. Lilly May's parents fell prey to bandits, and we don't know if they are still out there. You will be safer in numbers."

The preacher spoke up. "Maybe one of us men should accompany the ladies."

Adam nodded. "If it's possible, I don't see why not."

Adam's mother joined the conversation. "I've been thinking we should become meal companions and share our cooking fire. Soon enough we'll be scrounging for fuel. Mrs. Brown, would you and the good preacher like to combine your food with ours and have meals together? That way we can cook, eat and clean up all at the same time."

The preacher's wife smiled. "That would work wonderfully for us. And please call me Betty."

Grace smiled her agreement and then turned her attention to Maggie's father and brother. "We can cook your meals, too."

"That's mighty kind of you, ma'am, but..." He stopped and looked at Maggie for help.

Maggie touched Grace's arm to get her attention. "That's sweet of you to offer, Grace. Pa and I discussed this earlier, and I have already agreed that he and my brother should have the meals with us for the remainder of the trip. I'll be happy to get their food supplies together, also."

The older woman smiled. "Good, we're a family now so I think this is going to work out perfectly." She turned her smile on Maggie's father, whose blush deepened.

Preacher Brown chuckled. "Now that we've got that settled, I'd like to talk about our spiritual wellness." Once all eyes turned to him he continued. "I'd like to have Sunday services tomorrow and maybe a nightly devotion, if we can."

Everyone nodded their approval.

For the first time, Maggie noticed the small pile of books beside the preacher. She watched as he picked one of them up. "I hope you don't think me forward, but I thought perhaps you might all like a new Bible." Before they could say anything, he pressed on. "Betty and I packed a case before we left and we'd like for you to have them."

Adam walked to him and took the one the preacher held out. "I would love one, thank you."

Mrs. Brown quickly handed Grace and Maggie one each as well until everyone in their party held a Bible. Maggie took the Bible with joy. Her father had assured her there was no room for extra books in the wagon and had insisted they only carry one Bible on the journey, his. Now she had one for herself and could read it as they traveled. She'd always enjoyed reading and memorizing God's word.

Adam stood. "Is there any other business we need to conduct tonight?"

Each person looked to the others, but no one spoke up.

Maggie fought a yawn that threatened to overcome her face.

Grace caught sight of it. "Son, if the ladies are no longer needed, we'd like to retire."

He nodded. "Gentlemen, we need to discuss guard duty and who and when we will be standing guard."

Maggie turned to leave. She was tired and ready for a good night's sleep. Her day had started with her being alone and feeling at a loss for her life. Now she had a new husband and mother-in-law, and best of all, a child to love.

Chapter Five

Adam sat astride his horse and watched the sun rise over the horizon. For the first time in over a month, he did not find himself preparing for a day of scouting. He yawned and rolled the tension from his tight shoulders. He'd had the first night's watch and when Preacher Brown came to relieve him, Adam had offered to take the second watch, too.

The good preacher had simply shrugged and returned to his wagon and nice warm bed.

Adam's mind hadn't been able to relax. Thoughts of the previous day continued to race through his brain like a rabbit running from the wolf.

Adam's life had changed the day before. He'd gone from being just a son to being a husband and new father. The night had been filled with plans for the future. They swirled through his mind, begging to be constructed into reality. But now he had Maggie to consider and what she wanted out of life.

His father once told him when he was a growing boy

and had taken an interest in girls, "Son, treat the women in your life like gold. They keep families running and when they are bone-tired, they continue to work to make our lives easier. God made them to be helpmates to man, but we got the better of the deal. You earn a woman's respect and love, and you will be set for life."

He hadn't thought of his father's words in years. Adam knew they were true, right up there with his father's other words. "You respect your mama and when the time comes and I'm no longer around, it's up to you to take care of her in her old age."

Adam missed his pa and his great advice. Movement from the main wagon drew his attention from those thoughts.

His gaze followed Wilbur Smith, the replacement scout for the larger wagon train, as he headed out. Like him, Wilbur went scouting on Sundays. Not necessarily to scout out the land before them but to make sure that they were still safe from nature and humans. Adam knew that Cannon would be on the alert for bandits and had asked Wilbur to search for signs of them.

Once more, movement caught Adam's attention. Brutus sat a few yards away from his wagon. The dog had something between his paws and was eating. Curious what the big dog had caught, Adam rode toward him. When he was a few feet away, he saw that Brutus had hunted down a rabbit for breakfast. Adam thanked the Lord that they wouldn't be solely responsible for Brutus's meals. Being as large as he was, Adam had feared the dog might turn to skin and bones.

Brutus looked up and tilted his head as if asking Adam if he was needed.

"Go ahead and enjoy your breakfast, ole boy. Everything is fine." Adam guided Shadow back to camp.

Maggie stood beside the fire, cooking. Lilly May sat a few feet away banging a spoon against one of their tin cups. Even as he ate, Brutus watched over them. Adam grinned. At first, he'd thought the dog would be a hindrance but now realized that the animal was another form of protection, one that he appreciated.

She looked over at him and smiled. "Good morning." Maggie turned to stir something in the cast-iron pot.

"Good morning. What's for breakfast?"

His mother answered as she came around the back of their wagon. "Oatmeal, bacon and biscuits."

Preacher Brown looked up from the Bible he'd been reading. "Sounds like a meal fit for a king."

His wife laughed. "You say that now, but they put me in charge of the biscuits."

"Then they are in for a real treat." The preacher smiled up at her and winked.

She playfully slapped at his arm and giggled.

Adam wondered if he and Maggie would ever be that comfortable with each other. "Do I have time to go put Shadow away? Or should I wait and eat it hot?"

"You have time," Maggie answered. "Would you mind stopping by my pa's wagon and telling him and Martin breakfast is about ready?"

"Will do." Adam rode to the back of their small wagon train and slid from the saddle. The men had created a rope corral for the horses and oxen. The Browns also had a wire pen for the six hens and a rooster that they'd brought along. He wondered how long the fowl would last on the trail. So far, they had survived.

Martin stood in front of one of the oxen. He had a piece of cloth and was gently resting it across the animal's nose. His gentle voice spoke against the beast's ear.

Adam pulled his horse into the corral. "Good morning."

"Morning." Martin took the cloth from the oxen's face.

Adam tied Shadow's reins to a low tree branch and began to unsaddle the horse. "I noticed the other day that you tied a cloth over your animals' noses. Is that to keep the dirt out of their nostrils?"

Martin nodded. He handed Adam a brush. "It was Maggie's idea. At the beginning of our travels, she noticed that a lot of dust gets kicked up into their faces as we follow the trail and the wagons ahead of us. She felt sorry for the animals and said that a damp cloth over their noses would cool them and keep the dirt from entering their noses and lungs."

Adam marveled at his new wife's compassion for the beasts. Normally the travelers didn't realize the importance of keeping their animals healthy until later in their journey. Adam returned to his brushing and replied, "I reckon she's right. We'll see about doing the same for our animals."

Martin grinned. "I think you will find that Maggie is very compassionate and smart."

"I've no doubt that you are right." Adam finished brushing Shadow's sleek black coat. He looked about the corral and made sure that the ropes were secure between the trees and other items they'd placed to keep the animals safe. "Maggie said to let you and your pa know that breakfast is ready."

"I'll let Pa know. He went down the river a smidge to wash out a couple of shirts." Martin started to leave but turned and faced Adam. "My sister has been through a lot in the last year, so please be patient with her. She's a good woman and will make an excellent wife, in time."

Adam nodded. Only time would tell if Martin was correct in his assumption.

Martin turned to the river. "Tell her we'll be right there." And then he hurried off to find his pa.

Adam walked back to his wagon. He pondered Martin's words. What had his young wife been through? It was common knowledge that she was a widow, she liked to keep to herself and she was a generous person. Many times, she'd shared the greens and berries she'd found along the trail, but he didn't know her personally. Perhaps he could make use of the extra time they would have until he went back to scouting for the wagon train.

Preacher Brown and his wife, Betty, were sitting together on a piano bench beside the fire. Betty, a middle-aged woman with brown hair sprinkled with gray stands and pretty blue eyes, was saying a morning prayer.

Grace had found a box that she'd placed across from the Browns to use as a table. Lilly May and Brutus sat in the dirt at his mother's feet. Maggie handed out plates with a smile on her lips.

When she saw him, Maggie frowned. "Where's Pa and Martin?"

Adam missed the sweet smile she'd been sharing with the others. "They will be here in a few minutes."

Her family arrived just as she handed Adam a tin plate with oatmeal, bacon and a plump biscuit. "About time you two showed up," she scolded.

Her father chuckled. "Always on time, never late, daughter." He took his plate and placed a kiss on her cheek. "Thank you."

Once they were all seated and Maggie had gathered up Lilly May to feed her, the preacher said a quick blessing over the food.

Adam ate and watched as the others enjoyed their breakfast. He noted that the women talked quietly together and Lilly May ate like a newborn bird. The little girl smacked her lips and grinned up at Maggie as she swallowed the oatmeal. Once she'd finished that, Maggie gave the little girl a piece of buttered biscuit. Maggie wasn't eating. He looked about and saw a lone plate by the pot of oatmeal waiting to be filled. His new wife had put her needs aside to take care of the baby.

He hurriedly wolfed down his food and then returned to the firepit. Picking up the clean plate, he filled it and then returned to Maggie and their daughter. "Here, let me take care of her and you eat."

Maggie looked up at him. Her eyes grew large with surprise. The ladies stopped talking, and the men looked at him as if he'd grown two heads.

Had he said the words too harshly? That hadn't been his intention. He extended the plate to her.

A light blush filled her cheeks as she smiled and handed him Lilly May's plate and then took hers. "Thank you."

Her soft smile and warm voice made him happy that he'd taken the time to think of her needs. They hadn't been together for long but he couldn't help wondering why her gratitude affected him so deeply at this moment. Maybe he was just tired and imagining feelings that weren't really there.

Adam scooped up Lilly May and carried her to where he'd been sitting by the Browns. The little girl grinned up at him. Her chubby little hand clutched the bread tightly as butter ran between her fingers.

A soft thump drew his attention to Brutus, who had followed close at his heels and dropped to a resting position on the ground by Adam's feet.

He chanced a glance in Maggie's direction. She and the other ladies were speaking quietly. Just as he was about to look away, Maggie's gaze met his. Her beautiful blue eyes shone across at him. Adam swallowed the sudden lump in his throat.

Maggie enjoyed getting to know the other two ladies better during the early morning hours. Both were older than her. She had yielded to their wisdom as they talked about ways to make camping easier on all of them. Since there were three meals a day to plan for, each woman agreed to take turns cooking the larger part of the meals; the other two would prepare camp by setting up and breaking down, getting water, starting the fire and doing dishes just to name a few things. They all agreed that for now this was a good way to share the chores.

Grace had reminded them that some days lunch would be cold biscuits from breakfast with a slice of meat in them. She'd also told them that if they needed to change chores that it would be fine. The fact that she continued to call them family made Maggie want to prove to her mother-in-law that she would make a fine wife for Adam and a big help to her.

Maggie had insisted that the tent was her responsibility, even though the other two ladies offered to set it up or take it down, depending on which meal of the day that Maggie would be cooking. Maggie was grateful for their help with Lilly May but didn't want to burden them with an additional chore.

Betty had expressed her desire to help care for the child, saying she missed her grown children and the one grandchild her daughter had supplied her. Grace beamed happily at Lilly May and told Maggie that Lilly May was her first grandchild and she planned to spoil her rotten. Maggie agreed to take all the help she could get. It was wonderful that Lilly May would feel so loved after losing her parents.

With breakfast over, Maggie looked about their camp. "What can I help with now?"

"If you don't mind going to the stream and getting a fresh bucket of water, that would be nice. I'll take care of the baby while you are gone." Grace placed the newly washed dishes into the rear of the wagon.

"I can fill the barrel and then we won't have to worry about water until tonight." Maggie moved toward the large rain barrel that sat on the side of the wagon. She hated to admit that the only reason for offering to fill the big barrel was that it would take a little longer than filling the bucket. And would give her a few moments to wash the grime from her face and arms.

Grace stopped her with the words, "No, don't worry about the barrel right now. Just a bucket will do. Adam can fill the barrel later."

Disappointment hit Maggie harder than she'd anticipated it would. She nodded.

"I can do it now," Adam volunteered as he came around the back of the wagon.

"It's all right, Adam. Grace just asked for the bucket—I wasn't thinking."

"Nonsense." He picked up the barrel and came to her side with a grin. "But if you want to fill the bucket too, I'm not stopping you."

"That's a good idea, since we used most of the bucket water to wash the breakfast dishes." Maggie scooped up the empty pail. New hope of a few minutes away from the noisy wagons filled her.

Adam started walking away. Maggie hurried to catch up with his long strides.

"Besides, Cannon asked me to show you ladies where you can go to at the river. Now is as good a time as any. We have to stay separated from the others and that includes when you fetch water or do laundry." As if he realized she was almost running to keep up with him, Adam slowed his steps.

Maggie nodded. "I'm hoping we can come down after lunch to wash out our clothes. I'll show the others then."

They walked beside a small stream that broke off from the main river. "I think this will do just fine. We'll have fresh water and still be able to bathe and such without disturbing the main train's water." He turned to look deep into her eyes. "This is where I want you to bring the others."

Maggie nodded.

Adam shared a warm grin with her and then said, "Bring the bucket. I want to show you something."

He didn't give her a chance to argue but continued walking along the shoreline until they turned a small bend. Adam motioned for her to hurry and join him, then he led her into the woods.

She continued following him. "Where are we going?"

He sounded like a teenage boy when he said in a teasing voice, "You'll sec. Come on."

Adam walked even faster; he shoved tree branches aside for her.

Maggie almost felt like a naughty little girl as she hurried through the woods with him. They came to a ledge where water gushed down several feet, creating a pool. Fern and deep shade surrounded the water. He held out his hand for hers and held it tight as they cased down the embankment.

At the pool, Maggie exclaimed, "Adam, this spot is beautiful." She looked at the water and decided it wasn't as deep as it first seemed. A sigh of relief filled her. Since she was a child, bodies of water had made her nervous.

He set the barrel down and grinned at her. "One of the benefits of being a scout is that you learn where all the secret, peaceful spots are. Normally, I wouldn't show this location to anyone else but keep it to myself."

She didn't know if he was teasing or not but returned his grin.

Adam reached forward and tucked a strand of hair behind her ear. His eyes softened as he looked at her. His fingers lingered on her cheek.

Maggie wasn't sure she wanted to feel the thrill that raced through her veins at his touch and closeness. She stepped back and then bent at the knees where she could dip her fingers into the cool water. It felt wonderful. Did it taste as good as it felt?

Once more it seemed to her as if he'd read her mind when he said, "Taste it." He knelt beside her and, using his hands cupped together, he sipped the water.

Maggie noticed he kept his head up and his gaze continued to be alert as he drank. She mimicked his actions. After spending days following the dusty trail and fighting off mosquitoes, the sweet, cool water tasted divine. She leaned back on her heels, aware that the sounds of tired oxen, dogs barking and men yelling from one wagon to the other no longer filled her ears and that a peace seemed to drift over her. "I could stay here all day."

He chuckled. "And have my mother track us down? That might not be such a good idea."

She knew he was right and dipped her bucket into the water as he filled the barrel. Maggie really did wish she could stay in the little cove, away from everyone. The noise of the train could become overwhelming at times. This place was quiet, peaceful and felt comforting.

They started back the way they had come. Adam stopped where he'd told her to show the women. It was a nice place as well, but Maggie missed the feeling of being alone in the cove.

"Don't forget, this is where you and the women should come to the river." Adam moved the barrel from his left shoulder to his right. He took the heavy water bucket from her hands. "If you want, I'll ask Ma to watch Lilly May for a little while this evening and we can return to the cove."

Maggie wanted to go back and enjoy the peaceful inlet, but she wasn't sure if they were being fair to the others. "I don't know if we should," she confessed.

"Why? Because you don't want to be alone with me?" Adam seemed to look deep into her soul.

Once more she felt that surge of excitement at the thought of them being alone. Getting to know him and spend time with him was something she was starting to crave. Maggie pushed the thought aside and sighed. "No, it just doesn't seem fair keeping such a wonderful spot to ourselves."

He nodded. "I understand but if we share it with everyone, it will lose its specialness." Adam shook his head. "Does that make sense?"

Maggie knew what he meant and nodded. "It does."

"Think of it like this. Everyone has some place where they feel that they can be themselves. Let's just say that the cove is one of the places I can be myself." He took her right hand in his. "I'd like to share that place with you."

Maggie swallowed. Who was the real Adam Walker? Had he just admitted that she didn't really see him as he truly was? She wasn't foolish enough to believe people showed all their true emotions and feelings to others, and yet, that's what she wanted from Adam. To know the real man. To learn of other secrets he might be hiding.

She tilted her head to the side and studied him. Would her marriage to Adam be different from her first marriage? It was too soon to tell. Right now, all Maggie wanted was to get to Oregon. By then, he could decide if she was a wife he could trust.

Chapter Six

Adam questioned his own judgment. Why had he shown Maggie his secret spot? He'd found it during his last trip to Oregon but like many other secret spots along the trail had kept it quiet. It wouldn't be long before civilization found the various spots that offered him peace along the stressful trail and Adam didn't want to see them trampled and spoiled much like the grasses along the prairie.

Shortly after returning to camp, he'd shown another woman the spot. His mother. She'd been as thrilled with the cove as Maggie had. Adam had used that time to ask Grace to keep the cove their secret and to watch Lilly May so he could return with Maggie and share a few quiet moments with his new wife.

He'd used the excuse that he wanted to get to know his young bride. It wasn't a lie. They did need to get to know one another if their marriage was to succeed, just not in the romantic way his mother had assumed. He had no intention of trusting Maggie with his heart.

Now Maggie exited the tent and came to stand with them. "Are you sure you don't mind, Grace? I can stay and take a nap with Lilly May."

Grace patted her shoulder. "That's my plan. You two go on and let this old woman rest with the child." She walked to the tent and went inside.

Adam chuckled. He didn't doubt for a second that his mother would be sleeping within the next ten minutes. The Oregon Trail was hard on everyone, but it seemed to wear harder on the older folks.

Maggie and Adam stood facing each other. They were alone now. The Browns had retired to their wagon for a few hours of rest. Maggie's brother and father were checking on the livestock.

"Shall we go?" Adam asked as he held out his hand for her to take.

Maggie ignored his outstretched hand and took her apron off. "Let me put my apron away." She took her slow, sweet time hanging it on a nail at the back of the wagon.

He dropped his hand back to his side before she turned back around. Her gaze met his and Adam watched her lips twitch. Was that a smile itching to cross her face? "What if we come across something edible? Won't you need your apron to carry it back?" he teased.

She tilted her head to the side and allowed the smile to venture forth. "Maybe we should take a small pail, just in case." She scooped up one of the pails that sat beside the water bucket.

Adam waited until they were far enough from the wagon that the others wouldn't hear and said, "Thanks for coming back with me."

Maggie grinned. "I have been looking forward to it all morning. Maybe we can find some greens to fill our pail on the way back." She swung the pail and sped up her steps.

He caught up to her and asked, "Why did you decide to travel to Oregon?"

She shrugged. "My pa and brother are all the family I have left. It didn't make sense to stay behind in Missouri."

"I suppose not."

"What about you?"

Adam looked toward the river. He'd known that asking her questions would give her the freedom to ask some of her own. How much was he going to share? He didn't know. "It was time for a fresh start. I've saved enough money in the last five years to buy a small farm. My ma will be happy there."

Maggie stooped down and picked a little blue flower. She inhaled its sweet fragrance. "I think a farm will be a nice place to raise Lilly May."

They continued to the private pool. He held back branches once more as they made their way to the sanctuary. The sound of the waterfall greeted them. Adam helped her down the incline once more. "Have you ever lived on a farm?"

She sat down beside the cool water. Sorrow filled her voice as she said, "For a little while."

Adam sat down beside her. "Mind if I pull off my boots and socks? My feet could use a good soak."

A soft pink filled her cheeks, but she nodded her consent. Maggie dipped her fingers into the water and smiled.

The splash of the water cascading into the pool and the sweet serenade of the crickets filled his ears as cool water washed over his tired feet. The last time he'd been here he'd stripped down to his undergarments and taken a swim. For a brief moment regret filled him that he wasn't alone again. A bath would have been most welcomed.

A soft gasp drew his attention. Maggie had cupped her hands under the water and several baby frogs decided to swim in and out of her palms. Her blue eyes filled her heart-shaped face with shock and wonder as she looked up at him. A blond curl escaped the confines she kept it in and waved about her cheek. His new wife was a true beauty.

He returned her smile. "They are swimming about my toes, too."

"Really?" She peered into the water.

"This is the sweetest, coolest water I have had the pleasure of dipping my toes in, in a long time. You could take your shoes off, too. I won't tell anyone." Adam watched her face. Her expression said she'd love to, but her next words denied it.

"I best not." She looked back to the tiny frogs. "If I took off my shoes, I'd want to take a bath, and that is out of the question."

"Why? We are married you know."

She pulled her hands from the water and sat back on her heels. Sharp words slipped past her lips. "Yes, but it is not a real marriage."

Adam filled his lungs with air and nodded. She was correct. Theirs was not a real marriage. He pulled his feet from the water and began drying them with his shirt. It had been a mistake to bring her to the pool. There would be plenty of time to get to know her when they got to Oregon.

Maggie felt his attitude change with her words. Adam had gone from relaxed and teasing to quiet and alert. She wished she could take her words back, but Maggie wanted their marriage to be what they'd agreed upon. A marriage for the sake of Lilly May. Still, her words could have been kinder.

She closed her eyes. The crickets and water still offered solitude, but no longer did she feel as if she were in a mysterious land. Maggie sighed and stood to join Adam. "Go ahead and enjoy the pool. I'll look for edible greens."

"Wait."

Maggie stopped and looked at him. Really looked at him. Adam wasn't very tall. She'd guess him to be about five foot ten inches. His hat covered light brown hair. Deep brown eyes stared back at her.

He took a step toward her. "Look, I know we aren't a real married couple, but we can still be friends. If you want a quick bath, I can scout for the greens and give you some privacy."

Maggie looked to the inviting pool. Oh, how she'd love to wash the dust and grime from her face and arms. This was probably the only chance she'd have.

Before she could answer, he took the pail from her hand. "I'll be back in ten minutes. If you need me, I'll be a shout away. Far enough not to watch, but close enough to hear you." Then he turned and walked away.

Maggie stared after him. He entered the brush; she

could no longer see him. Her gaze moved back to the pool. A quick dip would be so wonderful. She looked toward where he'd disappeared once more and then began taking her shoes and socks off. What would it hurt to have a quick bath? After all, the pool wasn't very deep and her chances of drowning in the still water were slim to none.

Ten minutes later, she was back on the bank. If it weren't for the fact that her hair was wet, Maggie felt sure no one would have guessed that she'd just had a wonderful dip in a cool pool of water. She pulled on her last shoe and called out, "All done."

Adam returned with a grin. "My turn."

Maggie gasped. Surely he didn't expect her to stay while he took a bath.

"Come on—I found a rock you can sit on, and your hair will dry while you wait for me." Adam took her hand and pulled her in the direction he'd gone.

They slipped through the wooded area to a spot with a large rock. "This is where I waited for you." He placed both hands on her waist and lifted her up onto the rock. For a brief moment they were close enough to kiss.

Maggie looked deeply into his brown eyes and realized they had caramel flecks around the irises. This was the closest she'd been to any man since her husband's death. When he released her and stepped back, disappointment filled her at the loss of his closeness.

"I'll be back in ten minutes. Same rules apply. If you need me, call out. I'll be able to hear you." Adam went back the way they'd come.

Maggie noticed the pail of greens resting on the rock beside her. He'd done as he'd said and foraged for fresh greens while she'd bathed. She finger-combed her hair. Maggie glanced around at her surroundings and listened. Birdsong filled the air, insects hummed about her and once more Maggie felt as if she were in a mysterious place and dreaded having to go back to the wagons, the dust and the noise of camp life.

Then she thought of Lilly May and smiled. The little girl was more than enough reason to return to the wagon. Lilly May gave her purpose, a reason to keep moving forward in life and someone new to love.

"You should smile like that all the time." With one hand Adam was using his shirt to dry his hair and in the other hand he held his hat.

Maggie scooted over on the rock to give him room in the sunshine. She averted her eyes as he pushed his arms into the shirt and buttoned it. "I was thinking about Lilly May."

"Well, since you were smiling you must have been thinking happy thoughts." He pushed up on the rock and leaned back on his elbows.

"They were. She is such a sweet baby. Did you notice that she walked about this morning without falling? She's so tiny—I wonder how old she is."

"Her mother said she is fifteen months."

He grew silent and Maggie realized they hadn't talked about Lilly May's parents. She only knew that they were both dead and that Lilly May was alone in the world. Questions about them filled her mind. Instead of asking them, Maggie closed her eyes and enjoyed the peace that their privacy gave them. There was nothing that she or Adam could do for the Jameses now, other than give their daughter the best life possible.

After several long minutes, Maggie turned to face him. "Tell me about our new home."

Adam sat up. "Well, if all goes well, we should arrive in about four months. Last trip I filed a land claim on a patch of land just outside of a small settlement called Milton. I chose twenty acres beside a creek. It's beautiful, Maggie. This place reminds me of my land. There are trees everywhere. The creek is slow flowing most of the time and will supply all our needs for water."

Maggie smiled. "It sounds wonderful. Do you think the leaves will still be on the trees there come October?"

He looked deeply into her eyes. "It's pretty lush there so I believe so. But it will all depend on the weather at the time. We'll be living out of the wagon for a few weeks but with your help, we can have the cabin up long before the winter months set in."

She nodded her willingness to help him. Having grown up in town, working at her father's general store most of her life and then living at the farm her husband had provided for a short time, Maggie knew the life he offered would take lots of hard work, but she was willing to work hard to supply a home and family for Lilly May. "We can try to get the cabin up by November and we'll have our first Christmas in it come December."

Truth be told she'd loved living on Matt's farm.

She didn't want to think about her past life with Matt. So she said, "Pa and Martin are going to open a general store." She groaned inwardly when she realized she'd just told Adam something he already knew. He must think her an odd duck.

He merely nodded. "That's a lot different than farming."

Adam continued to study her face, making Maggie

feel exposed. This wasn't the first time he'd seemed to know what she was thinking. Her husband Matt had never seemed to know what she was thinking.

Maggie ran her fingers through her partially dry hair. They should be getting back but she wanted to spend more time learning his plans for their future. "It is, but I'd enjoy having chickens, a milk cow and maybe even a few kittens. We already have a good watchdog."

He pulled back and laughed. "That's true and I'm thankful for him."

"Tell me more about the cabin. What will it look like?" Maggie pulled her legs up and tucked her skirt about them.

"Well, I was thinking I'd make it two stories, that way we would have a sleeping loft. The kitchen and sitting area would be downstairs. Ma can have her own space under the stairs that lead up to the loft. We'll have the rising heat in the winter, and she'll be close to the fireplace." He grinned. "Ma hates being cold."

"I agree with your ma." Maggie pretended to shiver.

He laughed again. "Then we'll make sure to insulate the walls with lots of straw and mud." Adam lay back and put his hands under his head. He closed his eyes as if asleep and dreaming of the future.

Maggie could almost picture his house. She closed her eyes and imagined what it would look like. After several moments, she opened her eyes and asked, "What about windows?"

"I'm thinking there will be two. One in the loft and one in the sitting room. You and Ma can make curtains, but I want to add wooden shutters so that we will be able to close them up at night."

Maggie knew glass windows were a luxury, especially in a new land. "Will you put chicken wire over the windows or leave them open?"

"We can put wire over them. That will help with the insects but won't keep them out totally. Maybe, if we have enough money left over, we can order glass for them in the summer." He opened one eye.

She had the sensation that he wanted to know what she thought of his plans. "Well, wire is cheaper. We could double the amount of wire needed to cover each window and position it so that the holes would be smaller and only little bugs could get in. Then someday, when times are easier, we can invest in glass."

He closed his eyes and grinned. In a teasing tone he said, "You really are easy to get along with, aren't you?"

"I think so, but Martin would probably disagree with me." She laid her chin on her knees. "You know, I've always wanted a window in the kitchen. It makes doing the dishes more enjoyable."

Adam laughed and sat up. "I will add it to my list of windows."

He jumped down from the rock and reached up to help Maggie down. "We best be getting back."

Maggie placed her hand in his and allowed him to help her off the rock. She turned and grabbed the pail, refusing to acknowledge that a slight tingle remained on her fingers where she'd touched his. The greens were already starting to look a little wilted so she decided that perhaps she should add them to their eggs in the morning. They would make a tasty breakfast treat.

"For the sake of our parents, would you mind pretending this is a happy marriage?" Adam asked when she turned back around.

Maggie tilted her head and looked up at him, aware that he was about five inches taller than her. "What do you mean?"

"Ma has voiced her concerns about our marriage. She's worried that I'm unhappy." He looked at his boots, reminding her of a schoolboy who had just arrived late for class.

She cleared her throat. "Are you?"

"No, I'm not unhappy. I just hadn't planned on marrying, and honestly, I'm not sure how to act."

His earlier words echoed back to her; Maggie said them to remind him. "We can be friends. Isn't that what you said earlier?"

Adam met her gaze. "Yes, we can be friends."

"Then I don't see what the problem is. Friends talk, laugh and spend time with each other. I don't know why we can't do that." She wasn't ready for a deeper relationship. Her first marriage had taught her that she was not a good wife. In time Adam would get tired of telling her about his plans and go off on his own, just as Matt had done.

Maggie had no intention of having Adam take her heart with him. She silently prayed that friendship would be good enough for him, his ma and her pa because that was all she was willing to give. Maggie held her breath as she waited for his response.

Chapter Seven

Adam studied her face. She looked as if she might run if he disagreed. "Yes, I think friendship is just what we need." He took her hand in his. Adam wanted to be sure that she wasn't thinking they were going to have a real marriage. He'd shared his plans for their house but in no way did he plan on making it a home. "Just don't expect more."

Maggie nodded.

He felt the air leave her lungs and watched as a smile spread across Maggie's face. If he grew to be a hundred years old, Adam felt sure he'd never understand women. "Good. We should get back to the wagon. Lilly May might be awake now."

As they walked back to the camp in silence, Adam knew he should be pleased that Maggie had agreed that friendship was all there would ever be between them, but instead he felt alone.

Grace stood at the back of their wagon rocking Lilly May. Her face looked anxious. Adam immediately worried that the baby might be sick.

Maggie saw her too and hurried her steps toward the wagon. She called out, "Grace, is everything all right?"

His mother shook her head.

Maggie ran toward her.

Adam lengthened his steps. *Please, Lord, don't let the baby be sick.*

Maggie reached Grace first. Lilly May giggled and kicked her little feet, reaching for her new mother. Maggie ran her hands over the baby's forehead and face. "She doesn't feel like she's running a fever."

"She's not sick," Grace said, touching Maggie on the shoulder. She handed the wiggling baby to Maggie.

Maggie placed the little girl on the ground. Lilly May immediately grabbed on to Adam's leg and sat on his foot.

Adam met his mother's gaze. Something was still not right but thankfully it had nothing to do with Lilly May.

"But I thought something was wrong," Maggie said as she looked up at her mother-in-law.

Sad brown eyes turned back to Maggie. "Something has happened, not to Lilly May but over at the main wagon train."

Adam reached down and touched the top of Lilly May's head. "Tell us, Ma."

The older woman nodded her head. "We heard a scream and then several others. We could hear the women's cries and shouts for the doctor. We called across to find out what was going on. It was Mr. Cannon who a little later called back that they had found two of the children dead."

Maggie gasped.

"What happened?" Adam looked toward the other

wagons. He could see people moving about but children were no longer running and playing. There were no happy voices floating on the afternoon air.

"Mary and Elizabeth Short were fixing vegetables that they had found. They think the girls planned on surprising their mother with a pot of soup. Poor Mrs. Short has had a hard time adjusting to the new baby she's carrying and had lain down for a rest. When she woke up, she'd found her daughters lying beside the cooking pot. They were already dead." The last sentence came out in a sob.

Maggie picked up Lilly May, no doubt needing to hold her new daughter. She hugged a squirming Lilly May tight.

Adam spoke in a low voice. He didn't want to add to the women's distress but he needed to know why the children had died. "Ma?" When she met his gaze, he asked, "What killed them?"

"Water hemlock. The girls must have mistaken the roots for large carrots." She pulled a lace handkerchief from her sleeve and wiped her eyes. "I can only imagine how Mrs. Short is grieving."

The men and Mrs. Brown had joined them.

"I can't even go across and offer God's comfort." Preacher Brown looked across the way longingly.

"Maggie?"

She turned to look at her father. "Yes, Pa?"

Concern filled his voice. "Do you know what hemlock looks like?"

Adam knew why her father asked. Maggie had a habit of collecting edible vegetables for the cooking pot. He probably didn't want her to come into contact with the plant. If Maggie didn't know, Adam would tell them all. Sorrow filled him. Normally he would have warned the travelers that hemlock could be found in this area. But with Maggie's disappearance, finding Lilly May and having to move away from the others, he'd forgotten. Guilt twisted his gut.

She nodded as silent tears streamed down her face. In a small voice Maggie sounded like she was reading from a textbook as she answered, "Water hemlock has white flowers that look like small umbrellas. The roots are joined together and look like a hand with fat fingers. Like most wild carrots they are white. They even have a faint carrot smell but are very deadly. Just touching them can make you sick." Maggie walked to her father. Her voice returned to normal but he heard concern fill it. "They can kill the animals too, if they eat them."

Maggie's pa hugged her. "Thank you, daughter." He looked to Martin. "We'll go check on the livestock. Hopefully they haven't found any."

Adam was amazed that his wife knew so much about the plant. Most of the women who traveled the trail had never heard of the poisonous root. "No need for that, Mr. Porter. I didn't see any around here. Which makes me wonder where the girls found the plants."

Betty Brown walked to the fire and stirred a pot of beans. "Maybe the girls found them earlier yesterday and had decided that today would be a good day to surprise their mother." She sat down on the piano bench with a sigh. "Sadly, we'll probably never know."

The rest of the day was spent in thoughtful silence. Sadness hung about the camps as they prepared to leave early the next day. Martin and John Porter had the first watch duty.

Adam decided to take Shadow out for a ride and scout ahead a little way. He planned on returning before nightfall. He circled the wagons. Two men were digging graves on the left side of the larger wagon train. Adam sat on his horse and watched. Shadow shifted from one foot to the other. Adam recognized Mr. Short and Mr. Miller. During his four years of scouting for wagon trains he'd seen many graves being dug. Children's graves were the hardest.

Inhaling and exhaling deeply, he turned his horse away and allowed Shadow to race ahead of the wagon train. He'd scouted ahead the day before and knew that Lilly May's parents' wagon train was ahead of them. Sorrow filled him. So many had already lost their lives this trip and they still had four more months of traveling ahead of them.

His thoughts went to the bandits who had killed Lilly May's family. They were probably long gone. Adam couldn't help but wonder if they had contracted diphtheria also? There was no way of knowing. He took another deep breath. Filling his lungs with air tended to settle his emotions.

Adam stopped Shadow, slid from the saddle and walked the rest of the way to the river's edge. He closed his eyes and listened to the soft sounds of gurgling waters. After several long minutes, Adam prayed. He thanked the Lord that none of them were showing signs of the sickness, asked God to be with the Short family as they mourned the loss of their children and to continue to watch over them all as they traveled on to Oregon.

* * *

Hours later Maggie listened to the quietness of the evening. She knew that Adam dozed several feet away under their wagon. Since their marriage, that was where he slept. His soft snores filled her heart with peace. If he was snoring, he wasn't worried about the bandits.

Thoughts of the Short girls kept Maggie awake. She thought of reading the new Bible she'd received from Preacher Brown but she'd left it in the wagon. Maggie remembered the small book at the bottom of the bag Adam had packed for Lilly May. Thinking it was a small Bible, Maggie pulled the last of Lilly May's little dresses from the bag and sighed.

She felt as if it had been much longer since she and Adam had found the child. They'd had Lilly May two days and the baby already held Maggie's heart in her sweet little hands. How Mrs. Short must be grieving to have lost both her daughters.

Maggie pulled the small book from the bag. She held it close to her face to read the front cover. In fine print was the word Diary. It wasn't a Bible. Intrigued, Maggie opened it to the first page and read.

Hattie James's diary
April 15, 1860
Today David surprised me with this small journal. He's a sweet husband with a big heart. David suggested that since I love writing I should tell our story in the pages of this book. He calls moving to Oregon a grand adventure. I still think it too dangerous and worry about taking a child on the trail. But I agreed to come with the promise of a

new life on a small farm where we can raise our children. David doesn't know it yet, but we will have another baby in the fall.

Right now, we are sitting on the edge of the prairie. Independence is behind us. David says any day now the grass will start greening and we must be ready to go. Our wagon is handsome. David added six tall hoops to hold the canvas on top. It looks plump and white, much like a fresh-raised loaf of bread.

Inside I have neatly packed all our possessions. Our boxes of food, dishes, the water barrel and pots are in the back to make cooking quicker. Tools and my favorite rocker are in the front. We sold the other one. Two lanterns hang from the hoops, along with extra coils of rope, our canteens, tin pans and tin cups. It's as noisy as a peddler's cart. In the middle, between barrels of flour and beans, is a small nest where I can rest with Lilly May. David says he will be sleeping under the wagon at night so as to keep us safe. I hate the thought of him being outside during the night. What about snakes? Indians? He assures me he will be safe, but I can't help but worry.

Maggie wanted to go to the next entry but knew she needed to rest so closed the book. Maybe tomorrow she'd have time to read more of Lilly May's mother's diary. Her thoughts went to their first few days on this journey. Like Lilly May's family, they had left Independence, only the grass had been tall and green when they'd left. According to the date, Maggie's train had left almost a month later.

She made sure Lilly May was tucked tightly in her bed and then blew out the hanging lantern. Maggie thought about her daughter's real mother. She'd been expecting her second child. Lilly May hadn't just lost a mother and father but also a brother or sister. Before falling asleep, Maggie prayed for the Short family and then prayed that Lilly May would remain well and not get sick like her parents.

The next morning Maggie woke slowly. She could hear the beginning stirrings of their small camp. She glanced toward Lilly May, who, after a restless night, now slept peacefully. The poor baby had called out for her ma several times during the night. Maggie had spent most of the time offering soft words of comfort as she patted Lilly May's small back.

Careful not to wake the little girl, Maggie touched her little forehead and sighed with relief at the coolness of her soft skin. She eased back onto her own blankets and closed her eyes once more. Maggie forced her body to relax and told herself she'd get up in a few minutes. It wasn't like her to be lazy in the mornings. Was this how all new mothers felt? Exhausted from a child's restless night?

She heard Grace and Betty whispering as they prepared breakfast. Guilt ate at Maggie. Never in her whole life had she been slothful, and she wasn't going to start today. She pushed the blanket back and quickly prepared for the day.

A few minutes later, she left the tent. Brutus rested beside the door. He raised his head and looked up at her with soulful eyes. Maggie rubbed him behind the ears and then hurried to the fire, where fresh coffee awaited. It was funny—until they'd started this journey, she hadn't been much of a coffee drinker. Her beverage of choice was tea, but after a few weeks on the trail Maggie had come to enjoy the bitterness of the hot brew. She smiled at Grace, who handed her a tin cup. "Thank you."

"Did you sleep well, dear?" Grace asked.

Maggie poured the dark liquid into her cup. "When I slept." She smiled, knowing full well that the other two ladies knew of her restless night.

Betty turned the potatoes that were frying in an iron skillet. "It takes time for little ones to get used to new circumstances."

"I hope we didn't disturb you." Maggie took a sip and almost sighed. It was silly to enjoy a heated drink this much.

Grace shook her head. "No, I just know how babies can be."

Tonight, she'd move the tent a little farther from the wagon. The last thing she wanted was for Lilly May to keep the older woman awake at night, and if Grace could hear Lilly May then Adam could too and both of them needed their rest.

The bugle sounded at the larger camp, telling everyone it was time to get up and get started. Grace and Betty chuckled at the sound.

Mr. Brown entered the cooking area. "You laugh now, but wait until that summer sun hits us all and zaps us of our energy. Soon none of us will think the bugle an instrument of amusement."

Grace nodded. "I do believe you are right, Reverend."

Betty muttered under her breath, "Maybe, but I think we will still beat the young'uns up." She shared another grin with Grace.

Maggie made a mental note to rouse herself earlier. She didn't want the other two ladies to feel like she was lazy. The Bible had strong words about the sluggard. Her gaze moved to the preacher. He simply grinned and shook his head at the women before sitting down on the bench and opening his Bible.

Adam joined them. "Maggie, if you'll wake the baby, I'll take the tent down for you this morning."

"Thank you." Maggie handed him her empty coffee cup and returned to the tent.

Just before she entered, Maggie glanced to the fire, where Adam poured himself coffee in the cup she'd just handed him. That was something that a husband and wife shared. She slipped inside the tent, not allowing herself to linger on that thought, yet feeling a sense of warmth and belonging.

As quickly as she could, Maggie packed up her and Lilly May's things. She decided to tuck the diary into her apron pocket. Perhaps she'd be able to read the next entry while walking beside the wagon.

As she reached for Lilly May, Maggie's thoughts went to Mrs. Short. Today she'd leave her daughters behind, her only comfort being the baby she now carried and her sons. Maggie cuddled a sleeping Lilly May close and prayed that she'd be able to keep her safe for the rest of the journey to Oregon.

Chapter Eight

The wind swirled around the animals and people with a vengeance. Dust and dirt pelted Maggie and Lilly May as Maggie pressed against the wind. She'd chosen to carry Lilly May instead of allowing her to walk as they normally did. The little girl loved walking and was quite quick on her little legs. But fear that she might get hurt in the sandstorm caused her to keep the child in her arms.

Adam rode up beside her. "Let me take the baby for a while."

Even though her arms felt as if they were going to fall off, Maggie asked above the wind, "Are you sure?"

He pulled his hat up enough to see them better and nodded. As he reached down from the horse to take Lilly May, who screamed her displeasure at getting pelted by the dirt, he answered, "I'm sure. I'll tuck her against me and then ride a little farther from the train. That should cut down on the amount of dirt she's breathing." Adam's gaze met hers.

Maggie knew she had to trust him. The dust wasn't good for Lilly May's young lungs. She'd tried to put a damp cloth over her face to keep the dirt out of her nose, mouth and eyes, but Lilly May had wanted no part of it.

"I promise to keep her safe," he called over the wind.

She held the baby up to him. Adam did just as he'd promised. He tucked Lilly May against his side.

"You try to keep from breathing in the dirt, too." Adam spun his horse around and away from the dirt the animals were kicking up.

Maggie took the bonnet from her head and pressed it against her face, praying. The oxen cried out their frustration at the wind and dirt. Maggie prayed the wind would settle down soon.

Grace and Betty joined her as she pushed against the gale. Each held a cloth against their nose and mouth. Grace yelled, "When this settles down and we camp, I'm going to make us all masks to wear in case this happens again."

Maggie had been thinking the same thing. Early in their journey she'd made covers for their oxen's noses but hadn't thought about making them for her family, until today.

Maggie walked closer to the other two women. "I hope this wind dies down before we make camp. I don't know how I will set up the tent if it doesn't."

Betty agreed. "John is praying hard. If you listen close, you can hear him."

Grace locked arms with them and said, "Maybe we should join him. Doesn't the Bible say, 'For where two or three are gathered together in my name, there am I in the midst of them'?"

"Yes! It does," Betty yelled over the wind.

"Let's pray silently," Maggie suggested. "The wind is making it too hard to hear each other."

The other two women agreed.

Maggie prayed that the wind would calm. She prayed for her fellow travelers, the men driving the wagons and the animals that pulled the wagons. When she was finished, she squeezed Grace's arm and said "Amen" above the wind.

For the next hour the wind and dirt blew. Then it began to slow before coming to a complete stop. Shouts of joy filled both wagon trains.

Adam rode toward her with Lilly May tucked in his arm. Maggie saw the little girl smiling and chattering to him in baby gibberish. He stopped beside her.

Lilly May saw her and began pushing against Adam to get to Maggie. He helped the little girl into Maggie's arms and chuckled. "It seems our daughter enjoys horseback riding. She's been all smiles and very talkative since the wind died down."

Maggie cuddled her close. "Did she nap?"

"Nope. She should sleep good tonight." He grinned and then called to Josiah, "We are making camp here tonight."

She watched as Josiah led the wagons into a semicircle. He quickly jumped down and released the oxen from the wagon. Preacher Brown did the same. Martin and her father worked together and soon all the oxen were grazing close by with Preacher Brown keeping watch over them and the other animals.

Maggie called to the ladies, "I'll get the firewood." She set the little girl down in the grass for a moment, took off her apron and then picked the child back up. Using the apron as a rope, she tied Lilly May in front of her and then proceeded to collect the wood in record time.

Lilly May pushed away from her, saying her new words, "No, down."

"No, be still. As soon as we are done collecting wood, we can go back, and you can play with Brutus." Maggie picked up another stick.

"Dog?"

Maggie laughed. "Yes, you can play with the dog." She felt a moment of motherly love as Lilly May nodded and then laid her head on Maggie's chest.

As she entered the camp, Betty met her. She carried a big pot of leftover beans. "I have a spare apron if you want to use it as a sling for Lilly May." She grinned. "I'm a little thicker around the waist and my aprons have a little more material to tie."

"Thank you, that's very thoughtful of you." Maggie laid the wood down and began to build the fire. "I should have let her walk but I was in too big of a hurry. I keep thinking of her as a baby and want to carry her." She laughed. "That's silly, isn't it?"

Betty laughed, too. "Not at all—she is still a baby, just one that likes to walk and get into everything."

Grace measured out flour, lard and milk to make dough for biscuits. "I'll make a double batch so that we'll have plenty for tonight and tomorrow." She rolled the dough on a little table Adam had set out.

Over supper, the women listened as the men's conversation turned to plans for the morrow and various concerns about the livestock and wagons. After the meal, Adam and the preacher went to care for the animals. Her father muttered something about fixing a wheel on his wagon before he left the campsite. Betty and Grace set to work cleaning up.

Maggie sighed. Lilly May slept peacefully, wrapped in a blanket, in her arms. Maggie was tired to the point of exhaustion but knew she still had work to do before going to bed, mainly setting up her tent. She thought about waiting for Adam to return until her brother approached, carrying her tent under his arm.

"Where would you like to set up your tent tonight?"

Maggie smiled up at him. "You don't have to help me."

"No, I don't." He waited with a mischievous grin.

She stood. Her feet burned as if she'd grown more blisters on them. Especially her toes. "Well, if you insist." Maggie took him to a spot beside their wagon. She made sure that they would be a little farther away than the night before so as not to keep Adam and Grace awake, should the baby cry anytime during the night.

Martin cleared the area of rocks before setting up the tent. "Are you sure Adam will be all right with you being this far from the wagon?" He stepped back and looked at the distance.

Maggie didn't know how her new husband would feel about the distance. "I'll find out soon enough."

He nodded. "I'll go get Lilly May's drawer for you." Martin turned to the wagon.

Maggie saw him stop and talk to Grace for a moment, before reaching into the wagon and pulling out the drawer. Grace looked to where she, Brutus and Lilly May waited. Her mother-in-law frowned. It was obvious she didn't approve of the new location of the tent.

When Martin got within hearing distance she hissed, "What did you say to Grace?"

"I asked if I could get the drawer." He stepped inside the tent and set down the baby's makeshift bed. "Why?" He added a small blanket before moving aside.

"You saw the look she gave me." Maggie gently laid the baby down.

"What look?" Martin frowned.

A soft thud sounded outside the tent door, alerting Maggie that Brutus had taken up guard duty. "Honestly, Martin. Sometimes I think you are blind."

He shrugged his shoulders. "Do you need me to do anything else for you?"

Maggie had planned on getting her and Lilly May's bags from the back of the wagon too, but since Martin was offering, she asked him to do it.

Martin grinned. "Chicken." He hurried out of the tent, almost tripping over the dog.

A few moments later, he poked his head through the flap. He handed her the bedroll and bags. "Anything else?"

Maggie smiled. "No, thanks for helping me."

He nodded. "Grace said to tell you good-night—she's turning in now." Then he was gone.

She was glad not to have to go say good-night to her mother-in-law. Maggie was certain that Grace didn't approve of the location she'd chosen for the tent. She tied the tent flap closed and quickly changed into her simplest dress that she used to sleep in. Some might think her foolish for changing but she couldn't stand the thought of sleeping in the dirt-covered dress of the day.

Maggie lay in her tent, waiting for sleep. Her legs ached from pressing into the wind most of the day. The blisters on her toes burned. Slowly, the camp quieted around her. From nearby came the sound of snoring; she knew that it had to be the preacher because Adam had guard duty with her father.

Her thoughts went to the diary. Once the wind had started blowing, she'd known there would be no reading of it while she walked. Earlier in the day, Maggie had returned the book to the flour sack. Careful not to wake Lilly May, Maggie lit the lantern again and found the book.

She opened it to the second page and began reading.

Day 2

My feet burn so bad. I'm such a softy. Blisters developed midmorning and burst soon afterward. I'm not the only one with aching feet. The other ladies are all limping around. Well, everyone but Mrs. Hewit. She rode in the wagon all day refusing to walk. Everyone heard her complaints today as she wasn't quiet. Her poor husband and daughter had to do everything, drive their wagon and do all the chores. Anyway, Lilly May loves riding on the wagon seat with her papa. Makes me nervous. What if she were to fall? But her papa assures me that she is fine and that I shouldn't be carrying her all day. I wonder if he knows about the new baby. I don't think so, but he is very loving and seems to know everything

*about me. I'm learning really fast that not every
woman on this train has a sweet man like mine.
We can't help but overhear everyone's business.
Mr. and Mrs. Black don't get along at all. I overheard him calling her a fat sow! So mean. I also
heard her crying. I think tomorrow I'll try to walk
with her and remind her that in God's eyes she
is perfect.*

Maggie closed the diary. Sadness at the loss of Lilly
May's parents, who seemed to be deeply in love, tore at
her emotions. She also craved a love relationship like
theirs, would she ever have such devotion in her life.
Her thoughts moved to the people on the other wagon
train. Had they continued to Oregon? If so, would she
ever meet them?

The next evening, Adam and Cannon had met outside the two camps. The men stayed far away from each
other even though Adam had assured him that Lilly
May showed no signs of sickness. Adam understood that
the larger train couldn't be exposed if she were sick, but
since they were going to cross the Kansas River tomorrow, he'd really hoped they could rejoin the larger train.

The wagon master called across the way. "We'll
camp here tonight and use the ferry in the morning to
cross. It will take a couple of days to get all the wagons across and then the ferryman can come back for
your people."

Adam nodded his consent to the plans. He knew
the others would enjoy their time off from traveling.
When they'd finished talking, Adam turned Shadow

and headed back to the wagon train and Maggie. She'd been in his thoughts all afternoon; her kindness and intelligence were what drew his thoughts. Adam assured himself that he was not becoming attracted to his new wife. He refused to allow those emotions to form.

The camp was already bustling with preparations for the evening meal. His mother was rolling out dough for biscuits, Betty stirred something in the big pot she'd hung over the fire and Maggie was cutting up greens that she'd picked this morning as they'd traveled.

Martin sat in the dirt playing with Lilly May. Brutus kept his constant vigil beside them.

Martin looked up and asked, "Are we crossing the river tomorrow?"

Adam shook his head. "Not us. The bigger train is going first. Then we'll get to go after."

John Porter came around the Browns' wagon. "Why do we have to go last?"

Preacher Brown joined them. "Probably for the same reason that we are here and they are there."

Adam looked toward Maggie. Her eyes reflected the fear she felt. He assumed it was because of the river crossing. He looked away from Maggie and faced her father.

"Preacher Brown is correct."

"How long do we have to wait?" John asked. He crossed his legs and lowered himself to the ground beside Lilly May.

Adam watched as the older man rolled a small ball to the little girl.

"It will probably take a couple of days to get all the wagons across. Then the ferryman will start taking ours." He watched as Lilly May rolled the ball back to Maggie's pa.

Grace smiled at them all. "That means we have two whole days to rest. I don't know about you all, but I plan on using the time to relax."

Martin nodded. "It will also give us time to do any repairs to the wagons that we need to."

Preacher Brown spoke up. "I wouldn't mind slipping up the river a ways and washing off some of God's dirt and grime."

Everyone chuckled, happy for a time of rest before they had to make the dangerous river crossing.

Adam always dreaded this part of the journey. With each trip he'd made, it seemed someone died or lost everything they owned during a river crossing. He hated the thought that this body of water could take one of the people in front of him.

Maggie spoke, drawing his attention. "Is there anything special we should do to prepare for the crossing?"

He shook his head. "Not right now. This river isn't like the others we've crossed. They were more like streams than rivers. The morning we cross we'll have to make sure everything is tied down. Does everyone know how to swim?" Thankfully everyone nodded. Then his gaze returned to Maggie. He noticed she studied the ground as if hoping it would open up and swallow her. "Maggie? Can you swim?"

She shook her head. Her hands shook as she wrapped them into her apron. She kept her gaze glued to the dirt at her feet.

Martin laid a hand on her shoulder. "When we were

kids, she almost drowned. We've not been able to get her to go in farther than her knees since that day."

"I'll teach you how to swim." When she shook her head, Adam continued, using the one thing he knew would persuade her. "For Lilly May's sake you have got to learn. What if she falls in the water while we are crossing?"

Tears filled her eyes and her voice quivered as she consented. "All right. I'll learn."

Martin's mouth dropped open. It was obvious he'd tried to get her to learn before and failed.

Adam grinned at him. "You might want to shut your mouth before a mosquito flies in."

Everyone but Maggie laughed. She looked to Lilly May and nibbled on her bottom lip. Was she wondering if she could learn to swim? Or realizing how much she loved the baby?

Adam wished he could spare her the lesson. But he'd seen firsthand what happened when women and children didn't know how to swim or float down a river. Fear gripped him at the thought of losing Maggie to a watery grave.

Chapter Nine

The next morning, Maggie stood beside the river. Why couldn't it be calm and peaceful like the pool she and Adam had enjoyed only days before? She shivered at the rushing roar of the water. According to Adam, the area he'd picked for her lesson was calmer than where they would be crossing but not much.

He stood beside her. "I wish I'd known you couldn't swim when we were at the cove. It would have been much easier to teach you there."

What could she say? She'd never dreamed of asking him or anyone else to do that.

Martin had tried many times over the years to instruct her but she'd never gone deep enough. Even now she felt panic at the thought of going farther than knee-deep in the water.

When her pa had said they were going to Oregon, her biggest fear had been the river crossings. She had told herself that she'd be in the wagon and safe but now, after talking to the others, she knew this wouldn't always be the case. And should the wagon tip over, Maggie would be not only responsible for her own life but Lilly May's also. The thought terrified her.

She swallowed. "Should I take off my shoes?" The thought embarrassed her to her core, but shoes would make it hard to swim.

"No, if the wagon tosses you into the river, you'll still be wearing your shoes." He grinned at her. "We're both going to have soggy shoes and clothes to dry out by the fire tonight."

Oh, how Maggie wished she'd learned how to swim when Martin had tried to teach her. Dwelling on the past wasn't going to help her now. Taking a deep breath, she turned to Adam. "So how do we start?"

He took her hand in his. Warmth traveled up her arm. Adam turned her away from the water and faced her toward the wagons. He released her hand and stood beside her. "What I'm going to teach you first is how to dog paddle."

"Dog paddle?" Was he crazy? She wasn't a dog.

"Yes, dog paddle. Have you ever seen a dog swim?" He cupped his hands in front of his body and waited for her answer.

"Yes, but I don't understand."

"Do what I'm doing. A dog paddles with his front paws and kicks his hind legs. Like this."

Maggie wanted to laugh as his hands seemed to dig into the air in front of them, but she knew he wouldn't appreciate her humor so she simply did what he did. Still, she felt her lips twitch.

Adam reached out and cupped his hands around hers

until he had the shape he wanted. "Now, act like you are digging."

She did as he said, feeling more and more foolish. Maggie expected Martin to come running from the wagons at any moment laughing and telling her that Adam was simply fooling her.

"Good. Now we'll go into the water."

All humor left her. Maggie didn't want to drown. She remembered her lungs filling up with water. The lack of oxygen in her lungs had burned and the water hadn't quenched the fire. Maggie tried to push away the memory of sputtering and coughing as they forced the water out of her tired body. Fresh chills of fear swept over her.

Adam took her hands in his and forced her to look at him. "I know this is hard for you, but I don't want you to drown if you fall in the water."

The warmth in his voice gave Maggie pause. Did he really care about her?

Then Adam added, "Lilly May needs her mother."

Feeling even more foolish at her wayward thoughts, Maggie nodded, not trusting her voice not to embarrass her further.

He led her to the water. "Ready?"

Maggie swallowed. "Yes."

Adam walked beside her as they entered the cold river.

The water splashed them hard as waves washed downriver. At any moment, Maggie expected to be swept under.

Adam positioned himself between her and the downward flow. "Cup your hands, Maggie."

She did as he said and continued walking deeper

into the water. When it got to her knees, she stopped. A gentle tug from Adam had her going deeper. When it came up to her chest, her breath quickened to the point that she thought she might swoon.

Adam turned and placed his hand on her shoulder. "Stop here."

Maggie had no trouble obeying that order. She stopped and took several deep breaths.

Adam looked deeply into her eyes. "I need you to trust me. I am a strong swimmer and I won't let you drown. Even if your head goes underwater, don't panic. Trust that I will be here with you. Can you do that?"

Her voice shook as she replied, "I will try."

"Good. Now, if you do go underwater, just relax. You will feel my hands catch you. Don't try to grab me and pull yourself to me. Let me grab you. I promise I'll hold you. Agreed?"

Maggie wanted to tell him how crazy he sounded. If she went under the water, she didn't know what she'd do. *Saying* she wouldn't panic didn't necessarily mean she wouldn't. Still, she offered, "I'll try."

Adam smiled at her. "That's all I'm asking."

His gaze held hers and Maggie knew she could trust him, but could she trust herself?

He put his hands on her stomach and said, "Now here comes the trust part. I want you to lie down on the water. Use my hands as a guide."

Maggie felt the warmth of his hands through her wet dress. They felt strong. She looked at his arms and saw the muscles through his wet shirt. Maggie forced herself to believe him, to trust him.

She held her breath, closed her eyes and did as he asked.

"That's it."

She felt herself floating on the water and opened her eyes. Adam stood beside her with his hands still supporting her waist. Maggie smiled and released the air in her lungs, and then she went under the water with a sputter.

Adam scooped her up and pulled her to his side.

Maggie felt like a drowned rat. The warmth where their bodies touched felt electrifying. Could he feel it, too? She quickly looked into his face, searching for some form of acknowledgment of the excitement coursing through her veins.

"See, I told you I'd save you."

A big furry head swam beside them. Brutus barked to let her know he was there, too. Maggie was thankful for the big dog's interference. She didn't want Adam knowing just how his closeness seemed to affect her nerves.

Then it dawned on her, and she said in awe, "He left Lilly May."

Adam reached out and petted the dog's big head. "Yes, he did. Brutus has accepted all of us as his family. He's here to save you."

Maggie smiled until Adam held his hands out in front of her and said, "Try again." Then it slid from her face, and she took a deep breath. Why couldn't they stay here in the shallow end of the water and just— She paused her thought. What was it she wanted? She didn't have long to wait for her answer.

She wanted more special time with Adam.

But why? They'd made a pact for a loveless marriage, so what was she hoping for?

With Brutus at her feet, Maggie sat beside the fire drying her hair. As she thought back on the day, she realized she'd spent more time under the water than on top of it. Clearly she hadn't progressed enough with her swimming lesson.

Playing with Lilly May in the dirt, Grace looked up and smiled. "My son is a good teacher, isn't he?"

"Yes. And he has a lot of patience," Maggie admitted. Her gaze moved to where Adam and her pa were in deep, low conversation. "Do you think he's telling my pa what a horrible student I am?"

Grace chuckled. "Your pa's probably begging him to take you out again tomorrow."

Maggie looked to her mother-in-law and saw the mischievousness in her eyes. "Very funny. Surely I wasn't that bad."

"No, I was teasing. Adam thinks you'll be swimming laps around all of us by the time we have to cross the river."

She hadn't quite accomplished that feat, but by the day of the crossing, Maggie was impressed that Adam had taught her how to float, dog paddle and swim well enough to save herself and, if need be, Lilly May. Much as he tried, though, she still hated the water and had no plans of swimming for fun.

Now as she stood on the bank, the Kansas River ran deep and stormy. Preacher Brown and Betty had been the first of their group to cross. Her pa and Martin were crossing now. Maggie held her breath because it looked frightening, especially when the ferry was caught by the current. The raging waters threatened to take the wagon, animals and people downstream.

The ferry tipped dangerously as it twisted in the river, but the ferryman managed to steer it right with Adam's help. Her attention had been glued to the bulge and swell of his muscled arms, clearly visible with his wet shirt plastered to his skin. Adam had guided, worked and kept each wagon safe as they'd ferried across the river. As long as she could see his muscles working, Maggie knew he was safe, too.

Earlier in the day, one wagon from the bigger wagon train had capsized and all its contents had washed downriver. The owners had spent hours repairing their wagon and searching for their goods. Sadly, they'd lost more than they found.

Maggie prayed her pa and brother would not encounter the same fate.

Grace stepped up beside her, holding Lilly May. "I'm not sure if I can hold her much longer, Maggie."

Maggie took her daughter. Lilly May bounced in her arms, pointing at the wagons and babbling loudly. "I'm sorry, Grace. She's as jumpy as a cat in a room full of rocking chairs today."

Grace smiled. "That she is, but I think I have an idea how we can get her to stay in one place as we cross the river."

"How?"

"Now just hear me out before you decide if you want to do this or not." Grace's face had grown serious, and her gaze searched Maggie's.

"All right."

"I want you to tie her to me." Grace held her hand up to still Maggie's objection. "We can tie her hands and feet around my body. I'll sit at the front of the wagon in the wagon bed. You can sit on the seat where you can see us but also help the men if they need you."

"But what if the wagon topsides? You'll both be in the water." Maggie knew Lilly May needed to be with one of them and had thought she'd be with her.

Grace smiled. "Well, if it does, I'm sure you and Adam will save us. Besides, with her tied facing my front, I can try to float on my back until we are rescued."

"But she's not going to lie still. Lilly May will panic." Maggie hated the thought of her baby in the river, and she wasn't sure Grace could handle the child if she was kicking and pushing her grandmother.

Even now, Lilly May was pushing against Maggie and demanding, "Down."

"I understand, Maggie. That's why we are tying her hands and feet to me."

Maggie wasn't sure. She didn't want to hurt her mother-in-law's feelings, but she also didn't want to lose either of them, should they end up in the river. "Have you run this plan by Adam?"

Grace shook her head. "I just thought of it. But it makes sense. I know the backstroke and I'm the stronger swimmer of the two of us. Honestly, I don't think we'll end up in the river so we may be fussing over nothing."

Maggie had to agree. Grace was the stronger swimmer. She could feel her heart race as she weighed the decision. "Okay, Grace. I'll agree, provided we can get

Lilly May to let us tie her to you." She didn't know how that would happen.

A new twinkle entered Grace's eyes as she smiled. "We have a deal."

A scraping sound drew Maggie's attention back to the ferry that carried her pa and brother. They'd made it to the other side with no mishaps. Knowing it would take a few minutes to get their wagon ready to go, Maggie took Lilly May and Brutus away from the water's edge where the child could play with the dog while they waited.

Half an hour later, Lilly May laid her head on Maggie's shoulder and yawned.

Grace handed Maggie two long pieces of ribbon. "I think the men are about ready for us to cross. Give her to me."

Maggie did as Grace asked. Lilly May went willingly to Grace. The older woman gently shifted the child so that her legs straddled Grace's waist.

Had Grace been planning this all along? she thought as she tied the child to her mother-in-law. It wasn't time for Lilly May's nap. Had Grace given the baby something in her water to make her sleep? As she gently tied Lilly May to Grace, Maggie voiced her thoughts.

Grace was unfazed by the question. "Just a little honey and chamomile. It won't hurt her and she will be much easier to transport across the river."

Maggie agreed that honey and chamomile wouldn't hurt the baby but wished her mother-in-law had confided in her before giving it to Lilly May.

"Are you ready?" Adam called out from the back of Shadow.

Josiah answered, "Everything is tied down. We just need to get the ladies inside."

Adam turned to them and smiled. "You heard the man." His gaze moved to Lilly May. "I thought she would be wide awake and trying to cross the river without us."

"She'll be no trouble at all," Grace replied. "Now get down here and help your old mama into the wagon."

Adam jumped from his horse to do his mother's bidding and Maggie walked to the front of the wagon. "Do you mind if I ride up here with you?" she asked Josiah.

"I'm not driving the wagon. Adam is, but I'm sure he won't mind you riding up here with him." Josiah leaped from the wagon and then turned to help her up.

Maggie put her foot on the axle to climb upon the seat. She felt his hands on her waist and turned to protest. A young man shouldn't be holding her in such a manner.

All she saw was Adam. "I thought it might be more proper if I helped you up."

She didn't argue, simply accepted his assistance. When she was on the seat, she scooted over and allowed him room to join her. She gripped the seat with both hands and looked over her shoulder to the wagon bed where Grace sat with Lilly May cuddled against her, sleeping peacefully.

"Nervous?" Adam asked as he prompted the oxen upon the ferry.

Maggie took a deep breath and exhaled slowly. "I'm terrified," she admitted, holding on for dear life as the wagon swayed on the small river raft that they called a ferry.

* * *

Adam watched as Josiah led Shadow onto the ferry with them. The other animals had already made the crossing, even the Browns' chickens, which had squawked the whole way. He offered another silent prayer to the Lord for their safety.

"We'll be fine," he told Maggie, praying it was true.

The ferry left the shore, floating like an ark upon the water. The current caught the vessel and twisted it about. Adam caught his breath as fear threatened to snag him. Not for himself but for his new family. He struggled but stilled his concerns. He'd seen this happen before and knew how to turn the wagon in the same direction as the ferry. He wished they'd had a bigger ferry so that they could have secured the wagon to the boards, but they hadn't.

Adam wrestled with the oxen, holding them in place as they strained toward the highest corner of the raft. He heard Maggie gasp and knew she was hanging on to the wagon with all her might. Thankfully, the ferry leveled out on the water and the rest of the journey across went smoothly.

When they were on dry ground once more, he turned to Maggie. Her face was white but her smile warmed his heart. She'd been brave during the crossing, hadn't screamed or offered advice like many of the other wives had done on their voyages across the river.

Adam allowed the oxen free rein as they pulled their wagon a few yards away from the ferry, and took a deep breath. They would be camping on this side of the river tonight so there was no rush to get in line and begin their journey once more. He set the brake and looked at his pretty wife.

"You did it." She hugged him briefly, released him just as fast and then looked back inside the wagon to check on Lilly May and his mother. "Grace, thanks to your son we made it across safely."

The happiness in her voice warmed him more than the sun on a cloudy day. Adam decided to accept the rich feelings her praise gave him. He turned on the seat and pretended to look at his mother and new daughter, too. But his gaze remained on Maggie.

Her bonnet had fallen back, and her reddish-blond hair fell about her shoulders, thick and soft. He had to fight the urge to reach out and touch her.

Maggie's sweet scent floated on the light breeze. For the first time since their wedding, Adam allowed himself to appreciate her happiness.

"Grace, you really shouldn't have done it," Maggie scolded in a sweet voice.

He looked to his mother. She grinned, then shrugged. "She didn't make a peep the whole way across, did she?"

Maggie giggled. "No, but you still shouldn't have given her a sleep concoction."

Adam watched his daughter sleep soundly against his mother. "Ma?"

She pushed away from the bed of the wagon. "I only gave her honey and chamomile. It didn't hurt her, and she didn't fall out of the wagon."

Adam looked to Maggie. "And you were all right with that?"

Maggie looked as if he'd slapped her. "What if I

was? Does that make me a bad wife and mother?" She scrambled down the side of the wagon.

Adam saw the tears that filled her pretty eyes. He didn't think what he'd said had been so bad. Her happy mood had gone sour quickly. What had he done?

Chapter Ten

For the next few days, Maggie was polite but not as friendly as she once was. She seemed to have put up a wall around her heart. Adam prayed she'd forgive him soon for whatever it was that had hurt her feelings and made her angry.

His mother walked beside him as he led his horse beside the Browns' wagon. "Ma, do you have any idea what it was that I said to upset Maggie so much the other day?"

"No, son. She's been very quiet since we crossed the river, even with me." She paused and looked over her shoulder where Maggie walked beside their wagon. Then she turned back to look ahead with Adam. "Maggie does her share of the chores and takes care of Lilly May." Grace tsked. "I'm hoping she'll open up to me or Betty soon. It's not healthy for her to hold in her emotions. I'm sure that whatever you said reminded her of a past hurt. I saw it in her eyes right before she turned away."

Adam wasn't a man to pry but if Maggie was this upset about her past, then he needed to know what it was that troubled her. "Maybe I should take her for a walk this evening." He felt as if he should say something that would assure her that whatever troubled her, they could work it out.

"Adam! Grace!"

He turned at the sound of Maggie's cry. She was running toward them. Lilly May fussed and pressed against Maggie as if she wanted to get down and walk. Brutus raced beside Maggie.

Adam held tight to Shadow's reins and then ran to meet them. He could have ridden the short distance, but didn't want to take the added time to get on the horse and then to dismount once more. His gaze locked with Maggie's until he was within arm's reach. Then he noticed Lilly May. The baby's face was flushed, and tears streamed down her little face.

"She's sick, Adam," Maggie said over the baby's cries. The fear in her eyes tore at his heart. He took Lilly May from her arms.

Lilly May laid her head on his shoulder but just as quickly pushed away with a wail. She fussed and pushed against him. Adam knelt and placed her on the ground.

The little girl sat down with a plop and screamed her unhappiness.

Grace arrived in a huff. She reached out and touched Lilly May's pink cheek. "She's feverish. Let's get her to the wagon."

Adam scooped up Lilly May and walked quickly, aware that his mother and Maggie followed close on his heels. Shadow followed along. Brutus's large feet made a padding noise as the dog kept up with his ward. Whatever was wrong with Lilly May, Brutus intended to remain by her side.

As they passed the Porter wagon, Martin reached for Shadow's reins. "I'll take care of him. What's going on?"

Adam released the horse but kept a firm grip on the fussing little girl.

Maggie answered, "The baby's sick."

"Are we stopping?" Maggie's father called from the seat.

Adam shook his head. "No, keep going. If we need to stop, we'll catch up with you later."

Maggie's father nodded, then Martin said, "I'll tie Shadow up to your wagon and then go back and tell the Browns what is going on." He ran ahead pulling Shadow behind him to Adam's wagon.

Josiah saw them coming and stopped the oxen. He set the brake and joined them at the back of the wagon. "What's wrong?" he asked.

"Lilly May is sick," Adam answered.

Martin tied Shadow to the wagon and then turned toward the Browns' wagon.

Adam's voice stopped him. "Make sure you all keep up with Cannon's wagon train. Don't stop until they do."

Martin looked to Maggie.

Adam could see that her brother wanted to be with her, to support her, but that was no longer his job. He waited until Martin looked at him once more then gave a slight nod of what he hoped Martin would see as a promise to keep them safe.

Martin clearly understood. He returned the nod and

then set off at a run to catch up with the Browns and his father.

Adam returned his attention to the women and Lilly May.

"How long has she been running a fever?" Grace asked Maggie. She lowered the tailgate and motioned for Adam to set Lilly May down.

"Not long. She was fussy so I rocked her to sleep as I walked. But she didn't sleep long. The poor little lamb woke up crying and hot."

As soon as the baby was on the gate, Grace gently shoved her son to the side. "Let me look at her." She placed her hand behind Lilly May's back to stop her from falling backward as she cried out again.

Adam reached over and rubbed Maggie's shoulder as his mother stripped Lilly May of her little dress. He knew his mother would figure out what was happening soon. Back home, she'd helped many a young mother either give birth or treat their sick children.

Grace mumbled to herself. "She doesn't have any spots or bumps. Maggie, get a cloth. Adam, draw some water. I'm going to give her a quick sponge bath and see if the fever will come down."

Adam hurried to the water barrel on the side of the wagon and poured a small amount into a pail. He handed the water over at the same time that Maggie returned with a rather large cloth. Maggie dipped the rag into the water, wrung it out then handed it to Grace to wash the baby.

"What could cause this?" Maggie asked.

Grace answered with a question of her own. "Was she fussy before she went to sleep?"

Maggie nodded. Adam saw her blue eyes fill with tears as she turned to look at him.

He couldn't stop himself. He pulled her to his side. "Ma often answers a question with a question." He tucked her close and held her as his mother washed Lilly May's face and neck. If he could take away Lilly May's pain and Maggie's worry, Adam knew he would.

The baby cried loudly.

Grace took advantage of Lilly May's open mouth and felt her gums. The little girl clamped her mouth down and gnawed on Grace's finger. She grabbed Grace's hand and held tight to it.

"Praise the Lord, she's only teething," Grace announced with a smile.

Adam felt Maggie's body sag against him.

She looked up at him with a wide grin. "Thank the Lord. I was so frightened."

"So was I." He gave her a gentle squeeze then moved away from her. Adam wanted to hold her longer but knew he had to catch them up to the others.

Grace picked up Lilly May with her fingers still in the little girl's mouth. "We'll need to make her a chewy."

Maggie nodded happily and shut the wagon back up.

Adam had no idea what a chewy was and really didn't care as long as it made all the women in his life happy. He turned to Josiah. "You want to walk or drive?"

Josiah rubbed his backside. "If it's all the same to you, I think I'll walk a spell."

Adam grinned. The young man had been driving all day. Normally, they would have switched places earlier in the day and Josiah would have ridden a horse or walked beside the wagon, but today, Adam's thoughts had been more about his wife and less about Josiah's needs.

He turned to Grace. "Ma, do you want to ride with me?"

"No, but if Maggie doesn't mind riding, I'll give her back Lilly May and the baby can chew her fingers off." She grinned at Maggie, who immediately reached for her daughter.

Maggie gave Grace a hug as they exchanged the baby. "Thank you, Grace. I was afraid she was sick, and we'd have to stay separated from the wagon train even longer."

Adam turned to help Maggie up onto the seat. "You'll have to give Lilly May to Ma again and then I'll hand her back to you when you are safely seated."

"She's not going to like that," Maggie offered, pulling her finger from Lilly May's mouth.

To prove she was right, Lilly May let out an ear-piercing scream as she handed the child to Grace.

Adam turned to help his wife up into the seat. Her narrow waist fit nicely in his hands as he lifted her. He was almost sorry he had to let her go, but she'd sat down and then scooted over to give him room. Adam pulled himself up onto the seat and turned to take their daughter.

Grace grinned up at him. She gave him a slight wink as she passed her granddaughter to her pa.

Gnawing on Maggie's finger, Lilly May settled down. Beside her, Adam snapped the reins to coax the oxen to move. They had to catch up to her family's wagon and the Browns'. Maggie used the quiet time to think. For the past few days, she'd been trying to understand herself. She had snapped at Adam when she'd felt he was judging her, saying that she wasn't a good parent. Upon reflection she realized his tone hadn't been one of accusation as she'd first thought. It was the old hurts springing forward, making her respond with a sharpness that she now knew she shouldn't have.

She looked over at her new husband. "Adam?"

He glanced in her direction. "Yes?"

"I need to apologize for my outburst the other day." Maggie swallowed around the lump in her throat.

He didn't say anything.

Maggie tried again. "I'm sorry I snapped at you."

Again, he held his peace.

Maggie rocked Lilly May. She refused to say more. She'd said she was sorry but still felt guilty.

"Why did you get angry? I've been trying to figure it out and I'm not sure what I said that irritated you." Adam still didn't look at her.

She sighed. "When I was married before, I thought I was doing everything right. But I was wrong." Maggie looked off to the left, away from Adam. "Matt hanged himself in our barn." There, the words were out.

Adam turned on the seat beside her.

She felt his gaze on the side of her face. "Shouldn't you be guiding the oxen?" Maggie asked, hoping his attention would go back to the beasts and away from her.

"They will follow the others. I'm sorry your husband took his life, but I don't understand what that has to do with me. All I did was ask you if you were all right with Ma giving her chamomile and honey."

How could she explain to him all the insecurities

that now plagued her? "It won't make sense to you. I'm not even sure I understand myself," Maggie whispered.

"I'm willing to try to understand, maybe even help you understand, but I have to know what you are thinking." Adam shifted again, facing forward.

"Can I ask you a question?"

"I suppose so."

Maggie looked ahead as well. "You asked me if I could be faithful to you before we got married. Why?"

His jaw tightened. Adam pulled air through his nose and exhaled. He locked his eyes on the yoke of the oxen in front of them. Thick silence filled the air.

She began to think he wasn't going to answer her but then he spoke.

"Four years ago, I was working at a sawmill and apprenticing as a carpenter in the evenings. My boss had a beautiful daughter who I fell in love with. I asked Lynda to marry me and two days before the wedding, I walked in on her and another man. She broke my trust, and I broke off the engagement. I thought she would be faithful to me, but I was wrong."

Maggie laid her hand on his arm. "Oh, Adam, I'm so sorry."

He continued to look straight ahead. His jaw tightened even more. "I don't want your pity, Maggie. I asked for your faithfulness and that's all I want."

Again, Maggie felt as if she were between a rock and a hard place. Adam had answered her question, so it was her turn to try to explain why she'd reacted the way she had to a simple question.

Her throat tightened. She forced the words, "My husband said he loved me but, in the end, he left me homeless and filled with questions. What did I do wrong? Why didn't he trust me with the truth? Was I such a bad wife that he couldn't bring our problems to me? Or worst of all, was I such a horrible wife that he chose death over a lifetime spent with me?"

Maggie ducked her head. There, she'd told him. Now what? She felt her stomach clench as fear overtook her body. She was afraid that Adam would use how she felt against her. Once they made it to Oregon, would he demand that they dissolve their marriage?

Chapter Eleven

Jim Cannon rode his horse off to the right of their wagon. He stayed far enough away to be safe from illness but close enough he could call to Adam. "Your wagon is lagging behind. What's happened?" he asked.

Adam pulled their wagon to a stop once more, to talk to the wagon master. He wanted to reassure Maggie but didn't have a chance to offer words of comfort. Their conversation had been so serious and full of past hurts. He hadn't known what to say about her husband's death and knew deep down he'd handled the information wrong. Then he'd ended up sharing his own hurts and again not responding to hers the way a loving husband should respond. Now he'd lost his chance because the wagon master demanded answers.

He raised his voice to be heard. "We stopped because the baby is running a fever. When we examined her, Ma discovered she is teething. We are catching up to the other wagons now."

"Everyone is still healthy?"

Adam added a nod with the words, "Yes, sir."

"Only a couple more days and you can rejoin the wagon train."

Adam nodded. "Won't be soon enough for me."

He heard Maggie's sharp inhale of breath. Then she slipped from the wagon seat beside him, leaving him to ride alone. Adam knew he'd have to talk to her again and soon. Not voicing his understanding of how she felt had left her feeling hurt even more. Why did relationships have to be so complicated?

All afternoon, Adam tried to catch Maggie's attention. Either she was deliberately avoiding his gaze or couldn't bring herself to face him. When they stopped for the night, they ate with the others, and she quickly hurried to help the women clean up. Then it was time for him to go stand guard duty.

Frustrated and unsure how to proceed, Adam started to leave the campfire. His mother's voice calling him back gave Adam pause.

"Maggie is standing guard with you tonight. I don't know what is going on with you two, but I suggest you sort it out before we join the wagon train." Grace turned and walked away, leaving Maggie and Adam staring at one another.

He knew better than to disobey his mother so Adam did the only thing he could do. He took Maggie's hand in his and said, "Come on. There's no point to fight Ma once she has something on her mind."

"I don't understand what she's thinking," Maggie muttered, matching his one step with two of her own.

"She's thinking we aren't playing nice. Not acting

like two people who are trying to get to know one another."

"Well, she's not wrong."

He'd already decided that his new wife could be trusted. She'd proven over the last few weeks that she was a good mother, sweet friend, devoted daughter and a hard worker. Not once during the trip had her gaze moved toward another man on the wagon train.

After he'd told her of Lynda and her betrayal, Adam had stated to Maggie he didn't want her pity. All afternoon he'd thought about their previous words, and he realized that the look he'd seen in her eyes wasn't pity. It had been understanding. She'd been hurt too and seemed to understand his hurt.

That's when Adam decided to be honest with himself. Lynda had roving eyes. She'd flirted with everyone but had used her words to convince him he was the one she loved. Her father was desperate to see her married and had quickly agreed to their union. Only neither of them had anticipated that Lynda would betray him with his own brother.

Adam looked up into the night sky. "We'll sit out here for a while and then I'll take you back. Ma will be sleeping and will assume we are playing nice again as a happily married couple." That was what his Ma wanted, for him and Maggie to fall in love and have a happy life together. But Adam knew his mother would never get her wish. He and Maggie could be friends but he would always guard his heart.

He walked to a slight rise overlooking their campsite. "This is a good spot." Adam sat down and waited for her to join him. He could see both wagon trains and the animal encampment.

Maggie's soft sigh as she sat down filled him with remorse. He could have been kinder to her over the last few days. Adam knew he should have spent more time with her, especially after she'd opened up about her past.

She tucked her dress about her legs and then wrapped her arms around them. She rested her head on her knees. "Does she really expect us to be happily married?"

Adam sighed. "Eventually. Ma is a romantic. She believes that in time we will both forget our past hurts and find love with each other."

She turned to look at him. "Do you?"

"Do I what?" He knew what she was asking but Adam didn't want to hurt her feelings by telling her again that he had no intention of falling in love with her.

Maggie shook her head. "Please understand—I don't have any romantic feelings for you. So I'm hoping you believe that she is wrong, even though I don't want to lie to your mother."

Adam tilted his head back and glanced overhead at the crescent moon tracking across the sky. Why did Maggie saying she didn't have any romantic feelings for him bother him?

"We're not lying to her. She knows we don't love each other. Ma is just hopeful." He lowered his gaze to look at Maggie. "Do you want to always have this stony silence between us? Friends normally are friendly and kind to one another. You and I have been silent and distant even though we've said we want to be friends. It just isn't feeling very friendly right now. I know much of it is my fault and I'm sorry."

"No, I hate the silence, too." A sweet grin crossed her face. "Does this mean we are going to try to be friends again?"

He laced his fingers through hers. "I believe it does, and if we are hand-holding friends, no one will be concerned about our romantic relationship."

Maggie nodded. "Then hand-holding friends we will be." She turned her head quickly in the opposite direction.

Had she done so to avoid his gaze? Adam looked to their interlaced fingers. Maggie needed a wedding ring. It might help his mother to think they were happily married. He made the decision that when they got to Fort Laramie, he'd take her ring shopping. For his mother's peace of mind, not because he wanted everyone to know that Maggie was his wife.

Her gasp drew his attention. "I think there's someone down by the livestock."

Adam narrowed his gaze and looked to the livestock. Sure enough he also caught movement at the edge of his field of vision. A shadow detached itself from the darkness near the livestock enclosure.

"I'm sorry," Maggie whispered. "Maybe my eyes were playing tricks on me."

"No, I see him. No, wait, there are three of them." Though his eyes strained for a better view, it was impossible to make out the men's features. "I can't see who they are."

Puzzlement filled her excited voice. "But what reason would anyone have for being near the horses in the middle of the night?"

"No good reason that I can think of. Let's go check it

out." He pushed to his feet. "We'll approach them quietly until we get close enough to identify them. Best to be cautious. If they're bandits up to no good, I can guarantee they're armed."

Adam sensed the panic in Maggie at his words. He wished he could send her back to the wagon, but he couldn't let her go back alone. And he couldn't escort her. The others were counting on him to do his job, innocent people sleeping happily unaware of the danger lurking near the livestock. He said a quick prayer, asking the Lord to protect Maggie should this go wrong.

He led Maggie down the hill. There was nowhere to hide on the vast open prairie, no convenient boulders or shrubs to offer concealment, as they made their way toward the enclosure. Adam swallowed hard. All it would take was for one of the men down below to glance in their direction and he and Maggie could find themselves in the middle of a gunfight.

His mouth ran dry, and his heart pounded behind his ribs, not for fear for himself but for Maggie. She was in danger and all because his mother insisted that Maggie sit with him during guard duty. Although, he couldn't blame his mother. He'd secretly been hoping for a chance to spend time with her, even if it was uncomfortable.

Maggie's whispered prayer reached his ears. "Please, Lord, let there be a perfectly innocent explanation for those men being here."

Adam focused on the men. Their furtive movements unquestionably roused suspicion. As they drew closer, the intruders' purpose became evident. They were tying ropes around the necks of several horses, including Shadow.

Now Adam could confirm that at least two of the men were not members of their wagon train. The last man turned and ran for the tree line, leaving his partners behind. Something about the coward seemed familiar, but since Adam hadn't seen his face, he couldn't be sure.

"I don't recognize them." Maggie kept her voice low, ensuring it carried no farther than Adam.

Anger bled through his response. "Horse thieves."

Once more he heard the panic in her quiet murmur. "What should we do?"

Adam squeezed her hand. "We have the element of surprise and we can use that to our advantage. I want you to — "

The rest of his words were drowned out by Brutus's barking. The big dog sounded the alarm for both camps to hear.

"What's that mutt yapping about?" one of the bandits growled as he glanced around. Seeing Adam and Maggie, he yelled, "Someone's coming!"

His partner fired a shot, the sound cracking through the still night air.

Adam ducked, but Maggie stood frozen in place. In the next moment, he grabbed her arm and pulled her down to the ground beside him. He called out, "Hold your fire! I don't want to risk hitting one of the horses."

"I don't have any fire to hold," Maggie gasped back.

Then Martin dropped beside her.

"You ignoramus!" the lead bandit growled. "Now the whole camp knows we're here! Let's get out of here!" He tried to grasp the ropes around the horses' necks.

But the loud noise of the gunshot had unnerved the animals. They danced out of reach, thwarting his efforts. He glanced over his shoulder in the direction of the wagon trains' circles, where several men were emerging with lanterns in hand.

Muttering a curse, the bandit abandoned all attempts to regain control of the skittish horses. "Forget them. I'm not sticking around to be caught and hanged!" He beat a hasty retreat, his partner hurrying after him.

Adam helped Maggie to her feet. After quickly assessing that she had not been injured, he and Martin ran toward the horses.

"Whoa, easy." Keeping his tone soft and gentle, Adam climbed between the ropes that formed the temporary enclosure.

Maggie's pa and the preacher arrived and soon they had the animals under control.

Cannon arrived next. "What happened?" the wagon master demanded, breathing heavily after his run from the larger wagon train. He kept his distance, but his voice held his concern when he asked, "Who fired that shot?"

Adam explained in a few brief words as he took the ropes from his horses' necks. He jerked his head toward the three retreating figures, now barely discernible in the darkness.

"Will they come back and try again?" Maggie asked as she watched the would-be thieves hightailing it across the prairie.

Her pa answered, "It's unlikely. They'd be fools to try anything else tonight. The entire camp is now on alert."

Josiah held up his lantern. "Shouldn't we go after them?"

Cannon shook his head. "There's no need. They didn't take any of the livestock. Besides, they have too much of a head start." He nodded at Adam. "Good work running off those thieves, Adam."

"I didn't do it alone. Maggie's the one who first spotted them." Adam looked to Maggie and saw her brother had wrapped his arms around her shoulders.

The wagon master held his lantern aloft to read the face of his pocket watch. "It's almost midnight. Since you men assigned to the second watch are already here, we may as well change the guards now." No one protested, and he continued, raising his voice so that both his camp and Adam's could hear, "The rest of you folks head on back to your wagons and get some sleep."

The group dispersed and soon only Adam and Maggie remained. "We better get back, too. Thank you for alerting me to the horse thieves."

He held Maggie's hand as they walked back to the wagons. It trembled in his. "Do you expect more trouble?"

"No." Adam turned her to face him. "You were very brave tonight."

She looked down. "No, I froze when he shot at us."

He tipped her head up. "Have you ever been shot at before, Maggie?"

A shake of her head and her big eyes told him that she hadn't been. "Then you had every right to freeze. You didn't scream or run. I'm very proud of you."

For a brief moment, Adam relived the bandit's gunfire whizzing past them. His heart had jumped into his throat. Maggie standing as still as a stone had nearly stopped his heart. Because of the fresh memory, Adam pulled her to him and hugged her close. When she looked up at him, he leaned forward and gently touched his lips to hers. Warmth spread from his lips to his heart and Adam knew that kissing Maggie had been a big mistake.

Chapter Twelve

Their kiss was still taking up all the space in Maggie's mind the next morning when their small wagon train gathered around the campfire for breakfast. While she drank her coffee, she relived its sweetness. But she didn't know exactly what to think of it. Adam had kissed her and then hurried off, saying he wanted to check on the livestock one more time before turning in.

She'd hurried back to the wagon and told the women what had happened with the bandits. She'd held Adam's sweet kiss to her heart, not revealing to any of them how much she had enjoyed being in his strong arms.

Grace had wrung her hands and fretted that they both could have been killed. Her mother-in-law had become a sweet friend and Maggie hated that she had frightened her.

Now she stifled a yawn. The night had been restless and she hadn't gotten much sleep. Her mind hadn't let her forget the way his lips had captured hers. Almost as if he cared about her. No, she told herself. She couldn't allow herself to think that one gunshot in the dark would cause him to care for her as a wife for the rest of their lives. She didn't want to study her feelings for him any more than he'd want to study his for her. After all, they'd made an agreement not to fall in love. It wasn't right to wonder if she could keep that promise.

From under hooded eyes she watched Adam fork up the last bite of his breakfast and wash it down with a swig of coffee. "I'll get the wagon hitched up. We'll be heading out soon." He handed her his dishes.

Maggie's skin tingled where his fingers briefly made contact with her hand. Under the dishwater, she rubbed the spot in an attempt to erase the peculiar sensation.

Preacher Brown stood. "He's right. I better get us going as well."

Before heading away from the campfire, he paused to give his wife a sweet kiss goodbye. His behavior was pleasingly romantic, as he wasn't going very far and would be back by Betty's side in a matter of minutes.

It was clear the preacher believed a husband didn't need a reason to shower his bride of forty years with loving gestures. Betty's pink cheeks appeared to agree heartily. They shared a tender look filled with caring and deep affection.

Maggie felt as if she were intruding on a private moment and turned away. Her gaze landed on Adam as he worked with the oxen.

The contrast between them and the Browns was evident. She sighed, telling herself that was to be expected given the dissimilarities in their relationships. Betty and her husband loved each other, and it showed in their every action when they were together. She and

Adam had shared one sweet kiss and were friends. Only friends, even though they were married.

Maggie had always desired a marriage like the Browns', one of shared looks and warm embraces, but she didn't fool herself that she would have that with Adam. Just last night they had agreed to be friends and to keep love out of the marriage. Still, they had shared that kiss.

During the long hours of the night, she had deluded herself thinking otherwise, but from the casual way he treated her this morning, she knew it wasn't to be. Adam didn't see her as a true wife and helpmate. And he never would. Neither had her first husband.

She finished putting the dishes away, asking herself if she would ever find a man who truly wanted to share his life with her. Adam didn't trust her, neither had her husband. Something about Maggie made men think she wasn't trustworthy, dependable or someone who would give all she had to make a man happy. It simply wasn't meant to be.

Thankfully the rest of the day passed without incident. They stopped for a quick cold lunch then went right back to the trail. Betty and Grace walked with her in the afternoon. They talked about quilt patterns, and Betty explained that she and her husband planned on settling in the Willamette Valley, where he intended to build a church.

With dinner and devotions finished for the evening, Maggie went to her tent where Lilly May was already sleeping. The calm day was a sweet relief. It seemed to Maggie that they had had one scare after another since they'd found Lilly May.

She only had one more entry to read from Hattie James's diary and looked forward to settling down to finish it. She slipped into her nightgown and curled up in her blanket with the book.

The day wasn't dated. It seemed Hattie had lost track of days after her husband had become ill and they'd been left behind. She'd written that Brutus seemed restless and had taken to herding Lilly May more and more. Hattie hadn't discouraged his actions; the dog was only doing what he had been taught to do. Thanks to her husband David's training, Brutus was protecting Lilly May.

It's a beautiful morning. Thankfully the sun has come out. I was worried it would rain so much we'd never get out of these woods and back on the trail. David said that we will begin our journey again tomorrow. Thankfully he is well but still very weak. I'll need to help him with the oxen and driving the wagon, but I don't mind.

Last night I told him about the baby. He says he loves Lilly May but would really like a son to carry on the James name. I'd like that, too.

Something has upset Brutus, and Lilly May is crying. She probably wants me to rescue her from her overprotective pet. I will write more tonight.

Maggie closed the book. What had upset Brutus to cause Hattie to quit writing?

Since he'd been with them, Brutus hadn't shown any signs of being upset or of herding Lilly May, except the night with the horse thieves. Had he alerted the Jameses of the bandits? She didn't know but was thankful the dog had herded Lilly May to safety.

She laid the book back inside her bag. It would be a good record for Lilly May someday. When she was old enough to read it, she would learn more about her parents and their journey.

Maggie thought more about the diary before blowing out the lantern. There were still plenty of empty pages. Maybe she should write Lilly May's story after her parents' deaths. The little girl might someday want to read about how Adam had found the diary and then married her to give Lilly May a family. A home.

In the darkness, Maggie hugged herself around the waist. The little girl would grow up loved. She would be an only child, but she would never know of her new parents' loveless marriage. The thought saddened Maggie. Every little girl dreamed of love, marriage and a household of children to love her in her old age. A tear trickled down her cheek as it hit home that she would never live her dream.

Quarantine was over. Adam and the others were back with the main wagon train. It felt good to return to his old routine, but it also left him feeling lonely for his family. He spent all day scouting ahead, and most evenings he took guard duty or fell into his bedroll exhausted from helping all the different families.

His little party had decided to stay together as much as possible and help each other out. The ladies continued to cook for all three wagons and the men took turns taking care of their livestock. In a way, the Browns were now as much a part of his new family as Maggie's father and brother.

As he returned to camp after a long day, his gaze searched for Maggie and Lilly May. The baby's jaw tooth had come in the day before and she was all smiles and drool. His mother had told him there were still other teeth that would be coming in soon, which was the reason for all the drooling.

His mind often drifted to the kiss he'd shared with Maggie. She'd surprised him by kissing him back. So much so that he'd made a hasty escape and spent the last few days trying to decide how to take back the action. Friends didn't kiss, did they? There was that question again. He'd asked himself the question every day since their kiss, and he was no closer to an answer.

Adam told himself he had no intention of falling in love, and from past experience he knew that kissing and warm embraces were signs of affection that women read as love. They'd agreed to hold hands. But that kiss… He pushed the sweet memory to the side and focused instead on his surprise for Maggie. A pencil.

A few days earlier, Maggie had shared with the group over breakfast that she planned on completing Hattie James's diary so that Lilly May would know what had happened on their journey to Oregon. She'd said that someday the little girl could look back and get to know her parents; Maggie had smiled at him and said, "Both sets of parents." Maggie figured it would be one of the first books that Lilly May would be able to read on her own, when she was old enough.

Maggie's words had caused Adam to realize he hadn't followed through with his promise to Lilly May's mother. It wasn't that he had forgotten his promise to read to Lilly May every night, but up until now there were no books that she would understand. Fortunately, they would be arriving at Fort Laramie soon and he'd see if one of the traders had any children's books that he could purchase.

Thankfully, the fort had grown since the army had taken over it. Several stores, army barracks and a bakery were there the last time he'd come through. It wasn't a big fort, but it did what it needed to do, which was provide the settlers with more goods, fresh water and a blacksmith to help repair wagon wheels that had broken.

He wondered what Maggie would think of the Camp of Sacrifice. That was the name many of the settlers had given the last few miles of the trail before they reached the fort. People usually unloaded their wagons to ease the load for the oxen or because they had broken wheels and needed to walk beside their wagons. Often, they were the fourth wheel, and the wagon was simply too heavy for them to support. Usually, the only things left in a man's wagon were his clothes and whatever food he still had remaining. Everything else was left on the side of the trail.

Which brought him back to his thought about a children's book for Lilly May. If he looked through some of the items left behind, he might not need to buy one from the store.

As Adam neared his camp, Maggie looked up from the cooking pit and offered a soft smile. In response, Adam motioned that he was going to put the horse away and continued to do just that.

A little later, Adam walked back to camp. Everyone

was there preparing for the evening meal. He could smell a stew or soup cooking and knew that Maggie had gathered edible vegetables along the trail. She often found carrots and potatoes that earlier travelers had left behind.

Josiah met his gaze with a grin. "Is it true? Will we be at the fort tomorrow?"

Adam poured a cup of coffee. "Not tomorrow. It's still a distance away. We'll be going through the Camp of Sacrifice tomorrow."

"What's the Camp of Sacrifice?" his mother asked, looking up from the needlework she was stitching on.

"It's where settlers decide that their oxen are too tired to carry their full load and start pitching the larger items from their wagons."

"What kind of stuff?" Mrs. Brown asked.

Adam took a slow drink of the lukewarm coffee, then answered, "All kinds of things. I've seen bookshelves with books in them, dressers, chairs, and last year there was a piano sitting on the side of the trail, just as pretty as you please."

Preacher Brown shook his head. "What a shame to haul it this far and then have to leave it beside the trail." He closed his Bible.

Betty's gaze moved to the Brown wagon. "I'd hate it if I had to leave my piano."

"You have a piano in your wagon?" Adam was amazed.

She clapped her hands. "Oh yes. It is a beautiful one, too. I can't wait to unpack it and play it on our first Sunday in Oregon." Her joy disappeared. "It is a shame that others had to leave their prized possessions."

"True, but their discarded goods often help others. You'll see piles of items sitting outside the fort gates, too." He looked at Maggie, who ducked her head.

"I'm thinking of looking for any children's books that I can read to Lilly May when we get back on the trail." He paused and took another sip from the cup.

Josiah spoke up. "Do they leave any useful things that we can use on the trail?"

Adam sat down on a crate. "They give up all kinds of things. Last year a couple found a whole trunk full of spices, sugar, flour and some other edibles. We heard that the family used those items all the way to Oregon. I've also heard of men finding broken wheels that could easily be repaired."

"No kiddin'?" Josiah looked perplexed. "Why would they get rid of good items like that?"

Adam shrugged. "I'm not sure. Maybe that is God's way of supplying other folks what they need."

"Now that makes sense." Preacher Brown nodded.

Maggie finally spoke up. "If you can't find Lilly May books on the trail, do you think they will sell them at the fort?" She dished hot stew out into a plate, put a piece of corn bread with it and handed it to him.

Adam inhaled deeply of the aroma. "I'm hoping they will. I promised her ma I'd read to her every night but haven't had anything I can read to her."

Preacher Brown tsked. "Son, you could have been reading to her from the Good Book. She might not understand the words now, but she'll hear them, and they will be planted in her heart."

"Our grandmother used to say that to us, too." Martin took a plate from Maggie. "Do you remember all the verses we had to memorize when we stayed with her that summer?"

She laughed. "Yes, I believe I do."

Martin grinned at her. "Have you quoted any since we left Independence?"

Maggie began reciting in a singsong voice. "'When thou passest through the waters, I will be with thee; and through the rivers, they shall not overflow thee: when thou walkest through the fire, thou shalt not be burned; neither shall the flame kindle upon thee.' Isaiah 43:2."

She smiled and Adam's heart melted a little.

"Now it's your turn," Maggie said to Martin.

A mischievous grin pulled at Martin's lips. "'Jesus wept.' John 11:35."

"You would choose the shortest verse in the Bible," Maggie scolded, playfully.

Everyone laughed.

"True, but there are days that I feel like weeping and remind myself that even Jesus wept." Martin seemed to realize he'd revealed more than he'd planned and stood up. "Well, I have first guard duty tonight, so I best be on my way."

Adam was thankful he didn't have guard duty tonight and could enjoy some time with his family. As he ate, his thoughts went to what Preacher Brown had said. Why hadn't he thought about reading Lilly May some of the stories from the Bible? There were so many that children enjoyed, like Noah's ark, Jonah and the whale, Joseph and his coat of many colors. He finished eating and handed Maggie the plate in exchange for Lilly May. He smiled at them both. "I think Preacher Brown is right. I'm going to read our little girl a few passages from the Bible tonight before she falls asleep."

Maggie wiped drool from Lilly May's chin with her apron. "That's a good idea. You are welcome to use my Bible."

Something in her eyes made Adam feel warm inside. He didn't bother to remind her that Preacher Brown had given him a Bible also. He smiled. Would reading the Bible to Lilly May somehow draw him and Maggie closer?

Chapter Thirteen

Maggie watched as Adam carried Lilly May toward her tent. She wished she could go with them, but she still had chores to do.

Preacher Brown's voice snagged Maggie's attention. "Adam! Why don't you and Maggie start to read the Bible as a family? Now is as good a time as any to begin."

Before Adam could answer, Maggie spoke up. "We can once we get to Oregon. I have evening chores to complete."

Grace shook her head. "No, I think the preacher is right. I'll finish up here."

Maggie didn't know what to do or say. She needed to protest, but hadn't she just moments before wanted to go with them? "I don't know, Grace. That's not fair to you and Betty."

"Posh, child. We can finish this up and from now on you can take care of the noon meal cleanup, freeing you to spend time with Adam and the baby in the evenings." Betty gave her a gentle push toward Adam, who had stopped and simply stared at them.

Maggie wrung her hands in her apron. "If you are sure—"

Both Grace and Betty answered at the same time, "We're sure."

Betty giggled but Grace pressed on. "Now go before the child falls asleep without hearing one word from the Good Book."

Feeling as if she didn't have a choice, Maggie walked to the tent with her husband and child. To argue now would simply cause the others to think she didn't want to spend time with Adam and Lilly May as a family.

Adam handed the child to Maggie and held the tent flap open for her to enter first. Once they were inside, it was a little cramped, but Maggie managed to get the baby ready for bed while Adam started on Genesis.

His warm voice washed over her as he read, "'In the beginning…'"

This felt natural, warm and, as Betty had said, more like a family. Maggie held Lilly May in her arms and rocked to the sound of Adam's gentle voice.

He read the first chapter then stopped with a grin on his face. He whispered, "Seems Miss Lilly May has gone to sleep."

She'd been so enamored by the warmth of his voice, Maggie hadn't realized Lilly May had drifted off to sleep. She gently laid the sleeping baby down and turned to Adam. "Your voice is so soothing it's no wonder the baby fell asleep tonight without fussing."

Adam closed the Bible. "Does she normally fuss?"

Maggie pressed her pillow against one of the tent's

poles and then sat back against it. "Most of the time, yes. She still misses her ma, especially at night."

"Maybe it's her pa she misses at night." Adam looked to the sleeping baby.

"What do you mean?"

"Before she died, Mrs. James asked me to read to Lilly May every night because her pa had done so. I'm assuming he started as soon as she was born. More than likely, our little girl fell asleep to the sound of his voice."

She was surprised that Hattie hadn't written that in her diary. Maggie made a mental note to put it in the book as soon as she had a pencil to do so. "I don't remember my pa ever reading the Bible. Ma and Pa didn't take to Christianity until Martin and I were teenagers, so it's no wonder."

"Does he read it now?"

"I'm not sure. He used to, but since Ma's passing a few years ago, I don't believe that he has read the Bible." She shrugged. "Of course, I could be wrong. He may read after retiring for the night."

"My pa read to us every Sunday. The rest of the time we were busy working the farm." He looked up at the lantern. "He died when I was about ten years old. After his death, Cain—my brother—and I grew up fast. But I still read the Bible as often as was possible."

Maggie watched the flame dance in his eyes. She could tell he'd gotten lost in his memories, perhaps of his pa, so she kept her questions to herself. Grace had told her that she had an older son, Cain, but hadn't elaborated on why she wasn't with him instead of Adam. Perhaps it was because Adam was the baby, but Maggie had felt at the time that it went deeper than that.

His attention returned to her. "Like her pa, I intend to read to Lilly May every night from now on."

The declaration in his voice left little doubt that he would keep his word. "I know she will love that." Maggie looked to Lilly May's sleeping form. Their voices didn't seem to disturb the baby so she asked, "Are you going back to farming because your pa was a farmer?"

"That's part of it."

"What's the other part?"

Adam grinned. "I've grown used to being my own boss. When I worked at the sawmill, there was always someone else to answer to. Being a scout for the wagon trains offered more freedom and I've become used to doing what I want, when I want."

"And you can do that farming?"

She'd lived on a farm for a short time with her husband and she never had that type of freedom. There were always animals to take care of, a garden to tend, not to mention the house, laundry and cooking. Granted, Matt hadn't done anything on the farm. He was too busy gambling and losing everything. Was that the type of farming Adam planned on doing, too? Maggie was shocked at the bitter thought.

Adam chuckled, clearly unaware of her feelings. "More or less. I have enough money to buy the land and build the cabin. Ma and I have seed in the wagon. At first it will be hard work building and planting, and we won't have a lot of extra. I have no intention of borrowing money from the bank. We will 'owe no man any thing,' like the Bible says."

Maggie blurted, "Are you a gambler, Adam?"

He tilted his head to look more closely at her. "No.

Are you?" It was clear by the tone of his voice he had no idea why she was asking.

She'd never heard of a lady gambler. Was he joking? From the look in his eyes, she decided he wasn't. "No, but Matt was."

Adam reached across and took her hand. He leaned in closer. His warm breath brushed her cheek as he whispered, "I'm not your late husband, Maggie. I promise I don't gamble, and I never will, especially with the lives of people I care about."

He waited for something. Maggie wasn't sure what but nodded. It was obvious that he cared for Grace and Lilly May. She fought against admitting to herself that she wished he cared for her, too.

"I should be going. Tomorrow morning will be here before we know it." Adam eased out of the tent.

Maggie heard the thud of Brutus taking up guard duty.

Adam's low voice drifted into the tent as he commanded the dog, "Keep her safe, ole boy."

She knew he was talking about Lilly May. Even though he'd assured her he wasn't Matt, Adam didn't love her. Maggie blew out the lamp and fought down the knowledge that if she wasn't real careful, her heart could easily betray her and love Adam.

The Camp of Sacrifice was just as he remembered it. Adam pulled the wagon behind the one in front of him and watched as others did the same until they had a complete circle. Men were already dismounting their wagons and tending to the tired oxen. The women were looking in the direction of the items that had been left behind and trying to keep the children in check, promising they could all go see what treasures lay in the piles after dinner had been served and put away.

Cannon rode up beside Adam's wagon. "I see you are driving again. What happened to Josiah?"

Adam grinned. "I believe he and a certain young lady wanted to walk together."

"You know you'll have to scout ahead tonight then?"

He jumped from his wagon. "I'm aware."

As if he knew they were talking about him, Josiah walked up to the wagon, leading Shadow. "Here's your horse, Adam. Thanks for the free time. I'll take care of the oxen." Pink color filled the young man's cheeks as he hurried to do his job.

"You are much too easy on him." Cannon grinned, taking the sting out of his words.

Adam pulled himself into the saddle, aware of Maggie and his mother working side by side, preparing the evening meal. "He's young and we still have a way to go to get to Oregon Country. He might as well have some fun now, while he can."

Cannon's gaze followed his. "How are you and the missus getting along?"

"Now that's kind of personal, isn't it?" It was Adam's turn to grin.

The wagon master laughed. "Fair enough." He turned his horse to move on to the next wagon.

"We're getting along just fine."

It was true. They were getting along fine. She was acting the part of a loving wife and he was doing his job as a wagon scout. They didn't have that much farther to go until they got to Fort Laramie, and then he would surprise her with a wedding ring.

After leaving her tent that night, his mind had raced. The thought that she might find someone at the fort who took her fancy ate at him. What if she betrayed him with one of the soldiers or someone from another wagon train? Or even a trapper? Some of those men came from the mountains with the sole purpose of finding a wife to take back to their winter cabin.

Adam shook his head at the ridiculous thoughts. She would never give up Lilly May to move in with a stinky man who only came from his cabin a couple of times a year to turn in his furs.

To be fair to Maggie, she'd given him no reason not to trust her. Deep inside he believed Maggie wouldn't betray him. She was still stinging from the loss of her late husband, Matt. Even last night, she'd compared him to her husband. It was obvious that Maggie didn't trust men—him or anyone else. He hurt knowing she still didn't trust him to do right by her. It was just an even better excuse to get her a wedding ring.

Maggie noticed him watching her and walked toward him. To save her a few steps, Adam met her halfway.

In greeting she said, "Grace and I were talking, and we were wondering if we see something that we can use in the left-behind things, do you think we'll be able to get it?"

Adam couldn't imagine what the women would want from the pile of goods. "Well, if you find something, bring it to the wagon and we can decide as soon as I get back from scouting ahead."

"You leaving now?"

Was that disappointment he heard in her voice?

"In a few minutes."

She shaded her eyes as she looked up at him. "How long will you be gone?"

"Probably a couple of hours. Why? Is there something you need?"

Maggie shook her head. "No, but you must be hungry. You didn't eat much breakfast or lunch."

His stomach growled in answer to her statement. "I am a little, but I'll be okay until I get back."

She shook her head. "No, wait here." Maggie hurried back to their campfire.

He watched the graceful way she moved. Her dress was tattered about the hem, her shoes had seen better days and her bonnet's strings were practically worn through. Yet she walked with the style of a lady in her finest.

Adam mounted Shadow and did as he was told. He waited.

The smile she offered on her return challenged the sun in its brightness. "Your ma and I pulled together a cold supper for you." She handed him a cloth sack.

He'd been looking forward to a hot meal tonight. It was kind of her to want to feed him when he was hungry even if it did cheat him out of a warm full belly later tonight. Adam tied the bag to his saddle horn.

As if she read his mind, Maggie laid a hand on his thigh and smiled. "I'll set a plate aside for you, too."

Her eyes danced with mischief. How was it she'd read his thoughts?

As Maggie turned to leave, Adam remembered the pencil he'd forgotten to give her the night before. "Maggie?" He waited until he had her full attention and then reached into his pocket and pulled out the writing tool.

A big smile brightened her face when she saw what he had.

"I thought you might like this." He handed it down to her. Their fingers touched as she took the pencil.

Her cheeks turned a soft pink. "Oh, Adam. Thank you."

"You're welcome. I'll see you soon. Don't forget to keep my supper warm."

She stepped away from the horse. "I won't. Be safe."

Be safe. That seemed like an odd thing for her to have said. Only people who cared about other people said caring words like *be safe.* Maggie cared for him. Maybe not as a loving wife, but it warmed him to think that she cared at all. He headed out of camp with a grin on his face.

Adam had been in the saddle for about an hour when he decided it was time to get back to the wagon train. The trail was clear and the water good for the animals and people to drink. He'd just turned Shadow when a gunshot rang out.

Pain entered his shoulder and the pressure from the bullet pushed him backward. Only Shadow's training kept him in the saddle. The horse slowed his gait to give his master time to recover.

Laying low over the saddle horn and neck of his horse, Adam looked for cover. He saw a clump of trees and made for them. Shadow entered them and he slid to the ground, grabbing for his gun with his left hand. Thanks to the bullet, his right arm hung limply by his side as warm blood pooled at his feet.

Stupid! Stupid! Stupid! he silently berated himself. Why hadn't he been paying attention? He didn't deny the reason. He'd been dreaming about his farm and the life he and Maggie would someday have.

If he survived.

Chapter Fourteen

Maggie paced.

Where was he?

Adam had said he'd be back in a couple of hours. She twisted her apron in her hands. That was four hours ago.

Grace pulled on her arm. "Please, Maggie, sit down. You are wearing me out with all that pacing." She smoothed out the material for Lilly May's new dress and began hemming the little sleeve.

"I can't. He's late." She looked in the direction Adam had left.

Her pa spoke up. "Adam is the wagon train scout. He's doing his job, daughter. Now do as Grace said and sit down."

Out of respect for them both, Maggie sat and scooped Lilly May up onto her lap. "I know he's doing his job, but Adam said he'd only be gone a couple of hours."

Grace and her father shared a grin. Maggie knew that they thought she worried about Adam because she loved him but that wasn't the case. She cared about him, they were friends, but she wasn't in love with her husband.

The sound of a horse galloping toward the camp caused them all to stand up and look. Her pa grabbed his gun. Maggie could see the other men doing the same. Mothers gathered their children to them like hens gathering their chicks during a rainstorm.

Instinctively, Maggie and Grace started to the wagon. They'd been told to get in the wagon if trouble arose in the camp. It sounded like they were in for trouble now.

Grace scrambled into the wagon and Maggie handed Lilly May to her.

Betty poked her head through the canvas at the front of her wagon and called to her. "Hurry, Maggie, get inside."

Maggie was doing just that when she heard one of the men shout, "It's Adam! He's been shot!" She scrambled back down.

Martin raced ahead of her and grabbed Shadow's reins. The horse snorted and bobbed his head as several of the men helped Adam out of the saddle. Maggie could see that he'd tied one of his hands to the saddle with the reins.

The wagon master pushed through the throng of men and women. He immediately began barking orders. "Mary Jo, go get the doctor. The rest of you, let his missus pass."

Maggie hurried through the parted sea of people. She now could see that Shadow's shoulder blade was covered in blood. Where had it come from? The man or the horse?

Then she saw him, Adam, slumped between two men. His pale face pinched in pain. "I'm all right, Maggie." He groaned.

"Easy, men." Cannon instructed, "Take him to his wagon."

His right arm hung limply at his side. Blood covered his shoulder, sleeve and hand. How much had he lost? She hurried after the parade of men. They asked questions as they walked.

"Who shot you?"

"How many were there?"

"Did you shoot back?"

Maggie couldn't tell which man asked which question, and she really didn't care. What she wanted to know was how bad Adam was hurt. But no one asked that question.

She heard her pa ask, "Son, did anyone follow you?"

"I don't believe so," Adam replied through gritted teeth.

The wagon master issued more orders. "Daniels, Smith and Green, you men are on guard duty until further notice."

It seemed to take forever for them to get back to their wagon. Even though they had given Maggie room to see Adam, the men hadn't allowed her to touch him or help get him back. She felt useless.

The doctor, with his black medicine bag in his hands, waited beside Grace. Maggie quickly located Betty holding Lilly May off to the side.

They had turned a crate over and the doctor ordered, "Set him there. Grace, I need to borrow your scissors."

Adam's mother hurried to get them from where she'd been working on Lilly May's dress earlier. She quickly handed them over.

"This shirt has to be cut off. I'll do my best to salvage

it for you, Maggie." He quickly began cutting the shirt from Adam. He looked up and noticed all the people standing around, watching. "Go back to your business, folks. He's not going to die."

At that exact moment, Adam slumped over. Maggie hadn't seen her pa move so fast in a long time. The older man caught him from behind and held him up as the doctor finished removing Adam's shirt.

"Do as the doctor says, folks," she heard Cannon say behind them. "We'll let you know how our scout is doing in a little while."

There were grumbles but the crowd did as they were told.

Maggie felt as if she were frozen in time. She watched as the doctor seemed to move in slow motion. He finished cutting the shirt off and handed it to her.

"Put it in cold water. That will keep the stain from setting. You should be able to repair it so that he can wear it again."

She nodded. "Thank you."

With her brother and pa holding up her husband, she watched as the doctor began his examination. She was thankful he was unconscious when the doctor poked his finger into the bullet hole and dug around as if looking for something.

Even though he was out cold, Adam grunted in pain and tried to move his shoulder from the doctor's grasp.

"Did the bullet go all the way through?" Grace asked.

"No, it's lodged in his shoulder bone. We need to lay him down so I can get the bullet out." The doctor looked at Maggie for directions on where to lay Adam down.

She pointed to her tent. "Give me a minute and I'll make room for you both."

Grace shook her head. "No, child, he needs to go in the wagon. He may not feel up to walking tomorrow."

Maggie simply nodded. She knew that if anyone asked how she held up in a crisis, based on today's performance, they would say not well.

Martin spoke up. "I'll help you move him, Doc."

"Thank you, Martin."

Grace hurried ahead and climbed into the wagon, before moving things around to give the men room. Adam's face was as white as the wagon tops had been when they'd first set out on the trail. He looked as if death were paying him a visit.

Grace poked her head out. "I'm ready for him."

Maggie knew it was her job to care for Adam; he was her husband after all. But she also knew that Grace was his mother and would want to be there for her son. She looked to the doctor. It took all her strength not to insist she take care of her husband. Instead, she asked, "What can I do to help?"

"Get a pot of water boiling. I'm going to need to clean the wound once we get the bullet out." With no more instructions to give, the doctor and Martin put Adam in the wagon.

Maggie set about her task.

As she put the pot over the flame she heard the doctor's voice in the wagon. "Martin, I need you to stick around. I'm going to require your strength to hold him down while I dig out that bullet."

The old saying, a watched pot never boils, came to mind as everyone waited for the water to heat up enough for the doctor. At the slightest boil, Maggie pulled the pot from over the fire and hurried to the wagon with it.

"Thank you, Maggie." He took the pot and pointed back to the campfire. "You ladies wait out there. This shouldn't take too long."

Grace exited the wagon and resumed her sewing, her eyes closed as if in prayer. Maggie paced. She wanted to talk to Grace but didn't want to interrupt her if she was praying.

The preacher sat on the piano bench with Betty by his side, holding Lilly May. After about fifteen minutes, he stopped Maggie's pacing by saying, "Would you feel better if we prayed over him?"

Both Grace and Maggie answered, "Yes."

He didn't need any more prompting. Preacher Brown prayed. "Heavenly Father, we come before You this evening with thanksgiving in our hearts. We thank You that Adam made it back to the wagon train. We ask You to help the doctor get the bullet out with as little pain as possible. And for his speedy recovery. In Jesus' name, amen."

"Amen" echoed around the campsite.

Maggie noticed that the wagon master stood just outside the firepit's light. She walked over to him. In her opinion, if he cared enough to wait, he should be made to feel welcome. "Would you like a cup of coffee while we wait?"

He cleared his throat. "Thank you. That would be most welcome."

Her pa scooted over on the crate he'd overturned and motioned for the other man to join him.

Maggie poured him a cup of the hot coffee. "Has this ever happened before?" she asked, handing him the mug.

"Not in my experience." Cannon blew on the hot beverage.

Her pa asked, "How many times have you led a train to Oregon?"

"This is my fifth trip."

Maggie would have thought her pa had asked that question before they left Missouri. Hadn't he studied anything about the trail before dragging his small family out West? She didn't have time to ponder her question.

The doctor climbed out of the wagon, followed by Martin. They walked to where everyone was seated. Maggie and the others all spoke at once. Doc held up his hand to silence them. "Before you all start asking questions, let me say he's going to be fine. It took some work, and he's going to have a nasty scar, but the bullet is out, and he will live." He walked over to the washtub, set his bag down and proceeded to wash the blood from his hands.

The doctor dried his hands and then picked up his bag. As if talking to himself, he said, "Adam may have an ache in that shoulder for the rest of his life, but that bullet didn't completely shatter the bone, so we have something to be thankful for, besides his life." He yawned and turned to Grace and Maggie. "You'll need to keep the wound clean and him still for a couple of days." His gaze moved to Lilly May in Betty's lap. "And no lifting that baby for at least a month. He shouldn't lift anything over five pounds during that time."

Grace stood and folded Lilly May's dress then put it back into her sewing box. "We'll see to him."

Josiah spoke up. "I'll take care of Shadow, the team and the wagon."

"Mr. Cannon, I'll take his guard duties," Martin offered.

The wagon master nodded his approval. "I'm sure Wilbur Smith won't mind scouting for the wagon train again." He turned to Maggie and gave her some final instruction. "Adam will sleep for the rest of the night. I gave him morphine for the pain. He may need more tomorrow but after that we'll use something else to ease the discomfort."

"Thank you, Doctor." Maggie felt like crying for Adam. His pain must have been great for Adam to need morphine.

The doctor yawned again. "I'm going back to my wagon. If Adam starts to run a fever, come get me."

"Good night, Doc." The wagon master turned his attention to the ladies. "I'll let the folks know Adam is going to be all right." As he walked away, Maggie heard him mutter to himself, "At this rate, he's going to need to pay me for letting him tag along."

Maggie paid him no mind. She was only concerned about Adam and the fact that he could have died. She'd thought earlier her concern was because they were friends. Now she questioned her emotions. Was it possible Adam meant more to her than just a friend?

Chapter Fifteen

Maggie rested in the wagon beside Adam. Grace had insisted that Maggie be with her husband, and she'd take care of Lilly May. Maggie knew her bed mat was comfortable but still hated the idea of her mother-in-law in the tent and her in the wagon. It just didn't feel natural.

Just as the doctor had said, Adam continued to sleep. It wasn't the restful sleep she'd expected. He lay on his back and talked softly in his sleep. The name Lynda came from his lips several times. But Maggie couldn't make out much more than the words, "Lynda, why?"

Maggie could only assume that Lynda was Adam's ex-fiancée. As she lay there, Maggie had mixed emotions. Sympathy for Adam warred with her anger with the mysterious Lynda for breaking his heart, and confusion with herself for feelings of jealousy.

He mumbled something in his sleep and turned onto his side. A groan of pain escaped his lips when he landed on his injured shoulder.

Maggie gently turned him onto his back. "Shhhh, lie still." She wiped the hair off his brow.

In his sleep, Adam murmured, "Sweet Maggie." He repeated it as if speaking to someone in his dreams. After several long moments of silence, his soft snores filled the wagon.

She lay back down. Sweet? He'd called her sweet. The wall around her heart began to crumble as she realized that in his sleep, Adam had revealed that he cared for her.

Maggie looked at the adobe Fort Laramie with its high walls that completely enclosed it. "Are you sure we'll be able to buy supplies here?" she asked Adam, who stood beside her. A sling made from Grace's tied-together tea towels supported his injured shoulder.

"It may not look like much, but this fort has several stores to buy supplies, along with a blacksmith shop, a couple of livery stables and a bakery."

She grinned. "A bakery?"

He nodded with a big smile. "Yep." Adam laced his fingers within hers and tugged to urge her forward. "Let's get what you came for and then we'll have a piece of pie before we head back."

Maggie giggled. "I kind of feel guilty, shopping and eating pie when your mother is back at camp taking care of Lilly May."

She probably should feel guilty for having Adam almost exclusively to herself for the past two days, but she didn't. Since he'd unknowingly admitted he had feelings for her, Maggie felt closer to him. He might never think of her as a real wife, but she now knew he regarded her as a true friend.

Adam chuckled. "Don't feel bad for Ma. We'll take a piece of pie back to her and maybe a cookie for Lilly May."

The wagon master had promised to stay a few days and give the men time to visit the blacksmith and do any repairs their wagons required. The women would have time to replace any supplies that had been used up. They were camped about a mile from the fort and Maggie knew that Grace would be able to shop soon, too. The thought made her feel a little less guilty.

It had only been a couple of days since Adam had been shot but he'd bounced back quickly. The bullet hole was still raw and sensitive, but Maggie admired her husband. If he hadn't been wearing the sling that the doctor had insisted on, she doubted anyone would know just by looking at him that he was injured at all.

As they entered the fort, Maggie felt as if they had stepped into a small town. Men were engaged in all kinds of business. They laughed and talked among themselves like old friends. A few women entered a shop that looked much like a general store. Children ran from store to store, laughing and playing.

"What is it that we came for?" Adam asked as Maggie led the way to what appeared to be the largest general store.

She continued to hold his hand but now she was pulling him instead of simply walking beside him. "Tea and sugar. Not a lot, just some for tonight. We will be returning tomorrow to get the full order of what is needed for the rest of the trip."

From the look on his face, Adam stifled a laugh. "And I guess that the tea and sugar are top on your list and not Ma's?"

"Exactly. I haven't had a good cup of sweet tea in ages." Maggie released his hand and opened the door to the store.

Their senses were immediately assaulted with the smells of spices. She detected cinnamon, cloves and something else that she didn't quite recognize. The scent of tobacco and pickles also filled the space. The large one-room store was packed with food items and some articles of clothing, hats and even a row of boots. There wasn't a single empty shelf in the whole store.

She clapped her hands in glee. "Oh, Adam, it's so wonderful."

This time he did laugh. Maggie enjoyed the sound clear down to her toes. Adam's laughter filled her with such joy that she joined in.

"I thought I recognized that laugh."

Both Maggie and Adam turned at the sound of the man's voice. She didn't recognize him and looked to Adam.

No longer did a smile fill her husband's face. Instead, his jaw hardened, and his fist clinched at his side. Deep hardness filled Adam's voice as he demanded, "What are you doing here, Cain?"

Adam faced his older brother. Every nerve in his body stood on end due to the tension he felt. They'd not spoken in the last four years. Why had Cain shown up now? Why on the Oregon Trail? Had he somehow learned of their plans and followed them?

"I would imagine that's obvious. I'm doing the same as you, buying supplies for the rest of my trip to Oregon." Cain crossed his arms and allowed his gaze to travel over Maggie, from the top of her head to the soles of her worn-out shoes. "And who do we have here?" He stepped closer to Maggie.

Maggie stepped back. Before Adam could answer she said, "I'm Maggie Walker."

"Walker?" Cain's eyes shot from Maggie to Adam.

Adam reached out and took her hand. "As in Mrs. Adam Walker."

Cain whistled low, drawing the attention of several of the men in the store. "You did good for yourself, little brother. I'm glad to see you recovered from your last lost love."

His voice grated on Adam's nerves. He turned to Maggie. "Go find your tea and sugar, and I'll meet you at the counter."

Concern filled her voice. "Adam?"

"Aw, that's sweet. She doesn't want to leave your side." Cain looked over Adam's shoulder. "Where's Ma?"

Adam ignored his brother and offered Maggie what he hoped was a gentle smile. "Everything's fine. The sooner you find the tea, the sooner we can be on our way."

She nodded, then hurried to the counter to place her order.

He took a deep breath then turned to his brother. "Ma is back at camp. I'm sure she will be surprised to see you here."

"I'm sure she will." Cain dropped his voice. "Especially since I haven't seen her since you broke off your engagement to Lynda."

Adam wanted to cross his arms, but his shoulder throbbed under the bandages and sling. He ignored Cain's reference to Lynda. "Goodbye, Cain." He turned to leave but Cain's voice stopped him.

"What happened to your shoulder, little brother?"

Was it his imagination or was there pleased smugness in Cain's tone? Adam faced his brother and answered, "That's no concern of yours."

"I'd be happy to help you with your wagon, if you want me to join your wagon train." Cain grinned, like a possum in the henhouse.

Adam got nose to nose with him and ground between his teeth in a low voice, "Stay away from my family. We don't want you anywhere near our wagon."

Cain continued to grin but the emotion didn't enter his eyes. "We'll see what Ma has to say about that."

"Cain—"

Maggie interrupted his threat by calling sweetly, "Adam, I'm ready."

Cain laughed and stepped around him. He headed for the door, but just before leaving he walked to Maggie at the counter. "It was nice to meet you, Maggie." Only then did he smile at Adam and walk out of the store.

His brother was up to no good. When had he begun his journey West? Now Adam wished he'd kept better tabs on his brother. He paid for the tea and sugar, then took Maggie's elbow and guided her out of the store.

"So that was your brother?" She pulled her arm from his grasp and slipped her hand in his. "Let me guess— you two don't get along, now that you are adults."

He searched the grounds for Cain. Now that they were apart, he wished he'd found out what Cain was doing here. He'd learned his brother was headed to Oregon but not by what means. Was Cain serious when he'd suggested that he join their wagon train?

His gaze moved to Maggie. Her head was tilted back slightly so that she could see his face. What had she thought of Cain? Had she found him handsome? Lynda had. Who was he kidding? Every woman his brother had ever met fell all over themselves at his good looks. Would Maggie?

Where Adam had dull brown hair, Cain had coal black, and it shone in the sun like a new penny. He felt his brown eyes were boring compared to the brilliant blue orbs that looked out of Cain's face. The only things they had in common were their height and build.

"Is he joining our wagon train?" she asked, still staring up at him, waiting for him to tell her more about his brother.

"No. Well, not if I can help it." Adam began walking to the bakery. He'd promised Maggie pie and then they were going back to the wagon train.

"I see."

What did she see? He hadn't told her that Cain was the other man who had stolen his fiancée four years ago.

"I imagine Grace will be glad to see him." She smiled sweetly up at him.

Still, Adam could tell she had lots of questions about Cain. Questions he wasn't ready to answer. "I wouldn't be so sure."

Maggie stopped walking.

He turned to face her. His gaze moved about to see if anyone was watching them.

"Adam, she is his mother. I don't know why you are angry with him but please don't make your mother choose between you." Her eyes pleaded with him to do as she asked.

She was right. Cain was the firstborn son and Grace loved him. Even though he'd done little to deserve that love. "I won't." Even as he promised her, he wished he could prevent Grace from seeing Cain. If only they weren't going to be staying a few days.

A big smile filled her mouth and eyes. "Good." She started walking again. "Do you think they have black-berry pie?"

Adam wished he could change his train of thought as fast as she'd done. "I don't know."

"What's your favorite pie?"

He decided to push thoughts of Cain to the back of his mind until they returned to the wagon train and just enjoy this time alone with Maggie. "With black coffee?" he teased.

"Sure, or a tall, cold glass of milk." She giggled.

Adam pretended to be in deep thought. "Hmmmm, I'd have to say either pecan or cherry."

"Yum, both sound wonderful."

He held the door open for her. The fragrance of hot fresh bread and sweet pies filled the air that greeted him like an old friend. Parker's bakery was his favorite food stop on the Oregon trail.

Maggie entered the bakery and inhaled deeply. "And they smell wonderful, too."

A big robust voice called to her from the counter. "Come on in here, young lady, and have a seat."

Adam grinned. He wondered what Maggie would think of Jim Parker, the baker and owner of the bakery. Jim was a big man with large arms, wide chest and a white apron. His voice could stop a man in his tracks if the baker wanted it to.

Without missing a beat, Maggie smiled sweetly and said, "Thank you." She headed to the table closest to the only window in the room.

He followed her.

Jim asked, "Do you want a pot of coffee or just a cup?"

"We'll start with a cup," Adam answered as he pulled out Maggie's chair.

She grinned up at him. When he was seated across from her, she leaned forward and asked in a soft voice, "How can he offer a full pot of coffee to each table?"

Adam met her in the middle of the table. "As far as I know, no one ever takes the whole pot, but if they did, I imagine he has two or three pots in the kitchen."

Jim came to the table with two cups of coffee. After setting them down, he pulled a small paper pad from the front pocket of his apron. "I have apple, blackberry and pecan pie today."

Maggie ordered blackberry with a smile. She seemed to be all smiles today. Adam studied her face as she talked to Jim. Her eyes danced as the baker told her that he'd be making cinnamon rolls topped with melted butter in the morning if she wanted to come in early for a warm one.

When Jim left the table to get their pies, Maggie turned to Adam. "Grace said she'd like to come to the fort tomorrow morning. I wonder if Betty would like to come with us. It will be fun to shop together and then come here for a sweet treat before we return to the wagon train."

"Sounds like you ladies will have a good time tomorrow." He took a sip of his coffee.

She nodded. "In the morning, yes, but we already know we'll have to pack up the supplies and do laundry tomorrow afternoon." Maggie picked up her cup and held it as if she were warming her hands. She rocked it in between her palms.

Adam wasn't sure he liked the serious expression on her face. What had happened to the playful Maggie? "Is something wrong?"

She shook her head. "No. I was just thinking about the rest of our trip." Maggie took a sip of her drink. "We still have the mountains to cross, and I overheard a couple talking earlier and they were saying it will be even harder than what we've already traveled."

He reached out and took her hand. "This trip is what we make it. If we use caution and work together, we'll be fine."

She grinned at him. "I'm glad you've made the trip before."

Adam wasn't looking forward to crossing the mountains, but he didn't see the need to concern her about the hardships that awaited them. In his experience, this last part of their journey was the most difficult.

And the most dangerous.

The next morning, Adam got up early and headed for Fort Laramie before anyone woke up. His shoulder ached. It would have been nice to sit by the fire a spell and let the shoulder loosen up a bit, but he couldn't afford to wait. He needed to find his brother and persuade him to move on, not join their wagon train. If that didn't work, he planned on meeting Cannon and asking him not to allow Cain onto their train.

He searched the fort but didn't see Cain anywhere. After asking around, Adam learned that another wagon train had left earlier that morning. Instant relief and joy filled him. To his way of thinking, if he couldn't find Cain in the fort, his older brother must have left with the other wagon train.

His next stop was one of the small general stores that was inside the fort. When he entered the door, a hearty voice greeted him.

"Good morning, what can I help you find today?"

Adam walked farther into the shop. His eyes scanned the room. He was the only customer. Adam gave the big proprietor his full attention. "I recently got married and I'd like to buy a ring for my new bride."

The big man walked to the board counter and stepped around behind it. He brought out a small tray of rings. "You are timely. I have quite a few. They aren't wedding rings, but they are rings."

"Well, this is a surprise. I didn't expect you to have so many." Adam wanted a ring that fit Maggie. Not just in size but in personality, too.

"I get two or three with almost every wagon train that comes through here." The big man picked up one of the smaller rings and sighed. "Traveling to Oregon takes too many wives and mothers from their families. Their menfolk will often trade goods for the rings. Then there are the families who come through that don't have cash, and I trade their rings for whatever they need to survive the trail."

A small pinkish gold ring caught his eye. It had

leaves and flowers etched into the metal. Adam realized as he looked at the jewelry that he didn't know Maggie's ring size. He picked up the ring and ran his finger over the fine etching. It matched Maggie.

He held the ring out to the store owner. "I like this one but I'm not sure it will fit my wife."

"You are welcome to return it if it doesn't fit but you have to do so today." He wrapped the ring in a small piece of material and smiled. "You have good taste. This is a rose gold ring. I bought it before I left Missouri and had planned on giving it to my wife, but she fell in love with a different ring, so I decided just this morning to put it with these."

Adam was glad to hear it hadn't been given up by someone who had cherished it. He paid the man and put the ring in his pocket. His next stop was the bakery. He remembered that the baker made a batch of cinnamon rolls each morning but usually sold out early. Adam hoped to get one for Maggie to share with Lilly May.

Fortunately, the baker was dishing out the sweet rolls when he arrived and thankfully Adam was in time to get the last two. With the pastries in a brown paper bag, Adam started back to the wagon train.

His gaze fell on Maggie as she climbed out of the tent. She helped Lilly May out too, all the while shoving Brutus back. The big dog was happy to see his ward and mistress and his greeting was an every morning ritual.

"Good morning," Adam said as he bent down and gave Lilly May a hug and then a kiss on the top of her head.

The baby giggled and raised her arms to be held. He started to pick her up, but Maggie stopped him. "The doctor says your pa cannot hold you until his shoulder is all better," she told the little girl as she picked her up and smiled at Adam.

"I have a surprise for you this morning," he told Maggie.

"A surprise?" Happiness filled her face. "What kind of surprise?"

He held the paper bag out to her. Adam grinned. "Look inside."

Maggie, balancing Lilly May on her hip, quickly opened the bag and inhaled. "Oh, Adam."

A chuckle escaped his throat. It would seem his wife liked cinnamon rolls as much as blackberry pie. She carried the sweets to the back of the wagon and set them out on two plates.

"What have we here?" Grace asked as she peeked out the back of the wagon.

"Adam brought us breakfast." Maggie showed her the rolls.

"Son, you shouldn't have." His mother climbed down the rest of the way out of the wagon, mindful of the food on the tailgate.

He didn't have the heart to say that one of the rolls was for Maggie and the other himself. Instead, he smiled and offered, "I'll make the coffee."

Adam stirred the coals in the bottom of the firepit. They were still warm. He had a fire going and coffee brewing in a matter of minutes. Maggie and Grace were cutting the rolls in half and putting them on plates.

"Should we scramble eggs this morning, too?" Maggie asked Grace.

"Maybe later. We can have egg sandwiches for lunch, if that's all right with you."

"That sounds wonderful to me," Maggie replied. She looked up into the morning sky. "I hope it doesn't rain."

Adam enjoyed listening to the women chatter as they discussed the day. He poured a cup of coffee and returned to them. "Here you go, ladies. Who gets the first cup?"

"Give it to Grace," Maggie instructed. She sat Lilly May on the tailgate. "Why don't you sit and let me do the serving."

"Nope, I might only have one usable arm, but I don't intend to just sit around."

Grace took the coffee and one of the plates with half a cinnamon roll on it. She then went to sit on her crate and wait for the rest of them.

Adam went back for another cup of coffee. "Where is everyone this morning?" he asked as he poured the hot brew.

"Betty and the preacher are sleeping in. They ask that we not disturb them this morning." Grace grinned. "It's not often we get to sleep in."

Maggie turned to look at Grace. Concern filled her face. "Did we wake you this morning?"

Grace waved her hand. "Not at all. I'm a creature of habit. I woke at my regular time."

"What about your pa and Martin?" Adam asked, drawing Maggie's attention from his mother.

"They went to talk to Mr. Green this morning."

Adam wasn't about to ask what about, even though he was curious.

Thankfully, Grace had no reservations of doing so. "What about?"

Maggie carried Lilly May and her breakfast plate and went to sit down by Grace. She sat Lilly May down at her feet and handed the baby a small pinch of her cinnamon roll. "It seems Mr. Green has decided not to continue to Oregon and wants to sell one of his wagons full of goods."

Adam knew Mr. Green had been planning on starting a store in Oregon. If Maggie's pa succeeded in buying his goods, he and Martin would have their hands full taking care of more animals and another wagon.

"Hurry, Adam. We can't eat until grace is said," his mother reminded him.

He poured his coffee and when he went to get his plate he saw that a whole roll rested in its center. A grin filled his face. Maggie had shared her roll with his ma, leaving him with a complete one. Adam picked up the knife and swiftly cut it in half. The second half he cut into thirds then turned to join his family.

Once grace was said, he dug into his cinnamon roll. The sweet syrup coated his tongue. His gaze moved to Maggie, who seemed to be savoring her roll. His mother had eaten hers so fast that he had to laugh. "Slow down, Ma. You're going to choke yourself," he cautioned her, as she had done him so many times growing up.

Grace smiled. "It's so good. That man can bake."

Adam had to agree. As soon as Grace had finished the last bite of her half, he stood and shared the pieces he'd cut. Waving off the women's protests, he sat back down to savor his breakfast.

He imagined life on the farm. The three of them and Lilly May would enjoy many mornings sharing breakfast. Now that he knew Cain had moved on, Adam felt at peace.

* * *

Just when Maggie thought her husband could be no kinder, he did something as simple as sharing his breakfast. She smiled her thanks and then dug in. Lilly May ate hers fast as well. The little girl smacked her lips and reached for more.

As soon as they were done eating, the two women cleaned up the dishes while Adam played with his daughter. Maggie wondered if he still intended to buy a children's book to read to the little girl or if he would continue reading the Bible as a family each night.

"If you two will excuse me, I'm going with Katherine White into the fort this morning." Grace took her soiled apron off and donned a clean one.

Maggie sat back down beside Adam. Disappointment filled her. She'd assumed she, Grace and Betty would explore the fort this morning. *That's what happens when you assume*, Maggie reminded herself. Was Josiah's girlfriend, Penelope White, going with her mother and Grace? Instead of pouting, she decided to be happy for Grace and her new friendship with Mrs. White. "Have fun, Grace."

Grace laughed. "Oh, I intend to. Betty told me last night there is so much to look at in that fort." She waved and then walked away.

Adam took her hand in his. Maggie turned her attention back to him and Lilly May.

"I have another surprise for you." He stood and dug in his front pants pocket.

Another surprise? Maggie had no idea what more he could surprise her with.

He held something small in his hand when he returned to his seat. "I know our marriage isn't a true marriage, but I wanted to get you something that most married women want."

"What's that?" Maggie asked, curious as to what her husband thought she wanted.

He slowly started to unwrap the small package in his hands.

Maggie didn't realize she was holding her breath until he extended a dainty ring toward her. The small vines and flowers were stunning. The band shone in the morning sun. "Oh, Adam, it's beautiful."

"Try it on." He waited while she slipped it onto her finger. "Does it fit?"

"It's a little big." Maggie ran her fingers over the band. "I might be able to wrap a small piece of cloth around the underside of it."

Adam shook his head. "No, I'll return it."

"No!" Maggie didn't realize how much the ring meant to her until he said he would return it. In a calmer voice she said, "I want to keep it. It's beautiful."

He stood and smiled down at her. "You can keep it."

"Thank you." Maggie held her hand out and watched as the morning light caused the pink glow of the ring to sparkle and dance.

Maggie wished theirs was a marriage of love and trust. She wanted to kiss Adam and thank him properly for the beautiful ring, but she didn't think he'd take kindly to such affection.

Then again, why did he get her a wedding ring? To show he cared for her? To let everyone know that she was married? Her emotions were torn; Maggie wanted to think he bought it for her as an expression of love.

But she knew that wasn't the case. And she didn't want to fall in love with him, so why did it hurt to think he simply thought it was a pretty ring she might like?

Chapter Sixteen

Maggie hated to leave Fort Laramie. She'd enjoyed the shopping and relaxing. Mr. Cannon had allowed them to stay a day longer than he'd first scheduled. He had called a meeting and informed everyone to enjoy the extra day, as the rest of their journey would be filled with danger and added hardships.

She remembered Adam's words. "This trip is what we make it. If we use caution and work together, we'll be fine." She looked to where he walked beside the wagon. The doctor had cautioned him the night before about riding on the seat or on Shadow. He'd suggested that the jarring could open the wound and cause more bleeding.

Now that they were away from the fort, the wagon master had told them to carry as much water with them as possible and advised the women and children to collect buffalo chips to start their fires. Wood was as sparse now as water.

Lilly May giggled happily from the small wagon

Adam had purchased for her at the fort. Brutus trotted along beside his girl, while Maggie pulled her and searched for dried chips. The wagon was lightweight, with slats of wood on each side, tall enough to keep Lilly May from falling out. For added protection, Adam and Martin had attached material to securely tie the child inside and connected a canvas cover much like the larger wagons to supply shade for Lilly May. Maggie had made sure to put a soft yarn ball and a small cloth doll in for her to play with.

Maggie watched as Lilly May tossed the ball out of the wagon and Brutus fetched it back to her. Since she was so small, Lilly May couldn't throw it very far, but Brutus made a show of racing about and then going back to the ball. He would then drop it back inside the wagon for Lilly May to toss again.

Grace caught up to them. "That wagon was one of Adam's best purchases." She giggled. "Right up there with cinnamon rolls."

Maggie fingered the ring that Adam had given her. To her the ring was the best purchase Adam had made while at the fort, but instead of arguing she said, "I agree. She is safe and having fun with Brutus."

"Good thing I picked up another spool of yarn at the fort. That baby's ball is going to need to be replaced." She laughed as Lilly May tossed the toy out again.

"I wonder if we should wrap it in a piece of cloth. It would make it easier to clean."

Grace shrugged. She bent down and added another chip to her sack. "Either way, that dog is going to make it sopping wet with slobber."

"True, but as long as he's guarding and playing with

her, I don't mind washing the ball." Maggie looked forward again. She picked up another buffalo chip, thankful it was dried. "Are you nervous about this leg of our journey?"

Grace nodded. "Yes, all the women are. I wish we had more men to help get these wagons over the mountains."

Maggie wondered if Grace was referring to her son Cain. She didn't ask because she wasn't sure if Grace even knew her elder son had been at the fort. If she did, Grace hadn't mentioned seeing him, and as far as she knew, Adam hadn't told her.

Perhaps she should have, but Maggie didn't feel it was her place. And after seeing Adam's reaction to his brother, she didn't want to get involved. Maybe it was selfish of her, but she didn't want Cain putting a wedge between them. And telling his mother about his brother...well, it felt like that was exactly what would have happened.

"You and my son seem to be getting along well," Grace said.

"We are," Maggie admitted. She knew Grace expected them to be madly in love when they got to Oregon.

"I'm glad. Lilly May could use a brother or sister."

Maggie felt her cheeks burst into flames. The heat would surely turn them into a bright pink, giving away her embarrassment at such an intimate topic. She didn't know what to say.

Grace chuckled. "I'm sorry. I shouldn't have mentioned that, but can you blame an old woman for wanting more grandchildren?"

"No, I suppose not." Maggie glanced back at Lilly May.

The little girl chewed on her doll's arm. She yawned and then smiled when she saw Maggie looking at her. Drool dripped down her little chin, a sure sign that Lilly May had another tooth coming in.

Betty joined them. "I miss my family. It's too bad my daughter's husband didn't want to come with us." She carried her sack of buffalo chips out in front of her, keeping it at arm's length as if that would keep her clean.

"Did you send her a letter while we were at the fort?" Grace asked.

Betty smiled happily. "I did, but we'll probably be in Oregon by the time she gets it."

Maggie pulled her attention away from Lilly May. "I don't know. If that new Pony Express is as great as they say it is, she'll have it in a matter of days."

"Wouldn't that be something," Betty marveled.

Grace shaded her eyes. "Looks like we're stopping for the noon meal."

Sure enough, a few moments later, the wagons began circling up. The ladies all headed toward the wagons. They dropped their sacks into the back and hurried to set up camp.

Maggie oversaw the nooning meal. After breakfast was cleaned up, she'd made bacon sandwiches out of the fresh loaf of bread she'd purchased from Jim Parker's bakery. Her thoughts went to the tea she'd brewed earlier in the morning and put into mason jars. She'd dropped them into the water barrel with the hope that the tea would be cold when they ate.

She looked to the other women. "Should we serve pie for lunch? Or wait until the evening meal?"

"Let's serve it tonight when we can enjoy it with a hot cup of coffee," Grace suggested.

Betty grinned. "I have a small dessert for lunch."

Maggie wanted to ask what it was but there was no more time. As soon as the wagons were in place, the women went to work. Lunch breaks were short, and everyone had jobs to do.

Martin and Adam walked back to them. Martin lifted Lilly May out of her wagon. Adam told Maggie, "I'll keep an eye on her for you." He turned to his brother-in-law. "I'll be glad when I can lift my daughter again but until then, thank you for helping me with her."

Martin hugged Lilly May and then sat her on the ground. "Anytime. I like hugging her." Then he headed back to his wagon.

The little girl was allowed to toddle about the campsite with Brutus beside her when they stopped to make camp. Usually, all three of the ladies kept an eye on the baby, but today, thanks to Adam volunteering, they were free to prepare the noon meal, knowing she was being well cared for.

She knew Adam wanted to be helping the men with the animals. Maggie's heart went out to him as he walked behind Lilly May and the dog making sure no harm would come to their little girl.

Betty came to stand beside her. She set a plate of cookies on the tailgate of Adam's wagon. She smiled as her gaze followed Maggie's. "They sure are cute together." She turned her attention back to Maggie and the box of sandwiches. "That is a beautiful case. Is it a family heirloom?"

Maggie nodded as she pulled the ready-made sandwiches from her favorite wooden container. "It belonged to my mother." It was a square box with four-inch sides. She used it often and couldn't imagine ever parting with it. The box had been a wedding gift for her first marriage from Maggie's pa and she cherished it because it belonged to her ma.

Betty patted her on the shoulder. "You still miss her, don't you?"

"I do. You never get over the loss of your mother. But, because she accepted Christ as her personal savior, I know she is in Heaven, and I'll see her again." Maggie felt a tear slip from her eye. Using her apron, she wiped the moisture from her cheek.

Betty wrapped an arm around her shoulder. "I understand. I lost my mom when I was a wee child. You are right, we never get over losing our mother no matter how old we get."

Maggie wondered if Lilly May now thought of her as her mother or if she still longed for Hattie.

Grace set tin cups of tea beside Betty's cookies and joined the conversation. "How old were you when your ma died?"

Betty answered first. "About six."

Maggie sighed. "My ma died a few years ago. Thankfully I had Pa and Martin to help me get through her loss."

The three women stood still for a few moments, each silently reminiscing about their mother. Preacher Brown joined them. "Are you ladies all right? You look as if you've lost your best friend."

Betty lightened the mood by kissing him on the cheek and saying, "How can that be so? You're right here."

Both Grace and Maggie laughed at the odd expression on the preacher's face.

At the sound of their laughter, Adam took Lilly May's hand and joined them. Once everyone was seated, Maggie served lunch. She smiled at Adam as she sat down beside him to eat. Preacher Brown blessed the food and then everyone ate quickly. Nooning only lasted an hour, sometimes a half hour depending on how much ground they had covered that morning. Or what the weather looked like.

Brutus lay at Maggie's feet beside Lilly May. The baby gladly chewed on the fresh bread. The dog's ears perked up and he looked to the east. Adam and the rest of the men immediately took notice. A low growl formed in the dog's throat, alerting them that someone was coming toward them.

Adam stood and stared in the same direction as Brutus. After a few moments, he saw the horse and rider.

Pulling a small wagon attached to the horse, the stranger stopped a good way from the camp. Adam couldn't make out his face under a floppy brown hat. He watched as Cannon and Wilbur Smith rode out to meet him. Adam wished he were riding out with Cannon to investigate the newcomer, but once more his injured shoulder kept him from doing the job that he loved.

Brutus seemed to have decided that the men had the

situation under control, and he lay down next to Lilly May and rested his big head across her lap. His eyes watched the men.

From the corner of his eye, Adam saw Maggie give the dog the rest of her sandwich. Seeing that his family was safe with the dog, he said, "I think I'll go see what our visitor wants." He stuffed the rest of his sandwich in his mouth and picked up the cookie before handing Maggie his plate.

Martin handed his plate to Maggie, too. "I'll go with you."

Adam nodded. Martin was a good brother-in-law and friend. He always wanted to help, and Adam had to admit that he liked their conversations. Mainly because Martin wasn't a big talker.

When they were away from the others, Martin asked, "Who do you think he is?"

"Probably someone wanting to join our train. It happens every year. Usually after we've left the fort. They think Cannon won't turn them away." Adam had an uneasy feeling in his stomach. After his first run-in with Cain, his brother had disappeared. He'd hoped Cain had moved on with the train that had left the morning after their meeting. But what if he hadn't?

"Does he let them join?" Martin asked, just as they got to the edge of the wagons.

"It depends on their story and the wagon train's needs." Adam watched as Cannon nodded his head in approval. "Looks like this man has convinced Cannon to let him join."

Adam groaned as the three men returned to the wagon train and he saw the newcomer's face. His brother, Cain, waved a greeting. Why hadn't he warned Cannon not to allow Cain to join them? He sighed, because the only thing he could think of to say was that his brother had stolen the love of his fiancée four years ago and he still hadn't forgiven him. That sounded small and petty, but he couldn't shake his feelings, no matter how much he prayed about them.

When they got close enough for a greeting, Cain called to him. "Hey, little brother, looks like we'll be going to Oregon together after all." The smirk on his face grated on Adam's nerves. To everyone else it probably looked like a genuine smile, but Adam knew better. Once more his brother was getting just what he wanted and there was nothing Adam could do about it.

"So it would seem," Adam answered.

"We still have a few things to sort out, Mr. Walker," Cannon said.

While the wagon master continued talking to Cain, Adam whispered to Martin, "Can you keep my brother busy for a few minutes while I let our mother know he's here?"

Martin studied his face for a moment. Then nodded. "I'll see to it."

Adam walked back to camp. He wanted to hurry his steps but knew to do so would draw attention, and he didn't want the others to suspect he was in a rush.

Martin's voice drifted to Adam. "Come with me, Mr. Walker. I'll show you where we corral our horses."

Adam found his mother sitting with Lilly May. She was rocking the baby in her arms. Brutus lay at her feet. Adam felt certain that the Browns had gone to their wagon to lie down until they were ordered to travel. Mr. Porter was more than likely working at his own wagon. Not see-ing his wife, he asked, "Where is Maggie?"

"She's gone to the river for fresh water." Grace rubbed her fingers over Lilly May's forehead. "Who was the man?"

The little girl's eyes were closed and her breathing shallow.

Adam pulled a crate up beside his mother and sat down. "Cain. He's joining the wagon train."

Grace's head shot up. "My Cain?"

"Yes, Ma." He took his hat off and laid it on his knee. "I should have told you that Maggie and I saw him at the fort, the first day we were there." Adam ran his hand through his hair, wishing he'd told her earlier.

Tears filled her eyes and she stood. Grace placed Lilly May in his good arm.

Adam cradled the sleeping baby. "I should have told you, but after that first day, I didn't see him again. I thought he'd moved on."

Grace shook her head. Sadness filled her eyes. Tears choked her voice. "Adam, I know your brother hurt you and, son, I feel your hurt, but you have got to forgive him. The Bible says that if you can't forgive others, God can't forgive you. Adam, I don't want to lose my boys." She shook her head. "We still have time before we get to Oregon for you two to make amends. Please try, son."

He couldn't promise to forgive Cain. Instead, Adam laid Lilly May in her wagon. He pulled the top up to keep her out of the sun. He turned and told his mother what she wanted to hear. "I'll try, Ma." Deep down he knew God would have to work a miracle in him for him to be able to forgive his brother.

"That's all I'm asking." She stood beside the wagon and looked about. "Do you know where Cain is now?"

Adam nodded. "I believe Martin is showing him the corral." He watched as his mother headed in that direction. Why didn't she understand? Cain had betrayed him. He'd never shown remorse for his actions. If anything, Cain had been proud of what he'd done. It was as if Cain wanted to hurt him.

Adam wasn't sure why. They'd been close when they were younger but then Cain and their father had gone on a trip to get fresh grain and when they'd come back, Cain had been a different person. At first quiet and sullen. Then after their father's accidental death, Cain had become mean and manipulative. His being with Lynda before their wedding had been the knife that had killed Adam's brotherly love.

Maggie crossed into the wagon train circle. Water sloshed over the sides of the water bucket. "I'll be glad to empty this water."

He couldn't help but notice that the front of her dress was wet where the water had spilled as she'd carried it back. "Why did you fill it so full?" Adam watched as she took the bucket and poured it into the rain barrel on the side of the wagon.

"We've used a lot out of the barrel today and I want to make sure it is full before we move on, and since nooning doesn't last long I filled it to the rim." Maggie put her hands on her hips and grinned. "I've been drinking a lot of tea. Grace said I should slow down if I want it to last all the way to Oregon."

Adam loved it when she smiled like that. He could kick himself for allowing her into his heart. When had she managed to do such a thing? He'd thought when Lynda had betrayed him that he would never again let another woman get close enough to break his heart.

He silently prayed, *Please, Lord, don't let her betray me.*

Chapter Seventeen

Maggie could tell by the way Adam was looking at her that something was bothering him. Then Grace and Cain entered the campsite. She was clinging to his arm like a drowning woman. Only then did Maggie realize that Cain was the man who'd arrived earlier.

She looked from Adam to his brother. Her husband was by far the better looking of the two men but looks weren't what made the man. God did. And her husband had proven during their nightly Bible readings that he was a man of God.

When Grace saw Maggie, excitement filled her voice as she said, "Oh, Maggie! Have you met my other son, Cain?" Her joy filled her sweet face.

Maggie smiled, happy to see Grace's delight at having her son with her again. She nodded. "I did. Back at the fort."

"That's right, Adam did tell me you'd met. I am just so happy to have him with us during our journey, I forgot." She patted Cain's muscular arm.

Maggie looked to Adam. His displeasure showed in his hardened jaw and clenched hand. He was as unhappy with the news that his brother was joining them as his mother was joyful. "Adam?" She drew his attention to her. "Would you go with me to the river for a bucket of water? I'd like to fill Betty's water barrel as a surprise."

Adam turned his focus from his brother to her. "Of course." He looked to Lilly May's sleeping form. "Ma, will you watch the baby, or should we take her with us?"

Grace looked to the baby and smiled. "We'll be happy to watch her. You two kids go on. Your brother and I have a lot of catching up to do."

Maggie scooped up the empty water bucket, then grabbed Adam's hand. "Thank you. We won't be gone long." She led him away from his family.

They walked in silence. Maggie wasn't sure what to say. She knew he was upset about his brother, but she also knew he was going to have to start acting normal around the other man.

He took the pail from her and dipped it into the water. When he turned to face her, Adam sighed. "What am I going to do? With him on the train, I can't avoid him any longer."

"Maybe if you talked to me, told me why you and Cain don't get along, I could help."

Adam set the bucket down and ran his hands through his hair. "Remember I told you that my fiancée was unfaithful with another man?"

Maggie nodded, feeling deep in her gut that she knew where this was going. But instead of blurting it out, she felt Adam needed to tell her. Maybe in doing so it would be healing for him.

"Cain was that man. He stole my fiancée and never felt any remorse." He picked the water up. "We better be getting back. It's almost time to get back on the trail."

Maggie put her hand on his arm. "Adam, I'm sorry your brother betrayed you."

"Me, too." He started walking back to camp without her.

He might have begun to care about her, but Maggie instinctively knew that with Cain's arrival Adam had begun rebuilding the wall around his heart that only a miracle could tear down.

She couldn't stop thinking about that as they resumed traveling. Grace walked beside her once more. She talked nonstop about Cain and how wonderful it was to have him close again. Maggie kept her thoughts to herself. Other than Lilly May she didn't have children, and she had no idea how she would feel if Lilly May betrayed a second child.

"You disapprove, don't you?"

Maggie denied her accusation. "No. I don't approve or disapprove. I was just thinking it would be hard to be in your shoes. Both men are your sons, and you love them both."

Grace looked straight ahead. "With all my heart."

They walked in silence for several moments. Maggie looked back to make sure that Lilly May still napped. She hated that Adam and Grace were both hurting, not in the same way, but pain of the heart was pain of the heart. And they both seemed to be in a lot of pain.

Grace filled the silence once more. "I know what Cain did to Adam was wrong, but that was four years ago."

Maggie felt as if Grace was working through her

thoughts more than speaking to her. She continued to follow their wagon. Kids ran and played with the other dogs; other women walked together or alone. Adam had returned to the front of their wagon with Josiah. Other men walked beside their wagons. Traveling together had made them all like a large extended family.

"Maybe I should go talk to Betty." Grace smiled sadly at Maggie. "My emotions seem to be running away with me. Betty might have some advice about my boys."

She inhaled deeply, reminding herself that Grace needed advice that Maggie wasn't qualified to give. She hugged her mother-in-law around the shoulders. "Being a minister's wife, Betty might have encountered something like this before, and if she hasn't, she will keep your confidence. You are right to talk to her."

"Thank you for understanding, dear."

The Brown wagon was several wagons back, and Maggie watched until Grace came even with Betty, then turned around again. She couldn't stop her racing thoughts. Would Grace find a way out of her dilemma? Where would Cain end up? And most importantly, would Adam ever forgive his brother?

Over the next several weeks, Adam felt as if nothing had changed between him and Cain. He decided to talk to Cannon. Adam was tired of babying his shoulder; it was time to get back to work. As soon as they were camped and the animals were put away, Adam headed to the corral to get Shadow.

If Cannon wouldn't let him go back to scouting, Adam planned on riding Shadow for a couple of hours.

He needed time away from the camp and alone with his thoughts.

Cain had befriended most of the families in the train. If nothing else, his brother was quite the charmer. He seemed to work hard and for the most part stayed out of Adam's way.

"About time you got here." Martin stood beside a fully saddled Shadow. The horse pranced in place at the sight of Adam.

He stopped. "How did you know I'd come for him?"

Martin patted the horse's neck. "I might not be your blood brother but after the last few months, I feel like I know you like a true brother." He grinned. "And, brother, you've been restless all day. I figured you'd want a ride tonight."

That was the most that Martin had said at one time since they had met. "I feel the same about you."

"So, you replaced me with your brother-in-law." Cain stepped out of the shadows.

Adam looked to Martin. The younger man had straightened and balled up his fist. So, Maggie's brother didn't trust Cain either.

"Not now, Cain. I don't have time for your nonsense." Adam picked up Shadow's reins.

"You always did run, didn't you, little brother?"

Adam turned to face him and Cain took a step forward, his back ramrod straight, his arms tensed at his sides.

"Boys, dinner is about ready," Grace called out as she walked toward them. Her eyes took in the scene, and she frowned when she saw her son holding the reins. "Adam, where are you going?"

"I have some business with Cannon." He turned and, using his good arm, pulled himself into the saddle. "Please ask Maggie to keep a plate warm for me."

"All right, son." Then she looped her hand into Cain's arm and began walking back to the campsite.

Adam watched them go. Mealtime was always the hardest ever since his mother had insisted that Cain take his meals with the family. Maggie treated Cain like everyone else, but Cain watched her every move.

"I know he's your brother, but I really don't like him." Martin sighed. "I shouldn't have said that."

"I don't like him either," Adam said.

The two men shared a knowing look. "I'll keep an eye on the family while you're gone," Martin said as he turned for the campfire.

Adam hadn't thought about Maggie being alone with his brother when he was away from camp. If he went back to scouting, would Maggie fall for Cain's charm?

Shadow snorted and bobbed his head.

"You're right. The sooner we get going, the sooner I'll be back to the family." Adam headed to Cannon's wagon.

Cook looked up as Adam approached. "Good evening, Adam. What brings you this way?"

Adam liked Cook; he was Cannon's brother and partner in this wild wagon train business. "I need to talk to Cannon. Is he about?" His gaze moved around their camp.

"He's down by the river." Cook waved in the general direction.

"Much obliged."

He found the wagon master standing by the river.

Cannon looked tired. Running a wagon train full of so many people had to wear on the man. He looked to Adam. "What can I do for you, Adam?"

Adam dismounted. "I need to get back to work."

"Sounds good to me. Smith is a good man, but I've grown to trust and depend on you." He knelt and picked up a pebble. He rolled it between his palms.

"I appreciate you saying that." Adam knelt beside him. "Something bothering you tonight?"

Cannon pushed his hat back. "We're getting to the hardest part of the trail and I'm not sure about the men in this train."

Adam picked up a flat stone and stood. He skipped it across the water's surface. "I've been with you for the past two years and each year you say that."

"This time is different. The Porter men added another wagon and instead of lightening their load, they doubled it."

"I'm aware."

"Are you aware that Josiah and Penelope White got married at the fort?" His tired eyes searched Adam's.

"Nope, I wasn't aware of that."

"Or that the Carter woman is pregnant with their seventh child, and will probably deliver before we get to Oregon?"

Adam realized he'd been so wrapped up in his own problems, he'd neglected being the scout and support that the wagon master had hired him to be. He should have been aware of both those events. During the last two journeys he'd kept Cannon up to date on each family and assisted them as well as the wagon master. This time, he'd brought a baby to the wagon, gotten married, had to be separated from the wagon train where he'd spent fourteen days not doing his job and then he'd gotten shot while out scouting, leaving Cannon again to run the wagon train alone. He ran his hand through his hair. "I haven't been much help this trip, have I?"

Cannon stood and slapped him on the back.

Pain shot through Adam's shoulder but he forced his features to remain steady.

"Well, you're back at work now. We'll get them there safe and sound. Now, tell me about this brother of yours." He sent his pebble skipping across the water.

What could he say? That his brother couldn't be trusted? No, that was a personal issue between brothers, plus Cannon was wise enough not to trust anyone until they earned that trust. He'd keep an eye on Cain. "There's not much to tell. I haven't seen him in about four years."

"Because the Green family stayed behind at the fort I added Cain to the night watch to replace Mr. Green." Cannon picked up another stone.

He wasn't telling Adam anything he didn't already know. Adam might not have been aware of other people on the train, but he'd been very aware of his brother's every move. Still, he listened without interrupting because the wagon master had earned his respect a long time ago.

Cannon continued, "Since he doesn't have a wife or children, I'm sure Cain won't mind doing double duty. I'm trying to decide whether I should give him first watch or last. I've had him doing the middle watch."

Adam smiled at the thought of his brother being away from camp during the evening meal. "You should probably give him first watch. He always tended to fall asleep early."

"That's good to know. I'll do that, then. Anything else?"

"I'm sure he wouldn't mind watching the livestock a couple of nights a week, too."

Cannon gave him a wise look. "You didn't want him on this train, did you?"

"No, sir, I didn't. And I told him so at the fort." Adam heard the anger in his voice. Anger at his brother and at himself. He'd been preoccupied with Maggie while at the fort. Now Adam realized he should have made sure Cain had been on the other train.

"We'll keep him busy and away from you as much as possible." Cannon sighed as one of the little boys came running.

"Mr. Cannon! Pa needs you."

He gave a tired grin to Adam. "Well, duty calls. You can start scouting in the morning. I'm glad to have you back, son."

Adam pulled himself onto Shadow again. He rode the horse away from the wagon train. Was he being petty where Cain was concerned? Was his ma right in telling him to forget about the past and give Cain another chance? He still didn't understand why his brother disliked him. Adam closed his eyes and quietly prayed. "Lord, give me the strength to forgive my brother."

Chapter Eighteen

Adam filled the next few days scouting and reconnecting with the families on the wagon train. It felt good to get back into his job. He always left camp early and returned late. It kept him from having to watch his Ma fawn over Cain.

He'd made the decision to return early today. Soaked to the bone from the light drizzle that had begun to fall during the early morning hours, Adam listened to the families as they circled the wagons for the evening. Forcing their wagons and animals through the mud all day caused tempers to run high.

Josiah stood beside their wagon hugging an upset Penelope close.

Adam dismounted beside them. "What's wrong?"

Penelope hid her face from him and shook her head. Josiah sighed, then answered, "Mr. White has told Penelope that since she is married and too lazy to help out, she can move in with her husband." He used his head to indicate the trunk and bag at their feet.

"I'll speak to Ma and see if we can make room for her things in the wagon." Adam handed Shadow's reins to Josiah. "Take care of the horse and your wife. I'll tend to the oxen."

Though Adam had hoped Mr. White would allow his daughter to stay with her family for the remainder of the trip, he feared this would happen.

Maggie joined him at the head of the oxen. "I'll help you." She began working in silence with the smaller of the two oxen.

When her ox was free, she led him off to graze. Adam followed with the larger animal. From the set of her shoulders, Adam had the impression that Maggie was angry.

Maggie staked out her ox and then proceeded to return to the wagon.

"Maggie, hold up." Adam waited for her to stop and then finished tending to his ox.

She stood with her arms crossed and her gaze glued to the soggy ground. Rain dripped from her bonnet as she waited on him.

He walked to her and lifted her chin. Tears streamed down her face. "What's wrong?" He felt as if this was the most common question he asked these days. But this time he felt true concern. Dark circles under her eyes and her pale skin worried him.

"I'm sorry."

"What are you sorry for?" Adam dreaded her next words. Was she about to tell him she preferred Cain and wanted to end their marriage?

Maggie shook her head. "I'm not really sure, but whatever I did or said, I'm sorry."

More tears trickled down her face.

"You haven't done anything." Adam's confusion was real. He had no idea what she was talking about.

She wiped at her face. "Then why did you stop coming back at night? Lilly May misses her bedtime stories and her pa."

He pulled her to him and hugged her close. "Maggie, I'm the one who is sorry. When Cannon said I could go back to work, I didn't think you would mind. I come back but it's usually very late and then I leave during the early morning hours."

"Why? Can't you scout and return to have supper with us? Or stay long enough in the mornings for breakfast?" She raised her head and looked him in the eyes. "Have you been eating?"

The concern on her face made Adam feel special and like a heel all at the same time. He hugged her tight. "Yes, I've been eating." When it was just his ma and himself, he'd eaten with her, but since he'd gone back to work and wanted to hear the news and receive new orders each morning from Cannon, he'd started eating with Cook and Cannon like he'd done the previous years when he'd had no family to worry about. Now Adam realized he'd hurt Maggie's feelings and caused her unnecessary worry.

"Good. I was concerned it was me." She offered him a wobbly smile, then rested her head back onto his chest. "I thought maybe I did something to keep you away."

"Why would you think such a thing?" Adam rested his head on top of her wet bonnet.

"After a few days of being married to me, my first

husband would leave early and come home late." She took a deep breath.

Adam waited for her to say more but when it became obvious that she was finished talking he asked, "Why did he do that?"

"I didn't know it when I married him, but he liked to gamble and drink." She stepped out of his arms.

"I already told you I don't like either." He smiled at her, hoping to ease some of the past pain he heard in her voice. "I'm sorry my absence made you feel bad. I promise from now on I'll be home for supper and Bible stories." He took her hand in his.

A blush filled her cheeks. "Can I ask you for one more thing?"

"Sure."

"Will you move into the tent with me and Lilly May at night?" Her neck began to color with embarrassment.

"All right. But why?"

"Well, I don't want your brother to think I'm not a good wife." She spoke the words, then quickly ducked her head.

Why would Maggie want Cain to think she was a good wife? Had he been trying to get her attention? Had he scared her? Been mean to her? Anger boiled inside him. He needed to ask her, but would she answer any questions? And if she did, did he really want the answers?

Maggie knew she was being forward asking Adam to move into the tent. "I'm not asking you to do more than sleep there." That didn't come out right either. "I mean—"

"I know what you mean." Adam ushered them back to the wagon train, holding Maggie's hand in his. "Sleeping only and maybe talking." He cast a grin in her direction.

Maggie was glad that he didn't ask any more questions as to why she wanted him in her tent at night. If he had insisted on a reason, she would have had to tell him that Cain made her nervous. She'd seen his shadow outside her tent when everyone else was sleeping. What he was doing prowling about, she didn't know. But with Adam in the tent, his brother would stay away from her.

Thankfully the rain stopped as they continued to camp. Maggie enjoyed these few moments with her husband alone. Grace and Brutus were watching Lilly May, so she had nothing to worry about at the moment. Just as they stepped between the wagons and into their camp, she felt Adam tense beside her.

Josiah and Cain stood in front of them, engaged in conversation.

"What do you want for it?" Josiah asked Cain.

Maggie flinched at the hardness in Adam's voice as he interrupted them. "Want for what?"

The young man looked at Adam. "Cain has offered to sell me his wagon."

"And how do you intend to get your things to Oregon?" Adam directed his question to Cain.

Cain sat down on one of the crates. "My things are in the back of Ma's wagon."

"He's right, son. We moved them there today during the nooning." Grace flipped frying potatoes in a cast-iron skillet.

"Ma, there was barely enough room in there for you

to sleep without his stuff taking up even more of your space." Adam released Maggie's hand and walked to his mother.

"Nonsense, I still have plenty of room. I made room in one of my chests for his clothes." She patted Adam's arm. "There is nothing for you to worry about."

Maggie decided to say something. "You know, since we aren't charging Cain to keep his things in our wagon, maybe he'll consider loaning his to Josiah and Penelope until we get to Oregon."

Adam's eyes met hers. Something flickered in their depths that she couldn't quite make out. "I think that is an excellent idea."

A scowl passed over Cain's face. "I guess that seems fair."

Maggie knew her brother-in-law thought it anything but fair. "My pa has several small tents. I'll ask if we can give you one for a wedding gift. We should have done something to show our support of your marriage earlier."

Penelope looked up from where she was sitting. "Are you sure it isn't too much trouble?"

"No trouble at all," Maggie assured her.

The only thing that bothered Maggie was that since they'd left the fort, they'd taken on two extra mouths to feed. Penelope's family expected her new husband to supply her meals and a home, which he intended to do as soon as they got to another fort. Cain had arrived with a simple wagon and had promised to add meat to the cooking pot but thus far had not managed to fulfill that promise. Maggie had had to search more diligently for wild foods to supplement their food stores.

Grace turned from the campfire. "Dinner's almost ready. Maggie, will you go tell your pa?"

Maggie picked up Lilly May and tickled the little girl under the chin. "Lilly May and I will be happy to go get her grandpa and uncle, won't we?"

Lilly May giggled. "Ganpa."

"Yes, Grandpa." Maggie carried the little girl to her father and brother's wagon, Brutus right on her heels. She was thankful that Adam wasn't angry with her and that she'd managed to save Josiah and his new bride some money.

She found her family sitting by their campfire. Her pa was writing in the store ledger while Martin worked on a leather strap of some kind. "Grace said dinner's about ready."

"Thank you, daughter." He walked to the back of his wagon and tucked the book inside.

"Pa, Adam and I would like to buy one of the tents you have for the new store. Can we have it tonight?" Maggie handed Lilly May off to Martin.

Brutus watched the transaction with interest. The dog tilted his head from side to side. It was cute and very endearing to Maggie.

"Ma," Lilly May said as she patted Martin's whiskered chin.

"I'll be glad when you can say my full name." Martin tickled the baby and tossed her into the air.

Her pa climbed into the wagon and rummaged around inside. "What are you going to do with a second tent?"

Maggie called back, "We're giving it to Josiah and his new wife."

He handed her the tent. "Good thing I packed several of these. Your brother-in-law was by here earlier to buy a tent. Said he was tired of sleeping in the rain." He chuckled. "How a man can travel this far without at least a few comforts from home is beyond me. But I guess some do travel the whole way by horseback with only the clothes on their backs." He climbed down from the wagon. "Here, I'll carry it for you."

Maggie handed him the tent. She looped her arm in his and kissed him on the cheek as they began to walk back. Martin and Lilly May trailed along behind them.

"I heard Samuel this afternoon telling Penelope she needed to go live with her new husband." He tsked. "That boy should have invited her family to the wedding and not waited until after the wedding night to tell them she was married."

Her own marriage to Adam had been because her pa thought she'd disgraced the family by staying in a cave overnight with Adam and insisted they be wed. She could only imagine how embarrassed the White family had been to learn that their daughter had secretly gotten married.

Once back at camp, Maggie gave Josiah and Penelope the tent. Then she helped Grace serve the evening meal. She missed the Browns. Betty and the preacher ate their meals at their own camp now that they were back with the wagon train. For Betty, cooking for two would be much easier than cooking for nine.

Maggie looked to where Adam was holding Lilly May and spooning small bites of bean and potatoes into her birdlike mouth. He seemed happy to take care of the baby while she served the others. She enjoyed having him back.

Cain ate his meal and then left the group. With sad eyes Grace watched her older son leave the warmth of the campfire. Maggie wanted to go hug her and assure Grace that Cain and Adam would patch things up between them. Over the last few days, she and Grace had grown even closer, and now it hurt Maggie to see her mother-in-law's heartache.

Her pa stood. "Thank you for the meal, ladies. Martin and I need to get back to our wagon. I've got guard duty tonight and we need to get the harness mended before I go."

Everyone said good-night and then they left.

"Need some help getting that tent up, Josiah?" Adam asked as he handed a sleepy Lilly May to Maggie. Brutus bumped her leg as if to say he was still there.

"If it's not too much trouble," Josiah said.

Adam slapped him on the back. "Not at all."

Penelope looked embarrassed but followed the men to their place in the circle of wagons.

Maggie realized that the newly married couple had moved their few belongings to the end of the circle and would be the last to leave tomorrow morning. Had they done so to be alone? Or had her parents made her feel unwanted, making Penelope wish to be as far away from them as possible. Sadness filled Maggie. Tomorrow she'd make sure to walk with the younger woman and maybe they could become friends.

"Good night, Maggie." Grace climbed into the wagon and shut the opening.

Maggie sighed. She walked to her tent but stopped abruptly several feet away.

Cain had pitched his tent next to hers. She could see

his shadow moving about inside. Why had he put it so close to theirs?

Lilly May chose that moment to protest going to bed. It was as if the child had just realized that they were going into the tent.

Cain came out of his tent. "The little one not wanting to go to bed?"

Though Maggie wanted to step back, she held her ground. "She's started fighting sleep, but I think she'll sleep better tonight with her pa close by." She began rocking Lilly May side to side, and the little girl laid her head on Maggie's shoulder and yawned.

Cain seemed to straighten. "Oh, Adam is staying in camp tonight?"

Had she detected disappointment in Cain's voice? Once again she was thankful that Adam would be sleeping in the same tent as her and Lilly May. "Yes, he is."

Cain looked up into the night sky. Clouds still covered the moon and stars. "Where's my little brother now?"

Keeping her distance from Cain, Maggie walked to her tent. "He's helping Josiah. He'll be along shortly."

"Do you need me to help you get her to sleep? I'm pretty good with children." Cain stepped forward as if he were going to join her in the tent.

Brutus growled deep in his throat. Lilly May stopped sucking her thumb and looked from her pet to Cain. Could the dog sense Cain's intentions?

Maggie spoke sharply. "No, I've been putting her to bed long before you came along. I don't need any help."

He chuckled deep and low, keeping his eyes on Brutus. "That's too bad."

A chill traveled up Maggie's spine. Why was Cain acting this way? He knew she was already married to Adam. Surely, he also knew that there was no way she would betray her husband with him.

Maggie looked about, not for the first time fearful that they were alone. She reminded herself that Grace was in the wagon and would come quickly if Maggie called out.

His gaze followed hers to the wagon. As if he read her mind, Cain nodded and said, "Good night, Maggie." Then he returned to his tent.

Maggie entered their tent. Her heart raced at what she'd learned of Cain's character. To her way of thinking, he wasn't the nice man she'd first thought him to be.

She placed Lilly May on the floor of the small tent and then moved items around to make room for Adam. She placed the baby's bed between their sleeping mats and put their personal items at the foot of her bedroll. Tonight she was thankful for the canvas tarp that lined her tent. At least she wouldn't be sleeping in a puddle.

Lilly May began to fuss. Maggie quickly changed the baby into a dry nightgown and placed her in her dresser drawer.

"Pa?" Lilly May asked as Maggie tucked her soft blanket about her.

Maggie smiled. "He'll be here in a few minutes."

The little girl giggled her joy and squirmed under the covers. She turned on her side and put her thumb in her mouth.

Remembering how she could see Cain's shadow through the tent, Maggie blew out the lantern and quickly changed out of her damp socks and dress into drier clothes. She shivered as the warm fabric of the dress covered her cool skin. Even though it was now summer, the steady rain had left her feeling chilled.

As soon as she was dressed again, Maggie relit the lantern. Lilly May had used the dark to fall asleep. Maggie yawned and climbed into her own bedroll. Soon she felt toasty warm, and sleep pulled at her. She fought the slumber as she waited for Adam.

What was he going to think of Cain putting his tent so close to theirs?

Chapter Nineteen

Maggie woke early. She turned to check on Lilly May and found Adam looking at her.

He whispered, "Good morning."

Keeping her voice low, she answered, "Good morning. I'm sorry we fell asleep before you came in last night." She offered him a soft smile.

"It wasn't your fault. After I finished helping Josiah, Cannon wanted to talk." He sat up and the blanket dropped from his bare chest.

Maggie swallowed hard. "Is everything all right?"

"Yes, he wanted to remind me that we will be crossing the river today and after yesterday's steady rains the water is going to be choppy, making it harder on the wagons." Adam reached for his shirt and pulled it on over his head.

"We've crossed rivers before."

"True. Cannon wants me to ride ahead and assess the situation." Adam pushed the remainder of his covers away and reached for his boots.

Maggie breathed a sigh of relief that her husband hadn't completely undressed for bed.

"When we get to the river, promise me you will wait for me before attempting to cross our wagon. I've already told Josiah but he's apt to listen to other men and forget what I've said." He finished pulling on his boots before turning to look at her. "I need to be there."

She sat up and nodded. "I understand. We'll wait."

"Good. I'm sorry I don't have time to help you take down the tent and get ready to move."

Maggie grinned. "Don't worry about us. Martin usually comes to help me."

"I'll be back as quick as I can. Remember, wait for me." With that, Adam stepped out of the tent.

Maggie whispered, "I'll wait for you until the day I die." The words sounded strange in her own ears, but she knew in her heart, they were true. She loved her husband; it didn't matter that she might not be the perfect wife for him. Maggie vowed to be the best wife she could be.

Adam hated leaving her. With her hair falling around her shoulders, Maggie looked adorable. She'd always been pretty, but with a sleepy face and soft voice, she was beautiful.

Brutus stretched and then moved to the side to let Adam out of the tent. The dog used his massive body to bump him. Adam gave him a quick scratch behind the ears.

He frowned when he saw his brother's tent as he stepped out. He'd seen it on his return last night, but Cain had been on watch duty. Now his mother was already fixing breakfast and Adam didn't want to upset her by arguing with his brother, and he knew there would be an argument. But first chance he got, Adam intended to tell Cain to move his tent to the other side of their wagon. His plan was to tell his brother that with him on one side and Cain on the other, their mother would be better protected.

Making his way to the corral to get Shadow, he ran into Martin. "Morning."

Martin yawned. "Morning."

"On your way to help Maggie take down the tent?" Adam wished he was still there helping her, but duty called.

"Yep."

Adam almost laughed. Evidently Martin was even less talkative in the mornings. "Thanks."

Martin nodded and then continued on his way.

Shadow bobbed his head in greeting as Adam approached. Early mornings were a favorite time for Adam. He enjoyed feeding his horse and then getting him ready to ride. Other men came to the corral and cared for their horses, his brother included.

Adam was the first to speak. "I've been thinking. Instead of both of us sleeping on the same side of Ma's wagon, we should each take a side. That way we'll be able to protect her better during the night."

Cain grinned. "Plus, that gets me away from your lovely wife."

"Yep." Adam didn't plan on denying that he wanted Cain to stay away from Maggie. He pulled himself into the saddle. Without saying another word, he rode out.

The sun began to top the horizon when Adam got to

the area where the wagons would cross the river. Everyone knew that river crossings were dangerous, but they were even more so when the water was up and swirling. He'd crossed this river two times before, but it hadn't been up this high in the past.

Adam rode a mile in each direction, hopeful that he'd find a safer place to cross. Not finding any, he returned to the wagon train. They were slugging through the mud at a slow pace. He spotted Maggie walking with Lilly May on her hip. Brutus walked beside them.

Thankfully the dog was still in good health. He continued to hunt each morning while the ladies fixed breakfast. Brutus had proven very protective over both Lilly May and Maggie. Adam had noticed his brother didn't care much for the animal and seemed to keep a good distance from him. Yes, he was thankful for the dog and his protective nature.

Cannon spotted Adam and waved. The wagon master rode his horse to meet him. "Is it as bad as I thought?"

"'Fraid so." Adam wished he had better news. "The water's high and turbulent."

"Maybe we should camp beside it tonight and cross tomorrow." Cannon scratched the whiskers on his chin.

Adam nodded. "The water may recede some and make for an easier crossing."

"Perhaps." They sat for several long moments before Cannon spoke again. "Keep a watch out. One of the guards thought he saw someone moving about the wagons last night in the shadows but when he went to investigate, nothing was out of the ordinary."

Adam immediately became alert. "Do you think the bandits are back?"

"I'd hoped they'd moved on but who knows. Could have been a curious Indian, too. Might not have been anyone. It's just best to be alert for trouble." Cannon started back to camp.

Adam rode beside him. "Anything else I need to know about?"

"Just the normal stuff." He looked to the wagon train. "I'm tempted to retire after this trip, too."

"You say that every year." Adam laughed.

Cannon grinned. "True, but if I could find a wife as sweet as yours, I'd leave this trail behind and settle down." He kicked his horse into a gallop and went to call the nooning.

Adam helped everyone get settled for the noon break. When he got back to his own wagon, Maggie and Grace were handing out cold biscuits with bacon in them. He took his and thanked his mother.

When Maggie took her and Lilly May's lunch, Adam asked, "Maggie, would you like to have a picnic?"

Grace smiled. "I think that's an excellent idea."

"That will be nice," Maggie agreed. "Give me just a moment and I'll get things ready."

What was there to get ready? Adam didn't ask. He simply took Lilly May from Maggie and watched as she hurried to the wagon with Grace. His mother handed Maggie an oil tarp, a blanket and an empty milk jar. She put two tin cups in a flour sack along with two large chunks of cheese she'd wrapped in cheese cloth, then added their biscuits and bacon. Maggie carefully added the milk jar that she'd filled with water.

Maggie took the pillowcase from Grace. "Thank you for helping me, Grace."

Grace smiled. "Have a good time, child."

Adam shook his head. "Ma, if I had known it would make more work for you ladies, I would have waited until this evening to talk to Maggie alone."

"Nonsense. It was no extra work at all. Now get going before the wagon master tells us it's time to leave." Grace waved them away.

He carried Lilly May with Brutus trailing behind them.

"What did you want to talk about?" Maggie asked when they were a good way from the wagon train.

Adam shrugged. "Nothing really. I wanted to spend time with you and Lilly May, you know, as a family."

Maggie smiled. "That's sweet."

They walked a little farther. Adam looked back at the wagon train and decided they were far enough away to have a little privacy. "I think this is a good spot." He set Lilly May down and took the blanket from Maggie. "What do you think?"

"It's perfect."

He spread the oil tarp and blanket then snagged Lilly May before she ventured too far away. "Here you go, little one. Sit here and we'll eat."

Lilly May smiled, showing new teeth.

Maggie pulled out the food and water from the flour sack. She gave the little girl a pinched-off piece of biscuit. "There you go."

Adam accepted the food Maggie handed him and sat down, enjoying the light breeze that cooled them. Brutus put his nose to the ground and began smelling around in the grass. Soon the dog was off exploring.

Every so often he would turn and look to them then continue on.

Maggie sat beside Adam. "Do you mind talking about our farm?" She tore a small piece of bacon and gave it to Lilly May.

He swallowed a mouthful of biscuit and bacon. "What would you like to know?"

She tore one of the chunks of cheese into bite-size pieces. "Well, I wanted to tell you what me and your ma were thinking we'd like to do."

"Oh." He hadn't considered that Maggie and his ma would join forces to make the cabin into their home. "Well, go ahead."

She sat up on her knees. Her eyes grew bright and full of life. "We want two kinds of gardens. One for flowers and one for vegetables."

"When you say a flower garden, what do you mean?" He handed Lilly May a piece of cheese.

"Num." Lilly May started to scoot off the blanket with one hand on her cheese and the other reaching for grass.

Brutus barked his dissatisfaction of his ward being ignored.

"I see her," Adam called to the animal. He snatched up Lilly May and held her in his lap. His gaze moved to where Brutus rested in the grass. Feathers coated the prairie around the dog.

"Maybe *garden* wasn't the right word. We want to plant rosebushes under the windows and have different kinds of flowers around the front porch. Maybe some honeysuckle and tulips." Maggie held a cup of water up for Lilly May to drink.

"I like the idea of rosebushes under the windows. In

the summer they'll make the whole house smell sweet."
Adam felt water drip down his legs.

"That's what we were thinking, too." Maggie obviously didn't catch the teasing tone in his voice.

"What kinds of vegetables?"

Her eyes sparkled. "All kinds. I love tomatoes and peppers. Grace said she'd like cucumbers so we can make pickles. She said you like corn, so I was thinking we could do several rows. We'll have plenty of fresh and some to can for the winter. And potatoes, carrots, green beans and onions. Just think of the soups we can make and can." Excitement filled her voice.

Adam laughed. "Here I thought you were going to talk about the house."

"Oh, we've been talking about that, too. Grace would like her bedroom to be on the east side and I said ours could be on the west. And I want Lilly May's bedroom beside ours." Maggie paused to take a bite of her lunch.

Adam rocked Lilly May. "I'm not sure we can build all of that the first year."

"Yeah, we've talked about that, too."

He was sure they had. There wasn't much to do but talk as they walked beside the wagons. "What did you decide?" Adam asked. As they spoke, he gently stroked Lilly May's forehead like he'd watched Maggie do when she rocked the little girl to sleep. He was rewarded with a yawn.

Maggie offered him a sweet smile. "We're leaving it to you. Then when we start to add on, we'll know more about how the house will be set up."

He chuckled softly so as not to wake the baby. "I like that plan."

"We thought you would." Maggie giggled. "I like your plans for the house. Remember you told me them a few weeks ago."

Yes, he had. Adam was pleased she remembered.

"I wish we could visit that cove again. It was so cool and peaceful." Her face took on a dreamy look.

"We do have a river that runs by our land. I found a place that is secluded where we can swim and fish during the summer." Adam remembered the spot and smiled. It would be perfect on hot days to cool off in the water.

Maggie turned her attention to him again. "Is it as nice as the cove?"

"I'm sure we will make lots of memories there and it will be even better than the cove." Adam reached over and took her hand in his.

Her eyes softened and she leaned toward him. Adam found himself meeting her halfway. She smelled of sunshine. Her lips were inches from his. For the first time in a very long time, Adam wanted to kiss a woman. Not just any woman. Maggie.

He released her hand and cupped her face before claiming her soft lips. Maggie responded shyly. His heart melted just a little more.

"Time to go!" Grace called from the wagon train.

Maggie pulled back; pink filled her cheeks and neck. She quickly put everything back into the flour sack then stood.

Adam cradled Lilly May's sleeping body close. He didn't know if he should say anything about the kiss. When he stood and stepped off the blanket, Maggie quickly folded it and the tarp. "We should be going," she said, unable to meet his gaze.

He followed her back to the wagon. Once there, Adam laid Lilly May in her wagon, where she curled up and napped, and Maggie busied herself helping his mother pack up.

As he left, Adam couldn't stop thinking about the kiss they'd just shared. He'd enjoyed it and felt sure Maggie had, too. But he wondered if kissing her again had been the right thing to do. As far as he knew, Maggie hadn't changed her mind about wanting a real husband.

Chapter Twenty

Maggie spent the rest of the afternoon reliving her first meaningful kiss from Adam. Yes, they had shared a kiss, but it hadn't been like this one. It didn't feel nearly as special.

Their lunch together had been enjoyable. He'd listened to her talk of gardens and canning. She'd felt close to him, and the fact that he'd listened to her and planned their future together gave her hope that he appreciated her thoughts. She'd leaned toward him, why, Maggie didn't know, but when he'd kissed her...well, she felt warm and appreciated, like her feelings and opinions mattered.

"You've been quiet all afternoon," Grace said as she walked up beside her on the trail.

What could she say? "I've been thinking about when we get to Oregon."

It wasn't an outright lie; she had been thinking about her conversation with Adam that led up to the kiss.

"I've been thinking about that, too." Grace seemed to

be hesitant as she asked, "Would you be upset if I didn't come to live with you and Adam?"

"Where would you go?"

Grace inhaled deeply. "Please, don't mention it to Adam, but I'm thinking I'll go with Cain."

Shock shook Maggie. "Why?"

Grace twisted her apron in her hands. "Cain and Lynda never married and now he doesn't have anyone to care for him. Adam is blessed with you, and I know you will be adding to your family soon."

She forced herself to focus on Grace and not on the idea of having a family with Adam. "I don't think Adam is going to like that plan," she admitted.

"That's why I don't want to say anything until we get to Oregon. I'm hoping my boys will patch things up between them. Perhaps Cain and I will live in town, close to the farm." She looked hopeful.

Maggie didn't want to dash Grace's hopes for her boys. "I won't tell Adam your plans."

Grace cheered up. "Just think, we could be neighbors."

"Have you talked to Cain about this?" Maggie looked to where her brother-in-law was riding beside the wagon. He and Josiah were talking about something.

"Oh, no. I want to wait until my boys have patched things up between them."

"I'm not sure they ever will. Adam is still hurt by Cain's actions."

Grace sighed. "I know. I do wish he could forgive his brother."

Maggie wished he could as well. Forgiveness made people feel better. She'd forgiven Matthew for killing himself and leaving her a widow. His death had caused her pa to think the town was talking about them and made him decide to move to Oregon for a fresh start. There were a lot of things Maggie had to forgive her first husband for and it hadn't been easy. But she'd done it.

The rest of the afternoon was spent walking with her mother-in-law and talking about their futures in Oregon. They'd also discussed quilt making, crocheting, canning and sewing new clothes. If Grace went to live with Cain, would any of those things be shared or would Maggie be doing them alone?

They camped close to the river that they'd be crossing the next day. At first, they'd hoped to do laundry, but the river ran swiftly and Maggie was afraid they might lose the few clothes they had in the currents. Instead, each family spent the time securing their possessions in their wagons for the crossing. Adam put their tent up while the women cooked supper.

After the meal had been eaten and the dishes cleaned, one of the men got out his fiddle and played merry tunes. Cain brought out a deck of cards and the men played cards, all except the preacher. Maggie, Grace, Betty and Penelope used the time to mend clothes.

The wagon master called Adam and most of the men away to discuss crossing the river in the morning. Maggie watched Adam leave their campsite. She'd given him what she hoped was a sweet smile. They hadn't had time to talk since their picnic and their kiss. Maggie knew Adam had watch duty during the first half of the night, so they wouldn't talk again until tomorrow.

Lilly May grew tired of playing with her doll and

Brutus. Maggie carried the little girl to their tent to prepare for bed. Lilly May didn't protest; she was ready for
sleep and happy to be in her bed. Her deep breathing
told Maggie her baby had gone to sleep.

The sound of thunder drew her attention. A few minutes later the pitter-patter of rain sounded on the tent.

Maggie pulled out Lilly May's mother's diary and
flipped to the back. She didn't write in it every night
but felt that she should tonight. Unsure of what the date
was, Maggie simply wrote:

> *Much like your mother, I've lost track of the date.*
>   *We are camped beside a big river. We've had
> a lot of rain this week and the river we are to
> cross tomorrow is dangerous. We are all praying
> for a safe passage. Tonight, I walked to the wa-
> ter's edge, and it frightened me. The water is on
> the move. It seems to have a mind of its own and
> swirls debris into its depths. Adam, your pa, has
> asked me not to cross without him present. I've
> promised to wait, no matter what.*

Maggie stopped writing. What more could she say?
Tomorrow night she'd write about the crossing. She
yawned. Tired from the day's events, Maggie said her
prayers and turned out the light.

Her mind immediately reminded her of the kiss she'd
experienced with Adam. Not that she'd ever forgotten
it. She still wasn't sure what the kiss meant, if anything, though she spent what remained of the evening
thinking about it.

Maggie wasn't sure when she went to sleep but the

sounds of Grace cooking breakfast the next morning woke her. She immediately felt guilty for sleeping late. Quickly, she dressed and left the tent.

Brutus lay down in front of the tent door. With him there, Maggie knew Lilly May would be safe. She also knew that the dog would alert her to the little girl waking up.

"Good morning, Grace. How did you sleep?"

Grace turned the bacon in the skillet. "Not well. I'm worried about crossing that river."

"Me, too. I know we've crossed rivers before but this one feels different." Maggie poured herself a cup of coffee. What she wanted was a hot cup of tea but because she'd overslept, the tea would have to wait until tonight.

"Cain says it will be remarkable if nobody dies today." Worry etched the older woman's features.

Maggie sighed. Why did Adam's brother have to be so negative? Didn't he realize his words would cause his mother to worry? Lack of sleep could cause her to be careless during the crossing. Maggie didn't comment on Cain's thoughts.

She still feared the crossings too, but thanks to Adam teaching her how to swim, Maggie felt a little more confident than she had in the past. "Have you seen Adam this morning?" She looked about the camps that she could see from their campsite.

Grace dished up the bacon. "He left a little while ago."

Brutus stood and gave a soft bark.

Maggie hurried back to the tent, where she found Lilly May sitting up and rubbing sleep from her eyes. The little girl smiled when she saw Maggie. "Ma."

Maggie's heart jumped with joy. Lilly May had called her Ma. She smiled happily at the little girl. "Let's get you dressed so we can go eat." Maggie changed Lilly May and then headed out of the tent.

Adam met her outside the door. "I'll take down the tent today." He gave her a quick grin and kissed the top of Lilly May's head. Brutus brushed against his leg. He leaned down and rubbed the big dog's head. "Go get breakfast, Brutus. We have a busy day today."

As if he understood, the dog ran between the wagons and out of sight.

Maggie waited until Adam faced her again. She looked into his eyes and wished they were more of a family than just in name only. Heat filled her face at the thought. Words rushed from her lips. "Thank you." Then she hurried off to help Grace with breakfast. Only after she was by Grace's side did Maggie realize she forgot to tell Adam that Lilly May had called her Ma.

There was a sense of urgency as everyone ate the morning meal and cleaned up the campsite. Once that was done, Adam gave them instructions. "You ladies will ride in the wagon with Lilly May and Brutus." He looked to Penelope. "You, too."

Maggie knew they were going to be packed in the wagon like canned sardines. Hopefully they would be safe. She hugged Lilly May close. "When do we go across?"

"We are one of the first wagons. Cannon wants my wagon across so that I can help others cross."

Maggie nodded. She felt dread begin to build in her stomach.

Adam walked to her. He pulled Maggie close to his

side. "We'll make it. The rain has caused the river to rise but our oxen are strong, and Josiah and I have gone over every inch of our wagon to make sure it is river ready."

It felt nice to be nestled against his side. For a few moments, Maggie wished they could just stand here. She felt safe. And whether he knew it or not, Maggie felt loved. What would Adam think if he could read her thoughts? Would he say he felt the same? Or would he put distance between them?

Adam rode Shadow in the choppy water beside the wagon. The undercurrents pulled at Shadow, his wagon and oxen. His whole family was in that wagon, at least the ones who mattered the most to him. "You got this, Josiah," he called across the water to his young driver.

He slowed the horse down and came around to the back of the wagon. Maggie's white face looked out the canvas. "Are you all doing all right in there?" Adam watched Maggie bob her head. "Stay away from the edge. Don't fall out."

Maggie inched back inside the wagon.

Adam nodded. He returned to the side of the wagon and coached Josiah until the oxen began to climb up the slippery bank. A smile filled Maggie's pale face as the wagon pulled up on the bank.

He grinned at her as he followed the wagon. "We made it, and the wagon made it."

"Just as you said we would." Maggie smiled.

Adam nodded then went up the bank with the wagon. Maggie had made him feel important with just those few words. If she knew the fear he'd felt watching the undercurrents try to suck the wagon downstream, she wouldn't have been smiling at him with such trust.

Cook grabbed the oxen and pulled beside them. "Josiah, drive the oxen to where our wagon is waiting. We'll be spending the night here, so circle up and take care of your beasts."

"Yes, sir."

Adam nodded at Cook and went to find Cannon. The wagon master entered the water astride his horse. "Looks like the preacher and his wife are going to make it." He ventured farther out into the water. Adam followed.

He glanced over his shoulder to check on his family one more time. He could see his mother, Maggie and Lilly May standing outside the wagon. Brutus guarded them while watching the activities in the water.

Adam turned back to the task at hand. Now that his family was safe, he could focus on getting the other ones across. He heard a scream but couldn't see where it came from. The Brown wagon was almost ashore, the Merriweather family was in the center of the river, followed by the Short family a quarter of the way in.

People yelled all around them but Adam was able to distinguish John Porter yelling from the opposite shore. "Adam!"

Adam's gaze followed John's finger. His breath caught in his throat as he saw a plump woman bobbing downstream.

"Betty!" The anguished cry came from the preacher.

"I'll get her," he yelled to the preacher, turning his horse to ride to the bank. If he could race downstream, he might be able to fish her from the water before she drowned in the current.

A streak of white caught his attention. Brutus raced down the bank, his gaze on Betty. A howl filled the air as the dog voiced his need to save the drowning woman. His big paws covered the ground quickly.

Shadow climbed the bank while Adam hung on tight. As soon as they were on dry ground, Adam turned the horse to follow Brutus.

He checked on the preacher's wife in time to see Betty sink under the water. The weight of her wet dress was no doubt pulling her under.

Brutus had raced ahead of her. Adam watched as the dog jumped into the water and began swimming to Betty's last location. Adam slid from Shadow's back and jumped into the river as well. Immediately the undercurrent pulled him beneath the murky water. He fought to push himself upward.

As his head came up, he saw that Shadow had followed him into the river. He clutched the horse's bridle and held on tight as he looked about for Betty and Brutus.

The horse proceeded to swim back to the bank. Adam scanned the water. Where was Betty? Where was Brutus? He coughed up water.

Then he saw them. Brutus had Betty's dress in his mouth and was swimming for shore. Adam pushed away from the horse and swam as hard as he could to the dog. They were still too far away from shore.

Thankfully the horse wasn't giving up on his master. Shadow pushed against Adam and Adam grabbed the saddle horn and pulled himself up onto the horse, then reached out for Betty's dress.

As if Brutus understood the plan, he swam for Adam, tugging Betty behind him.

When they were close enough, Adam realized Brutus wasn't clinging to her dress but to her arm. The dog had clamped his teeth into the muscle and hadn't let go. He swam close to Adam's thigh and fought the current with his powerful legs.

Adam scooped Betty up out of the water. It took all his strength. His right arm burned but he continued to haul her up onto the saddle in front of him.

Brutus continued to hold on to Betty's arm. Blood mingled with the river water.

"Let her go, boy," Adam said as he pulled Betty across his lap with a grunt.

But the dog was gone. Adam prayed the undercurrent hadn't pulled him under.

Shadow began swimming back to shore. Adam clung to Betty, praying she was still alive. So far, she hadn't moved. As soon as they were on the bank, the doctor was there. He pulled her from Adam's horse and laid her on the ground.

The preacher ran over and watched as the doctor worked on Betty. "Lord, please don't take her." He repeated the prayer over and over.

"She's alive, Preacher," the doctor assured him. "As soon as I can get this water out of her and stitch up her arm, she'll be as good as new."

Adam released the pent-up air in his lungs and looked to the river. The Brown, Short and Green wagons were now out of the water. The others were waiting for Cannon to give them directions. Something Adam knew the wagon master wouldn't do until Mrs. Brown was back at camp.

He looked to the muddy water but didn't see any sign of Brutus. He couldn't help Mrs. Brown now, but maybe he could Brutus. Adam rode Shadow over to where Cannon stood talking to several of the men.

"Cannon, I'm going to scout down the river."

The wagon master searched his face.

There was no need to scout down the river. Right now, getting the wagons and families across was the job at hand. Adam knew the older man was trying to read his thoughts. After a moment of searching Adam's eyes, Cannon nodded his consent.

"I'll be back as soon as I can," Adam promised. Then he headed Shadow farther down the river. He had to find the dog.

Using all his scouting skills, Adam searched for Brutus. After about ten minutes, he saw a pile of white fur on the shore a little farther downstream.

The dog lay on his side, panting hard. Adam dismounted and knelt beside Brutus. He reached out and touched the dog's wet fur. Big brown eyes opened and looked up at him. Brutus whined and then closed his eyes again.

Adam collapsed on the ground beside him. He rubbed the dog's head and side. The need to return to the wagon train pulled at him but he couldn't leave the dog. If it hadn't been for Brutus, Betty would surely be dead. He feared the older woman was going to have a sore arm and possibly sore lungs, but she was alive because of Brutus.

The dog's breathing remained labored, but Adam continued to pet his wet fur and whisper to him. The big dog had saved Betty Brown, but at what cost?

Chapter Twenty-One

Maggie followed the crowd as the preacher carried his wife back to their wagon. The men were talking about how Adam and Brutus had rushed in to save Betty. She knew her husband was safe because he'd pulled Betty from the water. But where had he gone?

When they passed her wagon, Maggie stopped. Grace stood with Penelope and the baby. "Grace, would you like to go help with Betty? I'm sure she would be happy to have you close by," she said, picking Lilly May up and hugging her close.

Grace nodded. "I've been so worried. I would like to see for myself that she's well. Can you imagine falling into the water like that?"

"No, ma'am. I'm sure it is terrifying."

"I'll be back soon." Grace hurried toward the Browns' wagon.

Penelope twisted her apron in her hands. "Is Betty going to be all right?" Her gaze stayed focused on Grace's back.

"I believe so," Maggie answered. "Would you like a cup of tea while we wait?"

As if talking to herself, Penelope said, "My ma still has to cross the river."

"So do my pa and brother." Maggie reached for one of Penelope's hands. "Would you like to pray for their safe passage?"

Penelope squeezed Maggie's hand. "Ma is so angry with me for marrying Josiah in secret. I don't want her to die without me telling her I'm sorry I hurt her."

Maggie shifted Lilly May on her hip then bowed her head and prayed. "Heavenly Father, we thank You for the safe return of Betty Brown. And, Lord, we ask that You protect the rest of the travelers that have to cross the river today. Penelope and I have family crossing and we ask that You give them safe passage and give them the strength to get their wagons to the other side. We thank You for their safety and that of all the animals." She paused, thinking about Brutus and Adam, both of whom were missing. Taking a deep breath, Maggie pressed on. "And, Lord, please bring Adam and Brutus safely home to me. In Jesus' name we pray, amen."

Penelope echoed, "Amen."

Maggie gave her a hug. When they separated, she said, "We are all in God's hands. Now let's make tea. We can take a cup to Betty and Grace."

Lilly May pushed to get down. Maggie thought about Brutus's absence. She'd grown used to him being there to babysit her daughter.

"Down," Lilly May demanded.

Maggie set her on the ground. "Stay close to me,"

she commanded, reaching inside the wagon for Lilly May's doll.

Lilly May took the toy and smiled.

"I'll help you keep an eye on her." Penelope pulled the cow chip bag from the wagon as Maggie prepared the firepit. Working together, they soon had water boiling over the fire.

Thanks to Penelope, four mugs were lined up on the wagon tailgate. Maggie added tea leaves to the cups with a small amount of sugar. While they worked, she searched for the dog and Adam's return.

More wagons crossed the river. Maggie knew her father and Martin were scheduled to be the last two wagons to cross. Right then Penelope's family's wagon was crossing. The water rocked the wagon. Her mother and sisters couldn't be seen. Maggie assumed after Betty's mishap the other families had been warned to stay as far inside the wagon as possible.

She held her breath until the Whites' wagon made it safely to shore, and watched Penelope run to her family. Maggie watched with hope that the young woman's mother would forgive her. When her mother emerged from the wagon, the two women clung to one another while Penelope's little sisters clapped their hands. Maggie smiled. It looked as if mother and daughter had reconciled.

Maggie put three mugs on a slab of wood, leaving Penelope's on the wagon. It was likely that Penelope would be staying close to her family until evening and the tea would grow cold. She smiled. It was a good thing she liked cold tea, too.

Lilly May had tossed her doll to the side and was

now pulling herself up using the wagon wheel. Maggie scooped the little girl up with one arm. "I told you to stay," she scolded the little girl. Balancing the tea and her daughter, she walked to the Brown wagon.

The little girl patted the side of Maggie's face. "Pa?"

"I'm not sure where he is, but I'm sure he's fine," Maggie answered, praying she was right.

Surprisingly, Betty and Grace sat outside the wagon watching the activities. Betty's hair was still wet. A lap quilt circled her shoulders. A bandage covered her left forearm. She looked tired but otherwise healthy.

"It is so good to see you sitting up. I was afraid you'd be in bed after your ordeal." Maggie handed Grace the tray of teas.

"Oh, thank you, dear." She handed a cup to Betty, who took it with trembling hands. "This will warm you up, Betty."

"I wish Albert were here," Betty said, taking a sip from her cup.

Maggie rocked side to side with Lilly May; she'd never heard the preacher's Christian name. She tried to recollect if Betty had ever used it before. Funny, such a simple thing would catch her attention.

The little girl squirmed and pointed to her parted lips.

Maggie knew what Lilly May wanted. "You are always hungry. We'll eat as soon as all the wagons are on this side of the river." She set Lilly May down.

Betty smiled as the little girl walked to her and collapsed against her knees. "Hunger's a sure sign she is growing. There are morning biscuits in that basket." She pointed to the wagon's tailgate. "If you want to give her a little something to tide her over until supper."

"Thank you." Maggie opened the basket and un-covered several small biscuits. "Are you sure you don't mind?" She took one out and re-covered the bread.

"Not at all."

Maggie gave Lilly May one of the biscuits. Then, Grace handed Maggie a cup of the tea.

She took a sip of the warm brew. But Maggie couldn't enjoy it. As the other women talked softly, her thoughts went to her husband. Where was Adam? And Brutus? Were they all right? Or had something horrible hap-pened to them?

Adam held Shadow's reins as they walked beside Brutus. He could have ridden the horse but felt the need to assure the dog he was close by if he should need him. The dog was exhausted, his steps slow. He'd hauled a grown woman through the water to safety, gotten caught in the undercurrent of the river and been swept downstream. How he'd managed to get to shore, Adam had no idea.

They stopped several times to rest. It took much lon-ger to return than Adam had anticipated.

Brutus's ears perked up. Adam grinned. He too heard the sound of the wagon train ahead. "We're al-most there, boy." He bent down and rubbed Brutus's big head. "You've done a good job today." Adam looked the dog in the face. "Thank you."

For the first time, Brutus licked Adam's hand. As far as he knew, Adam didn't think Brutus had "kissed" anyone, other than Lilly May.

Adam continued walking. He noticed Brutus walking a little faster, too. The dog was going to be all right with a little rest.

Adam searched the camp for Maggie. She stood beside their wagon talking to Cain, with Lilly May clinging to her side. From this distance he couldn't make out their words.

Cain reached out and pulled Maggie to him in a hug.

He waited, expecting her to push his brother away. But, she didn't. It felt as if someone had thrust a knife into his chest. Why wasn't she resisting him? Had the woman he loved once again fallen in love with his brother? The thought tore through his heart. As it echoed in his mind, he pulled up short. When had he decided he loved Maggie? There was no other reason that he would be feeling such pain and betrayal if he didn't love her. Adam wanted to climb on his horse and ride away. Far away.

Brutus growled deep in his throat and then bounded toward them.

Maggie must have heard the dog because she pushed out of Cain's arms and turned toward the dog. Her gaze met Adam's and she smiled.

Was she really happy to see him? Or was she covering the fact that he'd caught her in his brother's arms? Just like Lynda. Bile rose in his throat. Adam fought the hurt and sickness.

Cain grinned over her head. A knowing smile crossed his brother's face as he rubbed salt into the unseen wound in Adam's heart.

Brutus pushed on Maggie's leg, drawing her attention from Adam. She bent over, allowing Lilly May to pat the dog. Maggie lowered the little girl to the ground beside Brutus.

Adam climbed into the saddle and turned Shadow before she stood up. He needed to get away.

"Adam!" Cannon called.

He waved. When they were within talking distance, Cannon continued, "That's the Porter wagons coming across now."

Adam looked toward his father-in-law's lead wagon. The old man's face was white with stress. "I'll go help."

He didn't wait for approval.

Shadow leaped into the water and swam out to the wagon. Adam saw Martin following his pa. He looked a little steadier, so Adam focused on John Porter.

"Adam, I'm having trouble keeping them steady," Mr. Porter confessed.

"Mind if I climb aboard and help?" Adam brought Shadow up beside the wagon. He didn't want to get too close in case there was an undercurrent that might pull the horse under the wagon.

"I'd appreciate the help," the older man admitted.

Adam took a deep breath and then slipped his feet from the stirrups. He tied the reins onto the saddle horn and then carefully worked his body so that he could dismount from Shadow onto the wagon without falling into the water. It was a tricky move and Adam prayed he'd make it.

He landed with a thud beside John. "Sorry, that was a little bumpy." Adam watched as Shadow swam back to shore.

"This whole crossing has been a little bumpy." Maggie's pa handed the oxen reins to Adam.

Adam couldn't agree more. He urged the oxen through the turbulent waters of the river.

When they were safely on shore, Adam sighed with relief, handed the reins to Mr. Porter and then hopped down. "Pull in behind the Short wagon." He pointed John in the right direction and then turned to check on Martin.

Maggie's brother brought the oxen to shore with no trouble. He looked down at Adam. "I hope the rest of the river crossings aren't as bad as this one was."

"Me too, but only time will tell."

Martin nodded. He guided the oxen to line up behind his father's wagon.

Now that everyone was ashore, Adam's mind returned to his brother and Maggie. Cain would always try to come between Adam and anyone he loved. Maggie had promised to be faithful to him and yet he'd seen her hugging Cain. He needed to think.

Cannon rode up. "We're camping here. Mrs. Brown needs time to recover and everyone else could use a rest after today's crossing."

"I'll scout the trail. The rain might have left us a few surprises." Adam looked to the wagons that were now completely circled up. Kids ran about playing, the men were working on their wagons and fires had started, suggesting that the women were preparing an early supper.

"Are you all right, Adam?" Cannon rested his arms on the saddle horn and waited.

It wasn't like the wagon master to ask such a personal question. "Yep."

"You're sure?" He pushed his hat back on his head. "You haven't been yourself since Cain has joined us."

Adam couldn't deny his words. He hadn't been the same. Cain's presence had brought back hurtful memories, doubt in himself and now distrust in Maggie. "My brother and I don't get along. But that has nothing to do with how I'm doing my job."

"I didn't say there was anything wrong with the way you are doing your job. I'm asking as a friend. Is there anything I can do?"

He didn't want Cannon or anyone else thinking he needed help. Besides, what could the other man do? "I'm fine, Cannon. I appreciate your concern. Would you go by my wagon and let the women know I'm scouting ahead and I won't be back tonight?"

Cannon bobbed his head once. He straightened up in the saddle. "If you find anything out of the ordinary, get back here." The wagon master returned to the wagon train.

Adam hated that he'd been short with his friend. He needed to get a grip on himself. Taking a deep breath, he set out to scout the trail. What else was he going to do? Regardless of what happened in his personal life, Adam knew he was obligated to get these people to Oregon.

Chapter Twenty-Two

Maggie knew Adam had seen her and Cain. She hadn't invited his hug but didn't know how to get free quickly. The fact that Adam had seen it and immediately reacted by leaving her alone with his brother broke her heart. She'd thought they were closer than that. That he would judge her immediately spoke volumes of what he thought about her as a wife and as a person who kept their word.

Lilly May fussed when going to bed. For the second night in a row her pa hadn't come to read to her and say good-night. "Pa?" she asked again.

"I'm sorry, little one, Pa is working."

Hearing the words didn't give Lilly May comfort. Maggie read her the Bible story about Peter walking on the water and how he had to keep focused on Jesus or he would sink. The story was more for herself but Lilly May seemed to enjoy it. Maggie rubbed Lilly May's little back until the baby went to sleep.

She didn't feel like sleeping. She stepped out of the

tent. Thankfully Brutus was there and back to his old self. He stayed close to Lilly May.

Martin waved at her from the firepit. He cradled a tin cup of coffee. It had been a while since she had had time to visit with her brother alone. Maggie smiled and joined him.

He handed her a second mug.

Maggie accepted it and sat down on the crate beside him. She took a sip of the drink and was pleasantly surprised to discover it was tea. "Where did you get tea?"

Martin grinned. "At the fort."

"But you don't drink tea." She took another sip, closed her eyes and savored her comfort drink with joy.

"Nope, but you do." His eyes danced over his cup. "And if I'm not mistaken, your tin is already almost empty."

Her brother knew her well. Maggie opened her eyes and nodded. "I'm afraid so."

"You share too much," Martin teasingly accused.

She remembered when they were children and their pa allowed them to get a little candy each; she always shared hers with other children. But not Martin. He only shared with her when hers ran out. Now that they were older, she realized he'd stretched out his candy until they went back to the store and Pa was feeling generous again. "Perhaps you are right."

They sat in comfortable silence for several minutes. It was still early. The sun hadn't set yet, but the camp had already quieted down. Everyone was bone-tired. Maggie wondered what her brother wanted to talk to her about and knew she'd have to be the one to ask. Trying to sound British, Maggie asked, "What brings you bearing tea this fine evening, kind sir?"

"Oh, that's terrible. You really should practice that accent." He shook his head as if he couldn't believe she'd brought back her childhood dream of having high tea with the Queen.

She waited for him to say more. When it was apparent Martin was stuck for words, she asked, "Well?"

He set the cup on the ground and turned to face her. Martin lowered his voice, aware that Grace slept in the wagon behind them. "It's Adam. You know I wouldn't get into your business if I wasn't concerned."

Fear raced through her heart. She'd not seen him since the day of the river crossing. "Is he all right?"

Martin waved his hand in dismissal. "He's not hurt physically but something has changed."

She swallowed and lowered her voice as well. "He thinks I've betrayed him."

This time it was Martin who looked shocked. "How?"

"The other day he saw Cain hugging me."

"What in thunder were you doing hugging Cain?"

"Shhhh!" Maggie shook her head. "I wasn't hugging him. But to an outsider I'm sure that's what it looked like."

Martin sighed in exasperation. "You just said he saw you hugging Cain."

"No, I said Cain was hugging me."

"To men, there isn't much difference, little sister."

"Oh, for pity's sake, shut up and listen." Maggie took a deep breath. "I was walking back to our wagon from the Browns when Cain called me to come where he was. Lilly May was fussing—it was her nap time—and

I didn't want to stop for him, but after all he is Adam's brother. So, I went to him." She looked to Martin, who was listening intently. "Lilly May was shoving away from me wanting down, but I didn't want her to get into any of the mud puddles, so what did I do, I stepped into the gooiest mud puddle around. I was stuck. Cain laughed and came to help me out. When I tried to step forward, my boot stuck and Cain grabbed me. With one foot in the mud and Lilly May fussing, I couldn't move away from him, and Cain didn't let go immediately. It was very awkward because I had to demand that he release me." When she finished, her lungs felt as if she'd run a race and had lost.

Martin nodded. "And Adam saw all this?"

"I'm not sure how much he saw. I didn't even know he was around until Brutus joined us. When I looked up, Adam was watching us. Before I could say anything, he turned to leave, and the wagon master needed his help with Pa's wagon."

"Everything will work out. This trail does things to people, but Adam is a good man and once you explain, I'm sure he'll understand." Martin picked up his cup. Maggie stood too and he hugged her. When they parted, he said, "Let me know when you run out of tea. I've got plenty to share with you."

Maggie smiled. "Thanks. You really are a great brother."

He laughed. "Just keep telling yourself that."

She shook her head, knowing he understood what she was saying. "Good night, Martin."

"'Night."

Maggie sat back down. After talking to Martin, she

felt as if the camp were smothering her. She walked to the side of the wagon and got the rope. Brutus looked up with sad eyes.

"I'll be right back, ole boy. I just need some fresh air." She looped the rope over his head and then tied the other end to the wagon. "You are a good boy and I don't want you to think I might fall in the river like Mrs. Brown. I need to know you are here protecting Lilly May." She patted his head and then stepped between the wagons.

The river water now drifted calmly over the rocks. Its sound soothed her frayed emotions. As she walked, Maggie had the feeling someone was following her. She looked over her shoulder but saw no one. It was still early, and the night guards would be keeping watch; they probably had already seen her. What she needed was to splash cold water over her face and wash the grime of the trail from her throat.

Adam had spent the last two days avoiding his wagon and Maggie. He'd had a couple of meals with Cook and Cannon, and even a roasted rabbit tonight over a campfire away from the wagon train, but he missed his family. He missed Maggie. Deep in his heart Adam knew he was in love with his wife.

He'd run what he'd seen through his mind over and over. Adam prayed and asked the Lord to give him guidance. Even now as he sat on top of the rise, looking at the wagons circled below, his mind replayed both events, the one with Lynda and the one from the other day.

Lynda's face had shown her guilt and shock at being caught with his brother, but Maggie's showed signs of relief and joy at seeing him. Why hadn't he seen that before? Instead, he'd focused on Cain's gloating features and allowed his heart to be bruised once more.

Adam eased Shadow down the embankment. He'd report to Cannon that the trail was clear but that he'd seen signs where a camp had been set up a couple of nights earlier. It appeared to be a cold camp, but just to be safe, he'd report it so that the men would all be alert when they passed through that area.

He'd almost reached the wagons when he spotted Maggie walking to the river. His heart jumped at the realization that he could have a few minutes alone with her to apologize for his behavior since Cain had joined their wagon train. There were several things Adam wanted to say to her before he told her that he loved her.

Something moved in the shadows behind Maggie. Even though night would soon be upon them, the sun hadn't set yet. Adam's heart leaped in his throat. Were Indians or bandits trailing after his wife? He started to urge Shadow into a full run when he recognized her stalker.

Cain.

Adam slowed Shadow down. Why was Cain following her? Had they planned a private meeting? Had he been wrong in thinking their shared hug had been innocent?

His heart warred with his thoughts. Hadn't he just moments before decided to trust Maggie? He continued to follow slowly, keeping out of sight, much as his brother was doing ahead of him.

Cain had always resented him; Adam really didn't understand why. When they were kids, he had followed his big brother everywhere. Now, as he thought back, Lynda wasn't the first painful infliction Cain had caused. He'd been mean, conniving, and many times Adam had felt the pain of Cain's cruelty, both mentally and physically.

At that moment, Adam made the choice to believe in Maggie. He dismounted from Shadow and tied the horse to a tree. Adam took a deep breath then proceeded to get close enough to Maggie and Cain to hear them, should Cain reveal himself to her.

Maggie turned to look behind her. She stood at the water's edge, weariness filling her eyes. "Who's there?"

Cain stepped from the shadows. "It's only me."

Maggie visibly relaxed. "You scared me. I thought you might have been a bandit sneaking up on me."

Anger filled Adam but he pushed it away. Maggie's relaxing didn't mean she was happy to see him, only that she was happy to see it was someone she knew. That's what he told himself. That's what he had to believe.

Cain laughed. "Not tonight. Tonight I'm just Cain Walker."

Adam inhaled sharply. What did his brother mean?

She tilted her head to the side. "What do you mean 'not tonight'?"

He chuckled as he continued to walk toward her. "I'm taking tonight off."

Adam exhaled, not liking the sound of that. It sounded like Cain was confessing to being one of the bandits. He prayed it wasn't so, but experience with his brother told him it was definitely possible.

"That's not funny. Why were you following me?" She crossed her arms and glared at him.

"Isn't it obvious?" Cain stepped closer.

Maggie stepped sideways from him. "No, it's not. I don't like games, Cain. We should be getting back to the wagon train."

He sighed as if he needed to make a confession. "All right, no games. I saw that you were finally alone, and I wanted to tell you that I love you. I've loved you since I saw you at the fort."

Red-hot flames coiled in Adam's chest. He realized it wasn't jealousy that burned deep; it was anger. Anger that his brother would be so brazen. Cain knew they were married.

She shook her head. "I'm not in love with you, Cain. I'm your brother's wife."

"You don't have to be," he told her. "We can leave the wagon train. We can leave tonight. I set up a camp a few hours away. We can go there tonight."

The desire to run out and pound his brother into the ground fought with Adam's common sense. It was a violent thought, and he wasn't a violent man. Unlike Cain.

Maggie inched around him. "Cain, I'm not going anywhere with you, tonight or ever."

Adam's heart went out to Maggie. She'd kept her word and been faithful to him. How had he ever doubted her?

Immediately, Cain's disposition changed. His voice hardened. "You are going with me."

She answered him in a firm voice. "Why? Why do you want me to go so bad? And don't say it's because you love me. We both know that isn't true." Maggie put her hands on her hips.

Fear gripped Adam. It grew in the pit of his stomach. He knew from this distance he wouldn't be able to stop Cain from grabbing her. Maggie was putting on a brave front, but he could see her lips tremble as she faced Cain.

Satisfaction filled Cain's face. "There's only one reason. Because taking you will hurt Adam. He'll hurt for years, like he did when I took Lynda from him."

Adam didn't care about Lynda. He knew his love for her had been that of a boy and not a man who knew the true value of a woman. Maggie had shown herself to be the woman he loved.

Maggie inched a little farther away. "Why do you want to hurt Adam? What did he do?"

A snarl crossed Cain's features.

Adam caught his breath, waiting for the answer.

"He was born."

Maggie shook her head. "You are mad."

"No, I'm not. Everyone loved me but then Adam came along. I was no longer the baby. Pa made sure I grew up fast while Ma doted on him as if he were a gift from God. When I turned thirteen years old, Pa took me fishing, told me he wasn't really my pa and that in a few years I'd have to make my own way. Can you believe that? I thought he was joking when he said he was leaving the farm to Adam. But he wasn't." His lips pulled back in a sneer. "I almost killed Adam by daring him to climb the highest tree in our yard with me and then I pushed him out. I felt sure the fall would break his neck, but all it did was break his collarbone. Ma made sure he was protected from then on. I moved on and waited until he was a grown man and then I reentered his life, much like I've done now. He was so in love that I thought taking Lynda would break him and make me feel better." He paused and grinned wickedly. "It did for a while, but then Adam took Ma and moved away."

Caution filled Maggie's voice as she asked, "And what did you do?"

He gave a wild laugh. "Why, I became a criminal. Joined a group of nice men and started searching the Oregon Trail for my sweet little brother. Only, the men weren't so nice, if you catch my drift. Anyway, I've killed before and I plan on killing Adam now. Hopefully he'll fight harder than Lilly May's parents did." He sighed as if he'd just thought of something. "Oh dear, I shouldn't have told you that. Now I have to kill you, too."

Adam willed Maggie to turn and run for the wagons. He moved forward through the trees, praying he'd get close enough to them to keep Cain from following through on his threat and killing Maggie.

She took a couple more steps back. She ignored his threat to kill her and instead said, "You shot Adam a few weeks ago too, didn't you?"

Cain nodded. He looked at her and grinned. "You are as smart as you are pretty. I was sure that shot would kill him, but it didn't. It's like he has nine lives." His eyes glazed over as if he was contemplating how many attempts he needed to make before his brother would be dead.

Maggie took advantage of his distracted state and backed up even farther. This time she moved faster but continued to face Cain.

Adam's heart pounded in his chest as she got closer

to him. Just a few more feet and she would be past him and he could come out, knowing she would be safe with him between her and his dangerous brother.

Cain glanced up at her. He advanced toward Maggie with long steps. "We need to be leaving before Adam returns." He reached out to grab her, but she was faster. She turned and ran.

As soon as she passed him, Adam stepped out of his hiding place. "Cain, stop."

Startled, Cain did just that. "Well, look who has come to save his wife." He pulled his gun from its holster.

Adam stood his ground. He prayed Maggie had continued to the wagon train. "What are you going to do? Shoot me again?"

"Well, I do have my gun out and you are standing in front of me. Now, let's see…which shoulder did I shoot you in before?" He rubbed the barrel of the gun against his whiskers.

Adam prayed his brother couldn't hear his rapidly beating heart. He forced a laugh from his throat. "I think you are forgetting, Cain. Shooting someone in the shoulder doesn't mean they are going to die. I mean, I lived through it once." Adam wanted to keep him talking, give Maggie time to get away. "Do you remember when we were kids and Pa took us hunting?"

A grin crossed Cain's face. "Yeah, I shot that big buck right between the eyes. Pa was proud of me that day."

Distracting his brother had saved him from a beating in the past, and Adam prayed it would do so again. "He was, and that venison tasted so good." Adam watched Cain go back in time to that day.

He took that opportunity to check on Maggie. She stood a few feet from him. Why had she stopped? He motioned for her to go to the wagons.

A shot rang out. Adam felt the fire explode in his chest and back. His body jerked but he kept upright. He faced his brother even as Maggie screamed. Intense pain dropped him to his knees.

Chapter Twenty-Three

Maggie ran and placed herself between Adam and his brother. "Cain, stop! I won't let you shoot him again." Maggie couldn't let him kill Adam. She faced Cain like a mother bear. Her love for Adam conquered her fear of dying at the hands of her brother-in-law.

He grinned at her. "Thanks for coming back. Now all I have to do is shoot you, too. I'll tell the wagon master that the bandits caught you two lovebirds out here and killed you." Cain raised his gun for the second time.

Maggie closed her eyes. She prayed silently that Grace would keep Lilly May and that the men from the wagon train would hear the shots and save Adam.

Her body jerked as the sound of a second gunshot filled the evening air. Maggie's eyes opened in fear. She looked to the front of her dress and realized she felt no pain and there was no blood on her clothing.

Her gaze jerked to where Cain had been standing. He now lay on the ground. Maggie's mind tried to piece together what had happened.

"Are you all right?" Martin stood a few feet away from Cain. He held a gun at his side.

Maggie nodded. Realization that Martin had saved her life hit her like a rock. She wanted to rush into his arms and thank him. But the sound of Adam groaning behind her had Maggie wheeling around.

She knelt beside her husband. He clutched his chest; his gaze rested on his brother. Maggie saw a group of men running to them. "Doc is on the way," she told Adam, praying that the doctor was one of the men heading toward them and that he had his medical bag.

Adam groaned between clenched teeth. Pain and sorrow filled his voice. "Is he dead?"

Maggie looked to Martin, who was kneeling beside Cain. Martin shook his head.

She answered Adam, "He's alive."

"Thank the Lord." Adam studied her face. He reached up to touch her cheek.

Maggie saw tears in his eyes before he passed out and his hand fell back to the ground.

"Let me see him." She heard Doc's voice approach behind her.

She moved back, afraid of what the future held. What if Adam didn't live? Could she go on without him? The pain in her chest was like none she'd ever felt before. She'd been sad and lonely after Matthew's death. But her heart hadn't ached like it was doing now.

"What happened here?" Cannon demanded. He looked from Martin to Maggie.

Martin straddled Cain's body to keep them from stepping on him. He moved out of the way so that men could get to Cain. "I'll explain everything when we get back to camp."

Doc glanced over his shoulder to Martin and asked, "Do I need to check Cain now, or can he wait until we get back to the wagons and I stop Adam's bleeding?"

"He can wait," Martin answered. "I shot him in the arm but when he fell backward his head hit a rock and knocked him out."

The doctor looked to the wagon master. "We need to get them back to the wagon train quickly."

Cannon nodded and then began giving orders to the men to gather up Cain and Adam.

Maggie began shaking. She couldn't stop. Her eyes filled with tears as she watched the men move swiftly and carry both Adam and Cain back to the wagon train.

Martin helped her stand. "He will be all right."

She folded herself into his arms. Words and tears flowed from her. "What if he's not?"

Her brother rubbed her back, much like she did Lilly May when the little girl was upset. "We'll cross that bridge if we get to it. Right now, we need to get back." Martin gently eased her away from him.

Maggie released him and nodded. "You are right. Grace will need me. With both her sons shot, I'm sure her mama's heart is hurting." Plus, there was Lilly May to consider.

Martin took a deep breath. "Promise me you won't leave the wagon train alone again."

The anguish in his voice made her turn to face him. "I promise." Maggie knew that without her brother's protective eyes on her, she would be dead now. "Thank you, Martin, for saving my life."

He reached out and hugged her to his side. "I am sorry I didn't get to you sooner. I could have saved Adam more pain."

They walked toward the wagon train, which was alive with activity. News had traveled fast, and people were rushing about. Preacher Brown stood with his head bowed. Maggie knew he was praying for the brothers.

"I still can't get over that Cain hates Adam so much that he would try to kill him." She stepped over the wagon tongue and into the circle of wagons.

Penelope and Brutus came running to her. She had Lilly May on her hip. Unaware of the events taking place, Lilly May laughed at the fun she was having clinging to the younger woman as she hurried to them.

"Adam is in your wagon and Cain has been taken to Mr. Cannon's wagon." She panted. "I'll watch Lilly May for you."

"Thank you." Maggie squeezed Martin's hand and then hurried toward her wagon.

She heard Penelope telling Martin, "Cannon wants you to come to his wagon as soon as you can."

Maggie stopped when she got to the wagon. The canvas was closed. Should she go in? Would there be enough room for another person in the cramped space? She leaned forward to open the canvas but stopped when she heard the doctor speaking in a soft voice.

"He's lost a lot of blood but thankfully this man has big bones. The bullet hit a rib instead of his lungs or heart." He cleared his throat. "But that means I have to go in to get that bullet out. We can't leave it—he could get lead poisoning."

Grace's soft voice responded. "I'll go find Maggie and let her know."

Adam would be having a second surgery on the trail. Maggie wiped the unbidden tears from her cheeks. She needed to be strong for Grace.

"He's stable for the moment. I need to go check on my other patient." The doctor pulled back the canvas. Seeing Maggie, he continued, "I assume you heard what I told Mrs. Walker?" He climbed down from the wagon.

"I did."

Grace's white face appeared at the canvas opening. "Maggie. I'm so glad you are here."

The doctor turned and helped Grace from the wagon. As soon as her feet hit the ground, he turned to Maggie. "Keep him comfortable. I'm out of morphine. If you have any whiskey, start administering it. That bullet has to come out and he's going to need all the help he can get to dull the pain."

Maggie nodded. "I will see to it, Doctor."

She climbed into the wagon. Adam lay on the mattress with his eyes closed. Thinking he was asleep, Maggie went about doing as the doctor ordered. She pulled a tin cup from the trunk where they were kept and then moved to the barrel that held the whiskey. With the brown bottle in hand, Maggie moved to his side.

Adam opened his eyes and saw what she had. He groaned. "I hate that stuff."

She opened the bottle and poured the dark brew into the cup. "I know you do, but the doctor says he has to take the bullet out and it would be best if you have this before he comes back."

Adam's face was pale. "How is Cain?" He tried to push himself up but realized that wasn't going to happen.

Maggie shook her head. "I don't know. Martin said he shot him in the arm and he hit his head on a rock when he fell." She held his head up and he drank from the cup.

When she pulled it away, Adam's voice was filled with sadness. "He really was going to kill us, wasn't he?"

"I believe so." She poured more whiskey into the cup.

Adam awoke. His first inclination was to call for Maggie. But he heard soft sobs.

Turning his head, he saw that his mother sat beside him.

"Ma?"

"Adam. You are awake." She wiped her eyes and felt his forehead.

He nodded. Aware that his chest felt as if it were on fire, he asked her for water.

"Of course, son." She moved to the back of the wagon and said softly, "He's awake and asking for water."

It seemed like forever to Adam before someone handed her a cup of water.

She hurried back to him and held his head while he drank from the cup. "I'm so glad you are awake."

"Where is Maggie?" he asked as she lowered his head back to the pillow.

"Putting Lilly May to bed. The little mite wouldn't let anyone else do it. Maggie hasn't left your side until now." Grace brushed the hair from his brow. "Can I get you anything else?"

Adam knew his ma well. Even though she tried, he

could sense something wasn't right. He couldn't remember much other than the doctor had managed to get the bullet out of his chest. His head felt as if it were in a fog. There was something he needed to remember, but what? Sleep threatened to overtake him again.

Then he remembered the reason he was lying in the wagon with fire in his chest. "Cain?"

His mother's lips trembled, and tears spilled from her eyes. "He's gone."

His head was starting to clear. "What do you mean 'he's gone'? Did he escape?" Adam wished he could rid himself of the confusion. How long had he been asleep after the surgery?

"No, he never woke up. Doc said his head wound was the cause." She dropped her head and wept for her lost son.

He couldn't believe that Cain was dead. Even though his brother had tried to kill him, Adam didn't want him dead. "I'm sorry, Ma."

She reached out and patted his shoulder. "It wasn't your fault, son."

Knowing it wasn't his fault didn't make Adam feel any better. For the past four years he had prayed he'd never cross paths with Cain again and now he wouldn't. Adam stared up at the canvas. So much had happened since they'd left Missouri. He had married, become a new pa, been shot, then Cain had joined them and tried to kill both him and Maggie.

Right now, Maggie was his only ray of sunshine. He'd heard her soft voice when he was half asleep. She'd prayed over him and had asked God to restore him to full health. Adam frowned. Had it been his imagination? Or had Maggie whispered she loved him in his ears?

The next morning, they buried Cain.

Adam's heart hurt for his mother and the loss of his brother. Even though they had never been close, and Cain had tried to kill both him and Maggie, Adam knew deep down he still loved his brother.

They stood beside the fresh grave. Preacher Brown prayed soft words over the solemn event while his mother wept softly beside him. Adam felt Maggie's small hand enter his.

Adam's chest burned and his legs felt as weak as a newborn kitten, but there was no way he was going to allow his mother to face burying her son alone. As if she felt his vulnerability, Maggie put her arm around his waist, offering her body as a crutch.

The preacher said, "Amen."

His mother dabbed her eyes and then looked to him. "Son, you are as pale as a sheet. We need to get you back to bed."

Adam knew she was telling the truth but dreaded climbing back into the wagon. He looked to Maggie, who hadn't moved from his side. "I'll be right there, Ma."

Grace nodded and left them alone.

Men came with shovels to finish burying Cain. Adam saw the large rocks that would be placed over the grave. He was thankful that the men were willing to take care of his brother's final resting place.

Cannon walked up to him. "Adam, why don't you

and the missus go on now. We'll finish up here and then be on our way."

Adam swallowed the lump that had gathered in his throat. "Thank you." He nodded to each man before leaving.

Maggie continued to stay close to Adam as they walked. She didn't protest as he took them away from the wagons instead of toward them. "I've been concerned for you," she finally said.

Adam moved from her side to face her. He wanted to tell her he loved her, that he no longer wanted a marriage of convenience. Now might not be the best time to tell her but he didn't care.

Clearing his voice, Adam looked deeply into her eyes. "Maggie, the thought of losing you yesterday was more than I could bear. I should have told you sooner that I love you."

Her eyes widened and she opened her mouth to speak but he stopped her. He was afraid she would say she didn't love him. Adam pressed on. "I think you love me, too. Why else would you put yourself in harm's way yesterday?"

"I do love you, Adam. More than I have ever loved any man in my life." She laid a hand on his chest. Her eyes begged him to believe her.

Adam covered her hand with his and swallowed hard. "When we get to Oregon, I promise to be the husband you deserve."

"You already are." Maggie raised up on tiptoes and kissed him. A sweet simple kiss that ended too soon.

Doc stalked across the grass to where they were. "Have you lost your mind? You should be lying down.

I've patched up a lot of men and I can tell you now that none of them were out of bed and kissing their wives the next day."

It was at that point that Adam's legs abandoned him. He felt himself sliding to the ground. Maggie hurried to one side and the doctor to the other. They supported him as they made their way back to the wagons.

Adam was aware of the doctor grumbling that he shouldn't have given him so much laudanum. Then he changed his mind and decided he'd give him more when they got back to the wagon. "Maybe that will keep him from wandering off," he muttered as if talking to himself.

He didn't care what the doctor did once they got back. Adam knew that he and Maggie were going to have a wonderful future. Maggie had said she loved him too, and she'd kissed him.

Epilogue

A cool October breeze washed across Maggie and Grace as they sat on the front porch of their cabin, rocking in their matching chairs. It felt nice to have some time to relax before supper. The past year had been hard, especially the winter.

Maggie's mind reminisced over the past year. They had arrived in Oregon at the beginning of October. It had taken Adam much longer than he expected to get well and regain his strength, and the cabin had been slow going up, even with her helping him while Grace watched Lilly May in the wagon.

Thankfully, Martin and her father had come to their rescue and helped them get the cabin built. It had been Martin who suggested they have a house-raising party and invite the new town folks to help. Her pa had supplied the food to feed the crowd that arrived, and Martin had supplied the logs.

Once the log cabin had been built, with enough bedrooms for everyone, Adam and Maggie had planned what they wanted to plant the following spring. Adam had also bought a milk cow, which thankfully supplied them with milk even in the winter months.

During those months Grace and Maggie had used their sewing skills to make new clothes for themselves and Lilly May. They also quilted bed coverings.

Maggie was thankful that her pa had a store, and that she could barter meals with him to get the cloth and supplies they needed. Truthfully, her pa had been very generous in his dealings.

With the arrival of spring, Maggie and Adam had worked side by side plowing a field and planting, and later they harvested. They were still harvesting fall vegetables. Grace and Maggie canned everything they could get their hands on. Maggie made sure to set aside jars for her pa and brother.

Maggie smiled as she thought about the other things that had changed during the year. Martin had helped their father set up his store but then surprised everyone with his decision to start the first sawmill in Cannonville, their new town named after the wagon master who had gotten them to Oregon safely. Josiah and Penelope had their first child, a little girl who looked like her father, only cuter. Most of the wagon train families decided to stay and develop the new town.

They now had a church, a doctor, a store, a bakery and a blacksmith shop. There was talk of hiring a schoolteacher soon. The children from the wagon train needed an education and their mothers were determined to have a school. Everyone missed Preacher Brown and his wife but the new preacher would be arriving soon.

Until then, the men took turns reading scriptures on Sunday.

The farm was between Cannonville and Milton. She loved Cannonville best because she felt as if her whole family lived there, even those that weren't related by blood but by hard work and the journey of the Oregon Trail.

Maggie cupped the small mound that was now her belly. She hadn't told Adam about the baby and was waiting until after supper to give him the good news. It hadn't been easy to keep her secret. The doctor told her earlier this morning that her baby would be healthy if she continued to work hard and eat right. Maggie planned on doing both.

Adam had proved to be the perfect husband for her. Where Matt had made her feel she wasn't good enough, Adam encouraged her to be herself and believe that she was a good wife and mother to Lilly May. Now she would be mother to Lilly May and another child come April.

She'd already written in Lilly May's diary about the new baby brother or sister she would see in the spring. Maggie had written that she knew Lilly May was going to be a wonderful big sister. And Maggie assured the little girl that her love for her would never change because of the siblings that she would soon have. She smiled with happiness at the thought of filling their home with lots of children.

Grace rocked in her chair. "When are you going to tell Adam about the babe?" She smiled knowingly.

"I never said I was with child," Maggie protested. She wanted to tell Adam first but from the twinkle in

Grace's eyes, her mother-in-law had guessed her condition.

The older woman chuckled. "I'll not give your secret away but I suggest you tell him soon. The ladies were whispering Sunday and you don't want one of their husbands telling him, do you?"

Maggie ignored the question. There were good things and bad things about knowing everyone in town and everyone knowing you. Everyone knowing your business was one of the bad.

Grace pushed out of her chair and stepped over to Maggie. She leaned down and hugged her around the shoulders. "We are all very happy for you. That's the only reason we were discussing it."

Maggie still refused to admit she was going to have a baby. Instead, she stood and hugged Grace back. "I'm going to go check on Lilly May." She opened the door to the cabin and stepped inside her home.

Lilly May's room was right off her and Adam's. She walked down the short hall and tiptoed inside.

Brutus looked up from his place on the rug.

Martin had made his niece her own bed. He'd built it much like the little wagon Adam had purchased for her at Fort Laramie. Only there were no wheels on the legs of the bed and the side rails were taller so that even if she woke and stood up, it was too high for her to fall out. Maggie stood beside it now looking at her napping baby. Soon Lilly May would be a sister.

She heard the door open softly but since Brutus didn't protest the intruder, Maggie assumed Grace had followed her into the baby's bedroom. She didn't look back, simply whispered, "Grace, I'm not telling you anything until after I talk to Adam."

"Talk to me about what?"

Maggie jumped. She hadn't expected Adam to be home this early. Her gaze moved to the sleeping baby. Lilly May hadn't been disturbed by them so Maggie grabbed Adam's hand and led him out of the room. She walked into their bedroom and shut the door. "What are you doing back so soon?"

He pulled her close and looked into her face. "That's a fine way to greet your husband."

Adam then proceeded to kiss her and tickle her at the same time.

Maggie loved this playful side of her husband. She twisted and turned until he released her with a sigh.

"No kisses, no tickles. What is it that my lovely wife is hiding?"

She pushed her hair from her eyes. "I'm not hiding anything."

"Well, that's good. So, what is it that you are going to tell me?" He tilted his head and studied her face.

Maggie had wanted to tell him in a romantic way but now she'd just have to blurt it out. She took a deep breath, reached for both his rough hands and said, "Remember when I told you I wanted to have a baby next fall?"

"Yes, but remember I told you God will decide when we have more children?" he countered.

She nodded. "You were right."

Adam looked perplexed. "I was?"

"Yes. God has decided we will have a baby in the spring instead." Maggie watched his face.

Adam grinned. "As in this spring?"

She nodded. "The doctor thinks the baby will come in April." Maggie pulled the material of her dress a little tighter around her waist to show him the baby bump.

He whooped and then grabbed her about the waist. Adam swung her around and around.

"Stop! You are making me dizzy." She laughed.

Brutus gave a sharp yip from the other room.

Adam continued spinning her around and laughing with happiness.

"Adam, Lilly May is awake." She laughed as he lowered her feet to the floor.

Grace called through the door, "I'll get her."

Maggie panted and felt a little sick to her stomach. "I don't think it's a good idea to swing an expecting mother about the room."

"Oh, I'm sorry." He searched her face. "Are you all right?"

She reached up and touched his face. "I am more than all right. I'm happy."

He rested his forehead against hers. "Me, too. I can't believe God is blessing us so soon."

Maggie shook her head. "Adam, we've been married for over a year now." Heat filled her cheeks as she hoped he'd understand what she was implying. "Babies come fast to happily married couples."

It was his turn to blush. Adam hugged her close. "Maggie, I am the happiest man alive. I'm so glad God brought you and Lilly May into my life when He did."

Her heart soared. Adam was happy to become a father again, pleased that she was his wife, and best of all Adam was a man of God. A man who treated his family well, loved them with his whole heart and protected them with his life. She was blessed and in love. What more could a woman ask for?

A smile parted her lips. Other than a houseful of children to love.

She looked up at Adam, who immediately kissed her. This was where she'd always longed to be. In the arms of a man who knew her value and loved her deeply.

* * * * *

Get 4 FREE REWARDS!

We'll send you 2 FREE Books plus 2 FREE Mystery Gifts.

FREE
Value Over
$20

Both the **Harlequin® Special Edition** and **Harlequin® Heartwarming™** series feature compelling novels filled with stories of love and strength where the bonds of friendship, family and community unite.

YES! Please send me 2 FREE novels from the Harlequin Special Edition or Harlequin Heartwarming series and my 2 FREE gifts (gifts are worth about $10 retail). After receiving them, if I don't wish to receive any more books, I can return the shipping statement marked "cancel." If I don't cancel, I will receive 6 brand-new Harlequin Special Edition books every month and be billed just $5.49 each in the U.S. or $6.24 each in Canada, a savings of at least 12% off the cover price, or 4 brand-new Harlequin Heartwarming Larger-Print books every month and be billed just $6.24 each in the U.S. or $6.74 each in Canada, a savings of at least 19% off the cover price. It's quite a bargain! Shipping and handling is just 50¢ per book in the U.S. and $1.25 per book in Canada.* I understand that accepting the 2 free books and gifts places me under no obligation to buy anything. I can always return a shipment and cancel at any time by calling the number below. The free books and gifts are mine to keep no matter what I decide.

Choose one: ☐ **Harlequin Special Edition** ☐ **Harlequin Heartwarming**
(235/335 HDN GRJV) **Larger-Print**
(161/361 HDN GRJV)

Name (please print)

Address   Apt. #

City   State/Province   Zip/Postal Code

Email: Please check this box ☐ if you would like to receive newsletters and promotional emails from Harlequin Enterprises ULC and its affiliates. You can unsubscribe anytime.

> **Mail to the Harlequin Reader Service:**
> **IN U.S.A.:** P.O. Box 1341, Buffalo, NY 14240-8531
> **IN CANADA:** P.O. Box 603, Fort Erie, Ontario L2A 5X3
>
> **Want to try 2 free books from another series! Call 1-800-873-8635 or visit www.ReaderService.com.**

*Terms and prices subject to change without notice. Prices do not include sales taxes, which will be charged (if applicable) based on your state or country of residence. Canadian residents will be charged applicable taxes. Offer not valid in Quebec. This offer is limited to one order per household. Books received may not be as shown. Not valid for current subscribers to the Harlequin Special Edition or Harlequin Heartwarming series. All orders subject to approval. Credit or debit balances in a customer's account(s) may be offset by any other outstanding balance owed by or to the customer. Please allow 4 to 6 weeks for delivery. Offer available while quantities last.

Your Privacy—Your information is being collected by Harlequin Enterprises ULC, operating as Harlequin Reader Service. For a complete summary of the information we collect, how we use this information and to whom it is disclosed, please visit our privacy notice located at corporate.harlequin.com/privacy-notice. From time to time we may also exchange your personal information with reputable third parties. If you wish to opt out of this sharing of your personal information, please visit readerservice.com/consumerschoice or call 1-800-873-8635. Notice to California Residents—Under California law, you have specific rights to control and access your data. For more information on these rights and how to exercise them, visit corporate.harlequin.com/california-privacy.

HSEHW22R3

Get 4 FREE REWARDS!

We'll send you 2 FREE Books <u>plus</u> 2 FREE Mystery Gifts.

FREE Value Over **$20**

Both the **Harlequin® Historical** and **Harlequin® Romance** series feature compelling novels filled with emotion and simmering romance.

HARLEQUIN
PLUS

Try the best multimedia
subscription service for romance
readers like you!

Read, Watch and Play.

Experience the easiest way to get
the romance content you crave.

Start your **FREE TRIAL** at
www.harlequinplus.com/freetrial.